"You're crying again."

Lillie swiped at her traitorous tears. What right did she have to feel sorry for herself? Her disappointments had been self-inflicted, unlike those she'd thrust onto Jase.

Before she knew what was happening, he'd drawn her into a loose hug.

"I know how hard you've been trying, Lill." He pressed his lips to her temple. "It's clear you're working hard to stay clean. This time."

Who knew two little words could sting as much as a cold slap?

Lillie tried to back away, but the powder room was small. She had nowhere to go.

"Like I said before, you're stubborn. You can beat this thing...if you want it badly enough."

Lillie felt like shouting, *If? This time? I've* already *beat it! I've been clean for more than a year, and I'm going to stay that way!*

It wasn't until he lifted her chin on a bent forefinger that she realized she'd said it all out loud.

"I know that, and I'm proud of you."

Lillie studied his face, searching for signs of sincerity. Or doubt. Relief flooded through her when a slow smile lit his face. She summoned every ounce of willpower she had.

Because if he kept looking at her that way—the way he had before she'd destroyed them—Lillie feared she might say something to mess up the little bit of *good* she'd just earned in his eyes.

Dear Reader,

Whether we've watched a loved one plummet to rock bottom, supported a friend whose family member has succumbed to the disease or been there ourselves, addiction has touched so many of us.

It's a complex illness, and like diabetes or cancer, ongoing management and support services can help people cope with their disease. There are plenty of effective treatments that can eliminate an addict's dependence on addictive substances.

My objective in writing *The Redemption of Lillie Rourke* was to give a glimpse into the mind of a young woman whose journey into addiction wasn't the result of peer pressure, depression or escape from a horrific past. Rather, Lillie had it all: a loyal family, caring friends and the love of Jase Yeager, a good and decent man.

If you or a loved one is grappling with addiction, I hope you'll seek help. It's out there, just waiting for you to benefit from it. These resources are a great place to start:

National Institute on Drug Abuse: nida.nih.gov; 301-443-1124

National Institute of Mental Health: nimh.nih.gov; 1-866-615-6464

Substance Abuse Treatment Facility Locator: findtreatment.samhsa.gov; 1-800-662-HELP

SMART Recovery: smartrecovery.org; 440-951-5357

Wishing you happiness and health,

Loree

HEARTWARMING

The Redemption of Lillie Rourke

Loree Lough

HARLEQUIN® HEARTWARMING™

ISBN-13: 978-1-335-63360-6

The Redemption of Lillie Rourke

This edition published by arrangement with Harlequin Books S.A.

For questions and comments about the quality of this book, please contact us at CustomerService@Harlequin.com.

Printed in U.S.A.

Loree Lough once sang for her supper. That space reserved in pubs for "the piano lady"? Well, that's where she sat, strumming her Yamaha in cities all over the United States and Canada. Now and then, she blows the dust from the old six-string to croon a tune or two, but mostly, she writes. She feels blessed that most of her stories have earned four- and five-star reviews, but what Loree is most proud of are her Readers' Choice Awards.

Loree and her husband live in a Baltimore suburb and enjoy spending time at their cozy cabin in Pennsylvania's Allegheny Mountains (where she has *nearly* perfected her critter-tracking skills). They have two lovely daughters and seven "grandorables," and because she believes in giving back, Loree donates generously to charity (see the full list at loreelough.com).

Loree *loves* hearing from her readers, some of whom have become lifelong friends! Find her on Facebook, Twitter or Pinterest.

Books by Loree Lough

Harlequin Heartwarming

By Way of the Lighthouse

The Man She Knew
Bringing Rosie Home

Those Marshall Boys

Once a Marine
Sweet Mountain Rancher
The Firefighter's Refrain

This novel is dedicated to every reader who has ever purchased a Loree Lough book. Without your staunch support, I'd probably spend my days alphabetizing my pantry and spice cabinet, color-coordinating my closets, and rearranging bric-a-brac and knickknacks in my display cabinets.

Acknowledgments

Sincere thanks to Dan Remington, Steve Balore, Susan Griffin and Jennifer Myers, whose willingness to talk about their former dependence on drugs and alcohol enabled me to better understand and describe the challenges faced by those coping with addiction. Thanks, too, to Emily Yost (Cognitive Behavioral Therapist), and Martin Wilson, PhD, for their insights into the mind and behavior of the addict.

CHAPTER ONE

RAIN SHEETED DOWN the grimy window and puddled on the blacktop, and a dozen identical buses lined up in angled parking slots.

Lillie watched as grim-faced passengers boarded, a few pulling wheeled suitcases, others hauling overstuffed backpacks. As they jockeyed for overhead bins, the scent of damp wool and denim filled the space. And, she realized, someone was eating a tuna sandwich. She hoped its owner would finish it soon, because inhaling the fishy odor wouldn't make the four-hour trip any easier.

"Are you saving this seat for someone?"

Lillie's gaze traveled from the man's haggard face to his frayed sweatshirt and holey jeans. Something told her he hadn't paid top dollar for the distressed look. The passengers waiting in line behind him seemed equally interested in her answer, so Lillie gathered up her jacket and purse.

"Don't worry," he said, settling in beside her. "I don't bite."

"That's good to know."

His right forefinger aimed at the straps of the backpack nestled in her lap. "I don't steal either, so…"

She relaxed her grip, but only a bit.

"Going all the way to Florida?"

"No." As the driver buckled himself in, she slid the backpack to the floor. "Only as far as Baltimore."

"Ah. A surprise Mother's Day visit, huh?"

Lillie nodded, watching the driver adjust his rearview mirror, fire up the motor and close the door. It had been dumb luck that she'd get home in time to celebrate the day with her mom. She'd missed the annual cookout last year, thanks to Rising Sun's strict don't-leave-the-grounds policy. And in all honesty, she hadn't been fully present the year before that, thanks to—

"My mom moved to Orlando couple years back. That's where I'm headed."

Another nod. Perhaps her nonanswers would send a *not interested in talking* message.

But he said, "Don't mind admitting, I'm not looking forward to it."

Lillie knew the feeling.

"Because last time I saw her, I was falling-down drunk." He winced, then hung his head. "I apologized. Promised I'd quit. But that look on her face…"

The look that said "I don't believe you." Lillie

cringed, remembering it on her parents' faces. Her siblings'. Worse yet, on *Jase's* handsome face.

Her seatmate sighed in frustration. Or maybe it was regret.

"That's what finally convinced me to sign into rehab—that look, I mean—and what kept me clean these past two years."

A recovering addict, going home to make amends, and to prove that he'd kicked the habit, once and for all.

Just like you, Lill. Except that he'd been sober a whole year longer than she had.

Of all the empty seats on this bus, why had he chosen the one beside her?

He held out a hand. "Gabe Sheffield."

"Lillie Rourke," she said, taking it.

She'd learned in rehab that to truly come to terms with drug or alcohol dependence, addicts had to admit their own culpability in the addiction. Lillie had managed to take full responsibility with the staff at Rising Sun, but wasn't at all sure she could pull it off with the people she'd hurt.

For one thing, her parents and siblings would have questions, and so would Jase. She owed them straightforward answers. What better way to practice dealing with the ugly facts than by confessing them with someone she'd never see again?

"I was in rehab, too."

"Yeah?" He studied her face. "You could have fooled me."

"Why?"

"You don't look desperate, or like you have something to prove."

During her final group therapy session, that was exactly what a fellow patient feared most. Until that moment, she hadn't given it a thought. Funny, because she felt both right now.

"Sixteen months ago," she continued, "I signed myself into Rising Sun. It was a really intense time."

"How long?"

"Seven weeks."

Gabe's brow furrowed as he considered her words. "You beat the addiction in less than the normal amount of time?"

"Yeah, I guess."

"Rising Sun, huh? Isn't that the place where movie stars go?"

Lillie knew how fortunate she'd been to have had Pete in her corner; his steady and generous contributions to the facility helped allow her to take advantage of the facility's groundbreaking treatments.

"Actually, a friend pulled some strings. I did odd jobs there in exchange for room and board and sessions with the staff."

"Cool." Then, "Did you get any autographs while you were there?"

She'd met a major-league baseball player, a well-known country singer and half a dozen Broadway stars. But she felt protective of their anonymity.

"All that matters is that I've been out for a year now, working pretty much nonstop, and saving to repay…everyone."

"Yeah, we tend to rack up some big-time debts, don't we."

Lillie bristled. She hadn't minded being treated like every other resident at Rising Sun, so why did it bother her when this guy assumed he and she were alike?

"So is Baltimore home, or just a payback stop?"

"It's both."

Lillie had grown up in the big old house that had become her parents' B and B. They didn't know it yet, but Lillie had no intention of accepting a salary for helping out in the kitchen, serving meals and cleaning guest rooms. And although they'd try to talk her out of finding another job to fill the hours when they didn't need her, that was exactly what she intended to do. Sending money to her siblings, the guys in the band and Jase's mother had been easy. Earning back their trust wouldn't be.

Jase? Jase would be another matter entirely.

She thought about what Jase had said that last night. If only there had been venom in his words, or if he'd ordered her to leave. Slammed a door. *Something.* If he had, she might have learned to live with it. Instead, when Jase found out that she'd stolen the band's money for a handful of pills, he had looked…

After all this time, the only word she could come up with to describe it was *wounded.*

Lillie closed her eyes and remembered how she'd gone through the well-rehearsed list of apologies he'd heard far too many times before. Promises that nothing like this would ever happen again. Claims that this time, *this time*, she'd get help. For the longest time, he'd just stared, grim-faced and slump-shouldered, then quietly ground out, "The guys have bills to pay, too, you know. When are you gonna realize your needs aren't more important than everybody else's?"

"Say, Lillie," Gabe said, breaking into her thoughts, "maybe you can help me make a tough decision. You know, since you understand things."

"I stink in the advice department."

He shrugged. "My older brother lives in Florida, too. It's the main reason our mom moved down there. He owns a landscaping company. Offered me a job and a place to stay. You know, until I get on my feet." Gabe paused. "But I don't know if that's such a good idea. I'm godfather to his thirteen-year-old son, see, and not to toot my own horn, but the kid's crazy about me."

Lillie thought of her brother's twins, who'd once lit up at the sight of her, and wondered if Sam had told the girls that their beloved aunt was a drug addict.

"You're worried that if you spend too much time around your nephew, you'll be a bad example?"

"Bingo."

The bus merged with traffic on 28th Street, and Gabe shifted in his seat.

"Your brother told your nephew…everything?"

"That's just it," Gabe said. "I don't know."

He looked as distraught as she felt. Disappointing people was tough. She'd certainly learned *that* the hard way.

"Well, even if the boy knows, that's not such a bad thing, is it? I mean, you made a mistake—"

"Lots of mistakes."

"—but you made things right, and stayed clean for a long time. What better example can you set than that?"

Who are you trying to convince, Lill? Gabe? Or yourself?

"Maybe…" And then, "So how'd you get into, ah, trouble?" He held up his hand again. "If I'm poking my nose where it doesn't belong, say the word."

Lillie reminded herself that this was the perfect

opportunity to practice the difficult "I was a mess and I'm sorry" speech before she had to deliver it yet again...to Jase, the one person she hadn't repaid. Yet.

She took a deep breath and let it out slowly. "A little over three years ago, my car was T-boned by a city bus."

"Holy smokes. How badly were you hurt?"

Lillie stared at the jagged white scar that crossed the back of her right hand, and instinctively covered it with her left. "There were seven operations..." To repair her shattered left leg and arm, and the ribs that had punctured her lung. Even after all this time, nightmares about the impact still had the power to shake her from deep sleep.

"Then I spent a month in an inpatient rehab center—the physical therapy kind—followed by months more of outpatient work."

"Holy smokes," Gabe repeated. "That's one brutal story." He paused. "Did the transit system pay the medical bills?"

"Yes, they were very accommodating."

"So the trouble started when your doctors put you on pain meds?"

"More like when they decided I didn't need them anymore."

"And?"

Admittedly, the pain had been excruciating, making it next to impossible to climb to her second-floor apartment—especially when hauling groceries—or to stand onstage for hour-long intervals or sleep more than an hour at a time.

"There were three doctors. My surgeon. My regular guy. And my shrink. Little did I know, they compared notes. And when they realized I was hooked on the meds, they cut me off."

"Harsh," Gabe said. "Wouldn't it have been better to wean you slowly?"

"Maybe." But given how totally dependent she'd grown, maybe not.

"So you had to find other ways to cut the pain..."

It should have been easy to admit. It wasn't. And so Lillie said, "What about you?"

Gabe shrugged. "Nothing as dramatic or understandable as a car wreck. No, I was the stereotypical spoiled brat with too much time on his hands and too much money in his pockets. Got in with the wrong crowd—although at the time they sure didn't seem like the wrong crowd—and the rest is history."

It wasn't unusual for recovering addicts to be tough on themselves. Unfortunately, the self-deprecating mindset, her counselors said, was responsible for more addicts relapsing than just about anything else.

"Still," she reminded him, "your mom inspired you to get help."

"She's only half the reason. I watched a pal

OD on crack." He grimaced and his voice trailed off, a clear sign that he'd recalled a raw memory. "I got real serious about rehab after that." He turned slightly. "So when you got off the prescription meds, what cut the pain?"

"Hydrocodone, mostly."

"As in Watson-387?"

"That, and half a dozen other types of pills supplied by my go-to guy." Although she hadn't touched drugs or alcohol since entering rehab, it shamed Lillie to admit that she'd washed down hydro, norco, vic, and more—with dry gin—and paid for it with money taken from those who cared most about her. Her sister and her husband. Her brother and his wife. Her parents. Her best friend. The guys in the band.

It had been humiliating, facing each of them, stammering through clumsy apologies, voice quaking and hands shaking as she returned every dollar. Though she didn't believe she'd earned their forgiveness, they'd been gracious, smiling as they told her to stay in touch and take care of herself. Had they meant it?

She'd saved the toughest encounter for last. Jase…

"Your friend," Gabe began, "the one who hooked you up with the Rising Sun people…is he a boyfriend?"

That inspired a smile. "No, Pete owns a pub in the Bronx. We met when my agent booked me to sing with his house band. I was barely eighteen, and he looked out for me."

"Like a big brother."

"Exactly." Pete was the first person she'd turned to after that last night with Jase, when it became clear that she'd gotten completely out of control.

"So—to quote my grandpa—you're footloose and fancy-free?"

Lillie had no idea how to answer him. Jase likely wouldn't want anything to do with her, other than to accept repayment of the money she'd taken. If that was the case, she'd deal with it, somehow… In all this time, she hadn't entertained thoughts of starting a relationship with someone new. He'd been her first true love, and he'd probably be her last. In her mind and heart, she hadn't yet earned the right to romance or happiness.

"This Pete guy, he's got connections at Rising Sun because he's a recovering addict?"

"Yes. They helped him kick his addictions, so when he inherited a lot of money, he donated a chunk to them. He'd been into the hard stuff. Heroin. Mescaline. You name it, Pete did it. And almost died when someone sold him a bad batch of H."

"Yeah, I can see how that'd scare a dude straight."

"That, and finding out he had a child."

"Whoa." Gabe nodded. "The whole set-a-good-example thing, like me." He reached into his duffle bag and withdrew two bottles of water. After handing one to Lillie, he said, "So you've been clean for a year?"

"Fourteen months." *And sixteen days...*

He unscrewed the cap, took several gulps. "You said you were on the road before this all happened?"

"Mmm-hmm. I was a singer. Hotel lounges, mostly, but now and then, my agent would book me with a band. I saw a lot of this country through bus windows." Until Jase, when she'd been more than content to stand on the same stage, singing into the same mic, every night for nearly a year before—

"Play an instrument?"

"Guitar. Practically the only thing I owned that I didn't sell for, well, you know."

"Yeah, I do." He picked at the bottle's label. "I have an Ovation. Belonged to my grandfather. And like you, it's one of a handful of things I held on to."

"Mine is handcrafted. It's a MacCubbin. It has a great sound." Jase had scrimped to give it to her the Christmas before she left for Rising Sun. While living at the center—and ever since—she'd taken the instrument from its plush-lined case only to change the strings and buff the Brazilian rosewood to a fine sheen. The calluses on her fingertips had all but disappeared, because she couldn't bear to hear the resonant tones that reminded her of the music she and Jase had made together.

"You going back to it now? Music, I mean?"

And think about the way she once shared a mic with Jase, creating perfect harmony?

"Absolutely not."

"I get it. Too much temptation."

Lillie had earned her keep at Pete's, serving liquor of every description, and managed to stay away from it. And yet she said, "Something like that."

Gabe yawned. "Well, I hope you won't think I'm rude or anything, but I'm gonna try to catch a few z's before our first stop."

"Good idea. I might do the same."

Moments later, listening to his soft, steady snores, Lillie closed her eyes. But she didn't expect to sleep, not with all those newly awakened memories whirling in her mind.

She was surprised when the lurch of the bus startled her awake.

"Hey, thanks for keeping me company. It was great talking with you," Gabe said, standing as she pulled her rolling suitcase from the overhead bin. "Maybe we can exchange numbers, do coffee if I ever get to Baltimore."

He produced an old envelope and a ballpoint, and not knowing how to say *not interested* without hurting his feelings, she accepted both. As she wrote her first name, Lillie was tempted to change a digit or two in her cell number. But starting her new life on a lie, even one that small, didn't seem like a good idea. So she handed back the pen and the envelope.

"Thanks," she said, "but..."

Gabe took it and, he must've read her hesitation because he said, "I get it." He shrugged. "Good luck to you."

"And to you."

She meant it, but if he ever did call, she'd find a reason to decline. She was in no position to start anything—not even a friendship—with anyone. Not until she had a better handle on who and what *she* had been...and what she'd done.

Besides, she wanted Jase, and no one else.

The admission gave her the strength to make a decision that had been a long time coming: she'd earn his trust again, no matter what it took.

"LILLIAN MARIE ROURKE, is that you?"

Only one person had ever called her by her full name. Heart drumming with joy—and dread—Lillie turned toward the robust voice.

"Dad! It's so great to see you."

"My, my, my," her dad said, gripping her biceps, "just look at you. Roses in your cheeks and sparkles in those big brown eyes. You look..." Liam wrapped her in a fierce hug. "You look healthy." He held her at arm's length again. "Are you happy, Lill?"

She was glad to be home, with rehab behind her. Glad to have put in hard, fourteen-hour days at work afterward. Lillie had saved a few thousand dollars, every penny earmarked to repay the last of her debts. Until then, she wouldn't truly be happy, so she didn't answer him directly.

"Where's Mom?"

"At the inn, planning your homecoming." He winked. "Here," her dad said, grabbing her suitcase, "let me take that. Can you believe I found a space right out front?"

Lillie followed him to the parking lot, tossed her backpack into the trunk beside the wheeled bag and climbed into the front seat. "You look wonderful," she said. "Have you been dieting?"

"Dieting? *Me?*" He laughed. "No, but I've started a new project at the inn. Turns out it's good exercise."

"A project?"

Liam started the car. "An addition."

"Ah, Mom's kitchen bump-out."

"And screened-in porch."

"With a terrace beyond it?"

"And a gazebo. *And* an arbor. I tell you, Lill, she's more excited than a bride on her wedding day. She has visions of hosting wedding parties. None of those eight-bridesmaids-and-groomsmen shindigs, mind you. Don't know where we'd put 'em all in a place the size of the White Roof."

Amelia had once dreamed of planning *Lillie's* wedding. It was all she could talk about after Jase proposed. Back then, her mother had looked into the possibility of renting an arbor for them to exchange vows under. They'd trim it with white roses and baby's breath. It would be a twilight ceremony, followed by a candlelight reception, complete with a string quartet, finger sandwiches and a four-tiered cake that Lillie would bake and decorate herself. Maybe, just maybe, it wasn't a completely impossible dream…

"You won't believe what your mother has done to that little room on the first floor of the turret."

"Let me guess… It's where the brides and bridesmaids will get dressed…" *Along with mothers of the brides...*

"A-yup."

Liam reached across the console and squeezed her hand. "It's really good to have you home, kitten. We missed you."

How long since he'd called her that? Not since… Lillie shook off the hard memory.

"I missed you guys, too."

"You're really okay, then?"

In other words, are you clean and sober, *for real*? "Yes, I'm fine. Fourteen months now." *And sixteen days.*

"What about all those aches and pains from the accident? They're gone?"

Translation: Pain meds had started her down the road to addiction; was it possible she'd make a U-turn at the first temptation? They'd warned her at rehab to expect varying levels of mistrust. *So much for the "forewarned is forearmed" theory*, she thought, doing her best to shake off the sting of reality.

"Oh, I have the occasional ache, but who doesn't? Don't worry, though, I've fought too hard to put that life behind me. Forever. Ever. Period. Even if more surgery is in my future. Besides, I worked in a pub for months and months and didn't so much as sniff a cork. So I passed the supreme test." Not to mention, she'd continue daily meetings with the new sponsor recommended by Rising Sun to stay on track, but no one needed to know that. "You're looking at the new me." She raised her right hand. "Honest."

Why did she suddenly feel sixteen again, explaining that she'd never stay out past curfew, ever, *ever* again?

"We just want what's best for you, is all. You had us real worried there for a while. But if you say you're cured—"

She hated to burst his bubble, but Lillie had to be up-front with him. "I wish there was a cure, Dad, but the fact is, I'm an addict. I'll always be an addict, even after I'm old and gray and rocking on Mom's new screened porch. But you have my word, I'll never *use* again."

There. It was out. Sadly, she'd need to repeat the little speech to reaffirm it for her mother and siblings. And Jase, whom she'd yet to apologize to. Something told her that no matter how many times she said it, the reassurance wouldn't get any easier.

Lillie squared her shoulders. "So how are things at the inn? Are you overrun with guests?"

"Actually, just one old couple this weekend. They'd booked last year. It's an annual thing for them, anniversary celebration. Once they check out, we'll shut down for the next couple of months, you know, so the contractors won't disturb anybody."

"Contractors? Since when do you let someone else wield a hammer in your house!"

"Since I won the lottery."

"Wait. The lottery? You're kidding!"

He held up his right hand. "As God is my witness. My ticket came in. After taxes, I raked in a cool half a million. More than enough to make all your mother's dreams come true. And even though you didn't cost me a dime, you're one of those dreams, you know."

They'd stayed in touch. Emails. Phone calls. FaceTime. Why was this the first she'd heard about something that big?

Stop thinking of yourself, Lill.

Her folks had worked hard all their lives and deserved a big break. She smiled.

He grabbed her hand again. "And now that you're home and healthy? Well, that's the cherry on life's sundae. Speaking of desserts, that's just one of the reasons she didn't come with me to pick you up." The car's interior rattled as he let out a piercing, two-note whistle. "That woman has been cooking and baking for days. All your favorites."

"That's sweet of her. But I hope she isn't ignoring her art because of me. She's still painting, right?"

"Not as often as she'd like, but yes, she adds a canvas to her gallery now and then."

"You mean she finally turned that old parlor room into a studio?"

"Yup. It looks good, I tell ya, and the guests agree. A few talked her into giving them lessons. They were happy with their paintings. You'd think that would inspire the cheapskates to buy one of hers, but no such luck."

"But they will."

"Right. There's always hope, isn't there."

She took the comment to heart, because hope was about the only thing Lillie had left.

"You're not still planning to get a second job, are you, kitten?"

The way Lillie saw it, she didn't have a choice.

Her parents had always been so generous and forgiving, and she didn't want to take advantage. "I'll look around, see what's available."

"Well, don't be in a big rush. Give yourself time to adjust to being back. Hasn't been all that long since you left the rehab center."

It had been more than a year. The minute her counselor felt it was safe for her to leave, she'd gone to work for Pete, waiting tables, scheduling the staff and pitching in wherever else she was needed. It was the least she could do since he'd refused to accept rent for the tiny apartment above the pub. Between her salary—and Pete had been more than generous—and tips, Lillie had saved enough to repay everyone.

Almost everyone.

"How are Molly and Matt?"

"They're good. Planning a world cruise once school is out."

She pictured her little sister, a miniature version of herself, married to a guy who could easily be a Ravens linebacker. Since he and Molly couldn't have children, they'd decided to save up and travel, instead.

"Wow. I can hardly wait to hear about this trip. And how are the Sams?" The fact that her brother Sam had married a woman named Samantha had, for years, been at the root of much good-natured teasing.

"They're great, too. Got a new dog."

"A mutt, like Beano?"

"No, she's a Yorkie. Or so their vet says. Clem's kinda yappy, but that's to be expected of a pooch you could carry in your pocket."

"They named her Clem?" Lillie laughed, picturing a tiny canine answering to the name. "Let me guess…it was Kassie's idea."

"She found her at the playground, shivering under the merry-go-round. Tucked the critter into her backpack, and the minute her mother got an eyeful of her, it was all over. They took pictures and tacked lost dog signs all over the place, put ads in the paper, posted on Facebook. But when no one claimed her…"

"No microchip?"

"Nope. But she has one now."

That didn't surprise Lillie one bit. Her sister-in-law, an in-home nurse, gave new meaning to the term *caretaker*. How she managed to work full-time, run a household, care for a cat and two dogs *and* keep track of the twins' playdates and soccer practices, Lillie didn't know.

"Do you mind stopping at the Flower Basket on the way home? I'd like to get Mom a little something."

"Why? It isn't her birthday." He glanced at her again, and feigning panic, added, "Is it?"

"Relax. No. But Sunday is Mother's Day. I got her a little something, but I know how much she loves orchids, so…" She shrugged. A bouquet couldn't make up for years of heartache and disappointment, but it was a start.

"I have something in my suitcase for you, too," she told Liam.

"Kitten, you didn't have to do that. I'm just happy that you're home and..."

His voice trailed off, so Lillie finished for him: "...home, and drug-free..."

He recoiled slightly at the phrase.

"You don't have to tiptoe around my addiction, Dad. If you or Mom have questions, feel free to ask. And if you have things you'd like to say, by all means, say them. I can take it. And anyway, you deserve the truth."

Nodding, he turned into the florist's parking lot. "Good to know." After rolling down the windows, Liam said, "Want me to come in with you?"

"Sure. Why not?"

Once inside the shop, Lillie perused glass shelves lined with floral arrangements, houseplants and orchids. She cupped the blossom of a purple pansy orchid and inhaled its delicate scent. "Is Mom still collecting orchids?"

He rolled his eyes. "Have you *met* your mother?"

Lillie removed the plant from its shelf and took it to the register. It surprised her when her dad slid a pale pink moth orchid onto the counter beside it.

"She's not *your* mother," Lillie teased.

He shrugged. "True, but she's a good egg. And gave me some of the best kids on the planet. So why not."

"You're a big softie, just one of a thousand reasons I love you."

Once outside, they gently placed the plants onto the floor of the back seat. After they were seated in the front, Liam said, "Did you mean it that Mom and I are free to ask questions?"

"Anything."

"Okay. Same goes for you, you know."

"I've always been able to talk to you."

"Not *always*."

Her therapist had warned her that from time to time, a comment like that would sting. The woman had recited a list of platitudes intended to help her cope when it happened: Consider the source. Whatever doesn't kill you makes you stronger. You got through rehab; you'll get through this. Lillie's least favorite cliché? *Don't try to go around the mountain; make it your home.*

During those excruciating months following the accident, Lillie had worked hard to spare her family and Jase the truth about her condition. Why worry them about things they couldn't control, like her never-ending pain? For the same reason, she'd kept her addiction a secret, too. If she could point to a specific time or event that made them see through her ruse, Lillie might have prevented the humiliating intervention. "You're not fooling anyone," they'd said. "Get help, or else."

Now, she said, "I know, Dad, but that was the old me. *This* me is very up-front about things." A nervous giggle escaped her lips. "You'll probably get sick and tired of hearing me 'fess up all over the place!"

Liam didn't respond. Instead, he exhaled a long sigh. "You still mad at me for getting that court order?"

When he realized how quickly she was going through the insurance settlement from her accident, Liam had seen a lawyer to gain control of her money. She'd fought him at every turn, because his actions would put a stop to her street drugs. He'd won, and she'd despised him for it. In hindsight, Lillie felt nothing but gratitude.

"I'd be lying if I said it didn't bother me at first. But time, and sobriety, helped me see that if you hadn't done it, I would only have wasted every dime. So no, I'm not mad. In fact, I'm relieved that you did it. You quite literally saved my life."

Another deep sigh, and then, "You don't know how pleased I am to hear that. It was the hardest decision I ever had to make. But that's all history now, thank God, and I'm glad we got it out of the way before we reached the inn." He squeezed her hand. "I can have things reversed now, if you want me to."

Lillie believed she'd kicked the habit for good. But she'd heard too many horror stories of people who assumed the same thing, only to fall back into old habits.

"Let's just leave things as they are for now," she said. "I've paid everyone back, except for you and Mom and..." *And Jase.* "And it isn't like I need the money for a world cruise or anything."

That, at least, produced a genuine laugh.

"So, how long before you'll call him?" her dad asked.

Lillie had to give him credit. He'd heard that little hesitation in her voice and knew exactly what it meant.

"I don't know." Of all the confrontations, that one scared her most.

"The longer you wait, the harder it'll be."

"He doesn't know I'm back, so there's no rush."

The look on her dad's face told her otherwise.

"But how could he know? I didn't know myself until a week ago, when I made the plans and called you guys."

"He... Jase sort of stayed in touch."

"Sort of?"

"Every time he calls or stops by, he says it's just because he wants to make sure we're okay. But we weren't born yesterday. We know he only wants a Lillie update. He's dating someone. This one seems nice enough."

This one? There had been others? Of course he wouldn't have put his life on hold, waiting for her to come back…

"You…you met them…these women Jase dated?"

"Not exactly. Ran into him at the movies once, at a restaurant another time. And there were a couple of chance meetings at the ice cream stand. I'll give him this: he sure knows how to pick the purty ones!" Liam chuckled. "No surprise there, when he started out with a beauty like you."

Again, her father cut loose with the ear-piercing whistle. Her heart ached at the thought of Jase with someone else, but she had only herself to blame. If she hadn't single-handedly destroyed their relationship, they'd be married, might even have a child by now. "Some of the people you've hurt will move on," the rehab psychologists had said. "You need to let them. Wish them well, and do the same, yourself."

Easier said than done, Lillie thought.

"Well, great." He didn't know it, but Jase had spared her the challenge of working hard to earn back his trust. "I'm happy for him."

"You're happy for him? Really?"

"Don't sound so shocked, Dad. Jase is a good man, and deserves the best that life has to give." *And God knows that isn't* me.

"I give it another month," her dad said. "Two, tops."

"Why? I thought you said she seemed nice."

"Oh, she's all right, if you're into leggy blondes. It's just that this thing Jase has going with—Whitney's her name—let's just say she's all wrong for him. You know your mother's talent for reading people? Well, she says it's healthy for Jase to sow some wild oats before he finally settles down. And I agree with her."

A twinge of guilt shot through her, because it didn't bother her one bit, hearing that this… this *Whitney* was all wrong for Jase. *If you had an ounce of decency in you, you'd want him to be happy.*

"What do you mean, she's all wrong for him?"

Liam shrugged. "She isn't you." He turned into the inn's drive. "So of course it won't last."

Another eddy of guilt swirled through her. And right behind it, a glimmer of hope.

Because oh, how she wanted her dad to be right!

CHAPTER TWO

"IT'S SO SWEET of you to do this for me, Jason." Whitney giggled. "You've been so sweet about chauffeuring me around that I don't feel the slightest bit helpless."

"Helpless? You?" Jase laughed. Somehow, she'd managed to keep her sweet and sensitive side intact, even while working with the associates and partners at a high-powered law office. Everyone in his life knew how much he disliked being called Jason, yet Whitney had never referred to him any other way.

"You really don't mind spending your entire day helping me run errands?"

She'd asked, and given him ample opportunity to say no. Wouldn't be right to hold her feet over the fire now, just because boredom had him counting all the things he could be doing instead.

"I know what it's like when your car is in the shop." Not exactly an answer to her question, but it beat hurting her feelings with the truth.

"I can't believe all this traffic! It's three in the

afternoon. On a Thursday. Why aren't people at work?"

"We aren't," Jase said, chuckling.

"No. No we aren't, are we. And I'm one hundred percent grateful that you took the day off, just for me!"

Her good-natured disposition was refreshing, especially compared with other women he'd dated: the librarian, who couldn't talk about anything *but* books; the boutique owner, who tried—and failed—to dress him like a Gatsby character; the PE teacher who ate nothing but nuts and grains…and expected him to follow suit; and the pièce de résistance, the cellist with the Baltimore Symphony Orchestra, who thought he'd appreciate sitting in her living room…while she practiced her portion of Johann Pachelbel's "Canon in D Major."

"It'll be so nice, having my watch back again."

Whitney giggled, a pleasant enough sound, but it didn't begin to compare with Lillie's musical laughter. Jase flinched inwardly. It had been months since he'd had a positive thought about Lillie. *Better clear your head, fool…*

"I rarely wear mine anymore," he said, steering into the right lane.

"I must seem like a dinosaur. Everyone but me uses their cell phones these days."

"Yeah, but when you want to know what time it is, all you have to do is glance at your wrist.

The rest of us have to find our phones." Whitney was one of the most pulled-together women he'd had the pleasure of knowing. So why did she feel the need to defend herself all the time?

Because you're doing something to make her feel that way. What, he couldn't say.

"At least this stop kills two birds with one stone." Whitney unbuckled her seat belt. "You know, since the Flower Basket is right next door to St. John's Jewelers."

In the rearview mirror, he saw a red SUV. He'd parked beside it enough times to recognize it as Lillie's dad's. Liam had probably decided to grab a bouquet for Amelia as an early Mother's Day gift. Jase backed into a space directly across from the shop's entrance as Whitney said, "I can't decide whether to get Patsy a green plant or a spray of roses."

Her best friend, who'd been at Johns Hopkins for nearly a week.

"I'm sure Patsy will be happy with either."

And that was when he noticed someone in Liam's passenger seat.

Not just someone.

Lillie.

His heart beat a little harder.

"I'm thinking a plant—" Whitney continued, one hand on the door lever "—so she can take it home with her. Which, unless she spikes a fever or something, should be in a day or two."

"Yeah. Mmm-hmm. Right," he muttered, watching as father and daughter exited the car.

The shop was cute—as flower shops went—and small. No way could he avoid running into Lillie in there. Or introducing her to Whitney. She'd been gone more than a year, no note, no call, not even a text message. For all he knew, she'd moved on, too. So why did he dread seeing her after all this time? And why was his heart beating double-time now?

"Wouldn't it be better to take care of your watch battery first? You know, so the plant won't sit in the hot car and, uh, wilt?"

That *giggle* again. And then Whitney placed her hand atop his on the gearshift. "It's May, Jason, and seventy degrees, not ninety."

"Yeah, but the sun is beating down like it thinks it's August. Only takes ten minutes for the truck's interior to reach one hundred degrees on a day like this."

She wasn't buying it. If he didn't do something quick, he'd find himself in the Flower Basket, introducing his could-be fiancée to his *ex*-fiancée.

Whitney made a habit of putting her cell phone into his console's cup holder, and he used it to his advantage. In one swift move, he backhanded it to the floor.

"Aw, man, sorry, Whit."

She frowned—or as close to a frown as the always-pleasant Whitney got—and leaning forward, said, "No harm done, Jason. The floor is carpeted."

For safe measure, he reached for it, too. But instead of retrieving it, he batted it under the passenger seat.

"Aw, man. I'm such a klutz!"

While she bent down, patting the floor mat in search of her phone, Jase looked up…

…and saw Lillie.

And his heart beat like a parade drum.

Her long auburn waves were chin-length now, and in place of her customary jeans, T-shirt and sneakers, she'd worn a gauzy calf-length skirt that billowed with every puff of the wind. She had on matching yellow shoes that looked like ballet slippers and a puffy-sleeved blouse with ruffles at the wrists. She still walked like a woman who knew where she was going, head up and arms swinging slightly. Marilyn Monroe–style sunglasses hid big eyes that couldn't decide if they were brown or green, and if he knew Lillie, she'd applied a hint of shadow and just enough mascara to showcase those long lashes.

"There," Whitney announced, "got it. Finally!"

He half ran to her side of the pickup and opened the passenger door. "First stop, jewelry store?" Taking her hand, he helped her to the pavement.

Grinning, she pressed a quick kiss to his

cheek. "All right, Jason, whatever you think best."

With any luck, Lillie hadn't seen the kiss.

With a little more luck, he'd figure out where *that* crazy thought had come from. Lillie was a part of his past. It had taken a while, but his life was on track again, and Jase aimed to keep it that way.

"Thank you," Whitney said.

"For what?"

"For helping me figure out what to get you for your birthday." She shouldered her purse and smiled up at him.

It took a conscious effort not to look into the flower shop, where by now Lillie and her dad were searching out just the right gift for Amelia.

"My birthday isn't until July."

"Oh, I'm not waiting that long. This old buggy of yours needs running boards. I'm five foot six, and I feel so short getting in and out of it."

"Ah. So my birthday present is really for you," he teased.

Lashes fluttering, Whitney said, "Can I help it if that's the way you choose to look at it?"

He followed her into the shop and breathed a sigh of relief when she marched straight up to the counter. Maybe he could talk Whitney into going to the florist in the Columbia Mall, too. That could work, especially if he suggested they grab a bite to eat while they were there.

His relief was short-lived, thanks to the sudden nerve-racking thought that Liam might want to buy jewelry for Amelia, to go along with the flowers…and Lillie might go into the jewelry story with him.

More determined than ever to talk Whitney into going straight to the mall, he leaned into the display case behind him. Whitney was asking for a new watch battery. She didn't use her hands, like Lillie always had. Once, he'd asked if some Italian blood coursed through the Rourke clan. She'd responded with a thick-brogued, "Yer ears must be on upside down, Jase Yeager! M'bloodline is pure green, I tell you!" And he'd grasped her wrists, pulled her close and kissed—

"What are *you* smiling about?" Whitney asked.

Standing up straight, he crossed his arms over his chest and said, "Told you it'd take longer than ten minutes to change your battery."

"The woman isn't sure it *is* the battery." She glanced toward the doorway that led to the repair shop. "I hope they're wrong. My grandparents gave it to me when I graduated from the U of M. I'd hate to think it's irreparable."

The University of Maryland was his alma mater, too. He'd started on a degree in communications. His dad had pointed out that it would limit his choices in the job market, though, and as usual, the old man had been right. The BA in business had been instrumental in helping him organize and grow his mother's company.

"I'm sure they can fix it."

"I'm sure you're right."

Standing close beside him, she rested her hip against his as she continued staring at the narrow doorway, arms and ankles crossed, just like his. Whitney had always been accommodating. No matter what he suggested, from restaurants to movies, from ballgames to staying home and watching old movies, she'd been agreeable. She was pretty. Hardworking and smart. He liked her. But…why couldn't he feel something more for her, something deeper?

She took his hand and aimed his forefinger at a bracelet, glittering under the bright overhead lights.

"Isn't that just gorgeous!"

She'd been hinting that their relationship had passed from "just dating" to serious. But not nearly serious enough for diamonds, he thought.

Jase grinned at her. "I suppose…if you're into glitz and glam."

She moved farther down the display case, pointing out earrings, pendants and anklets that matched the bracelet. When she maneuvered toward the rings, Jase pretended to scratch an itch beside his nose as an excuse to let go of her hand, because she'd zeroed in on a square-cut solitaire, nearly identical to the one in his sock drawer. The one he'd given Lillie shortly after her release from physical therapy. The one she'd returned after he called her on the carpet for taking the guys' money.

Whitney continued examining the glass cases until she reached the presentation of men's watches. "This one is nice, isn't it?"

He nodded, though he'd barely seen it. Jase was too busy remembering the night he gave the ring to Lillie…the week after her release from the PT facility and two weeks before her twenty-sixth birthday. They'd just finished a close-harmony rendition of an Eagles tune when he asked the audience to share in some good news… and held up the tiny blue velvet box.

Lillie's big eyes had grown round and wide as she stood, grinning and blinking under the spotlight. Then she'd grabbed the mic and faced the band. "I think he's trying to tell us we're doing 'Blue Velvet' next."

Jase smiled at the memory.

Whitney rapped on the glass counter. "Jason? Would you ever wear a man's bracelet, like this one?"

"Nah," he managed, his mind still fogged by the fond memory…

Whistles and applause had filled Three-Eyed Joe's pub. "Quit beatin' around the bush," the Muzikalees' drummer said into his mic.

"Ned's right," Spence agreed, playing a run

on his guitar. "Pop the question why don't you, so we can get back to work!"

"What about a necklace?" Whitney wanted to know.

"Nah," he repeated, "I'm not much into trinkets." He tried to focus on the thick gold chain, but what he saw was Lillie, opening the little box, smiling past glittering tears as she handed him the ring and waited for him to put it on her finger.

"Yes," she'd said matter-of-factly. Then, more emphatically, *"Yes."* And standing on tiptoe, she'd nearly knocked him over with a powerful Lillie hug.

When he kissed her, a patron yelled, "Atta boy, Jase! Atta *boy*!" And he'd barely heard the applause because—

"Have you ever considered wearing an earring?"

Jase shook his head, hoping to rid himself of those memories.

"Well? Would you?"

"Me? A pierced ear? Like a pirate?" He forced a laugh. "Have you *met* me?"

Whitney laughed, too, then exhaled a feminine groan. "You are *the* most difficult man to buy a gift for!"

"You know I'm not big on gifts." He pulled her into a light hug. "Besides, a little bird told me I'm getting running boards this year."

She blushed prettily and would have kissed him if the clerk hadn't said "Ms. Hendricks?"

Whitney went to the counter, and while she and the jeweler discussed the watch, Jase faced Route 40. Cars, trucks and motorcycles bulleted past. Then he noticed that his passenger window was down. Not partway, but all the way. Whitney must have accidentally hit the button while searching for her phone. "Payback," he murmured, and stepped up beside her.

"I left the truck window open and it looks like rain. Be right back," he told her. And without waiting for a reply, Jase palmed his keys and made his way to the parking lot…

…and crashed into Lillie, crushing a long-stemmed flower between them.

"Jase?" Her voice was barely a whisper.

He felt like an idiot when he replied, "Lillie…"

"Dad and I were just picking up a few things for Mom."

Liam, standing beside her, said, "Good to see you, son. What brings you all the way to Ellicott City?"

He transferred the keys from his right hand to his left and resisted the urge to glance into the jewelry store. "Just…just running errands. Sunday's Mother's Day…"

Lillie smiled as Liam chuckled. "Yeah," he said, showing off his bouquet, "we heard."

Jase stepped back, asking Lillie how badly he'd crushed her purchase.

She gave the orchid a quick once-over. "It's fine."

"Are you sure? Because I'm happy to go right back in there and buy a replace—"

Lillie silenced him with a tiny smile. "Really. Orchids are tougher than they look, kinda like the daisies Dad bought…" She winked at her father. "Because he thinks they're Mom's favorites."

While Liam chuckled, Jase remembered that once, they'd been Lillie's favorites. "They're tough," she'd say, "like me." The proof could be found on anything that would hold ink: envelopes, napkins, cash register receipts… Given enough time, the thing would be covered with doodles of daisies, jagged-edged leaves and curlicue vines swirling between the blossoms. But that had been before the accident.

Get it together, dude. "When did you get home?"

"I just picked her up at the Greyhound station. My girl, here, wanted to stop on the way home. Get a little something for her mom."

"Ellicott City is hardly on the way home to Fells Point…"

"I know," Lillie said, "but this place is owned by the parents of a girl I graduated with. Anyway, you know I like shopping at mom-and-pop stores when I can. Besides, no telling when I'll get a chance to go shopping, and I wanted to bring something nice to Mom. Dad says she's been cooking and baking for days to welcome me home, so..."

She'd never been one to ramble, not even when nervous, but Jase supposed a lot of things about her had changed in the year she'd been gone.

"Well, I think the flower is real nice. I'll bet your mom will think so, too."

She'd focused on something over his left shoulder, and Jase turned just as Whitney closed the distance between them.

"Well, it's all fixed," she announced, holding up a tiny black bag. Linking her arm through his, she pressed close to his side. "Turns out it was just the battery after all. You were right. I got myself all worried over nothing."

She fixed her gaze on Liam. "Mr. Rourke, right?"

Lillie's dad extended a hand. "Good to see you again, Whitney. And please, call me Liam." He drew Lillie into a sideways hug. "I don't think you've met my daughter. Lillie, this is Whitney."

Jase felt Whitney stiffen, and from the corner of his eye saw the slight lift of her chin.

"Lillie? *The* Lillie?"

Had Whitney intended to make it sound as though she knew all the gory details of Lillie's recent past? Because nothing could be further from the truth. Each time Whitney had pressed for information about former relationships, Jase steered the conversation in a different direction. Not to protect her so much as to spare himself the memories. Except once, early in their relationship, when she'd found a framed photo in his desk drawer. "You loved her a lot didn't you?" Whitney had asked, staring at it. When he didn't respond, she'd added, "So? What's her name?" Somehow, he managed to grind out "Lillie." Things got real quiet between them for the rest of that evening. But thankfully, the subject never came up again.

A fly buzzed by his head, rousing him from the memory.

"Yes," he said, "this is Lillie. We go way back." The image of the first time he saw her flashed in his mind. As manager of Three-Eyed Joe's and leader of the Muzikalees, he'd hired her on a probationary basis, thinking a girl singer would encourage a less rowdy crowd. From the instant she'd walked into the pub, Lillie had a positive impact on the place. The guys in the band quit cussing. People on the dance floor didn't bring their drinks with them. The bartenders and waitresses picked up on her sweet, upbeat demeanor, and served customers, even the surly ones, with smiles.

"Well, it's been lovely seeing you again, Liam, and meeting you, Lillie," Whitney said, "but Jason and I have a few more errands to run before we change for dinner at Sabatino's."

He'd all but forgotten their dinner plans. But the way she'd put it made it sound as if they were living together. And they most definitely were *not.* Lillie's eyes widened, exactly as they had when she pressed the engagement ring into his palm that night. Despite their history, he didn't like seeing her hurt.

"Sabatino's, eh?" Liam said. "That's one of our favorite restaurants in Little Italy."

Lillie, Jase noted, said nothing. *Their* favorite restaurant had always been Chiaparelli's, because they made great gnocchi.

"Well, good seeing you two," he said, shaking Liam's hand. To Lillie, he said, "See you around, kiddo."

If that look on her face was any indicator, Lillie was thinking, *Not if* I *have anything to say about it!*

"Does Dad have your contact information?"

Jase decided that mind reading wasn't among his hidden talents.

"Sure do," Liam said as Whitney pressed closer to Jase's side. "Why?"

When Lillie's big dark eyes locked on his, Jase had to remind himself to breathe. There had been a time when a look like that would have inspired him to—

"Good. I'll be in touch," she told him. "Is there a best time to call?"

"No, no, anytime's fine."

And with that, he let Whitney turn him around. Let her lead him across the parking lot, let her take his keys. The quiet *beep* indicated the doors were unlocked, effectively snapping him out of his reverie. If she offered to drive, well, he'd just have to draw the line at that.

She sat quietly for a few minutes, then said, "She's even prettier in person."

As he merged with traffic on Route 40, he silently agreed.

"How old is she?"

The question took him by surprise. "I dunno, twenty-seven, twenty-eight?"

"I should ask her what skincare products she uses. She doesn't look a day over twenty."

Should've seen her the night she left, Jase thought. By then, months of abusing her body with drugs and booze had taken a toll, painting dark circles beneath her eyes, turning her normally pink-cheeked, freckled face pale, dulling her once bright eyes. She'd lost some hair, too, and had taken to wearing knit hats and scarves, even in the summertime. And the tremors… She'd needed two hands to return the ring.

"Why do you suppose she wants to call you?"

To talk about a repayment plan? "We didn't

exactly part on a good note. I expect she wants to correct that. You know, for closure?"

He braked for a traffic light. Two more blocks, and they'd turn onto her street so she could dress up for the restaurant. Maybe his luck would continue, and she'd change her mind about eating out…

"When she calls, will she want to meet in person? To discuss…closure or whatever?"

"Guess we'll have to wait until she calls to find out. If she calls."

"If?"

Oh, she'd call, all right. And unless he was mistaken, it *would* be to discuss the money she owed him. In his mind, the balance was zero. He'd written it off ages ago. But…

"Anything's possible," he told Whitney, quickly adding, "Can we change the subject, please?"

When he pulled into her driveway, she sat, still and silent, staring through the windshield. It seemed like a full ten minutes before she said, "Would you mind very much if we skipped Sabatino's tonight?"

"Why?" *As if you don't know.*

She unbuckled her seat belt. "It's just… This has been a long week. I just need a good night's sleep."

He could have pointed out that it was only Thursday. That neither of them had worked today. But since she'd said it all without looking in his direction…

Jase felt like a heel. She was so uncomfortable she couldn't even make eye contact. He needed to take care from here on out. He didn't want to hurt her.

"I didn't mean for that to come out all mean and grouchy."

The look she gave him said "Oh, really." But she said, "Can you come in for a few minutes?"

He wanted to say no. That he was tired, too. What if that brief encounter with Lillie had made her add two and two…and come up with three's a crowd?

"Sure," he said, turning off the truck, taking his time while removing the keys from the ignition. "I'd like that."

"Leave the front door open," she said as he stepped into the foyer. "It's a gorgeous day, and the breeze will feel good."

The gray sky and the scent of impending rain didn't agree.

Whitney poured two glasses of iced tea and sat at the kitchen table. The instant he was situated, she said, "I guess that was really hard. Seeing her after all this time, I mean."

"Not really."

"You can be honest with me, Jason. No need to tiptoe around my feelings. I know that what you two had is over."

Jason. Again. Would she ever figure out how he felt about that?

"So you're okay?"

"Why wouldn't I be?"

She looked at him as though he'd grown a big hairy mole in the middle of his forehead.

"From what I've gathered, the breakup wasn't easy on you."

Jase had intentionally avoided talking about Lillie, as much to spare his feelings as hers. Because yes, the split had been difficult, for him *and* for Lillie.

"Who told you that?" he wanted to know.

"Your mom. And Dora."

He found it hard to believe his mother would bring the subject up. And even though Whitney worked at the same firm as his brother, his sister-in-law, too. He suspected Dora hadn't talked about it either. But why would Whitney make that up?

He swallowed a gulp of the tea. Concentrated on sounding cool and calm and completely in control. "How'd Lillie's name come up?"

Head tilted toward the ceiling and eyes closed, she groaned. "We… It just did, okay? Dora and Drew and I were having lunch one day. Drew admitted he was frustrated at how long it's taking to make partner, said the board's lack of commitment to the associates was getting on his last nerve. One thing led to another, and before I knew it, the conversation went from work, to family loyalty, to Drew and Dora's upcoming anniversary. And all of a sudden, Drew left the room."

Jase pretended not to have heard the family loyalty thing. "Seven years this summer." He was half joking when he added, "Drew isn't worried about the seven-year itch, I hope."

"No, no. At least, I don't think so. While we were alone, Dora told me that your mom keeps asking why she and Drew hadn't started a family yet. Dora said she'd grown super tired of answering the question. She said—and I quote—'I told her that my name isn't Lillie. Living the white-picket-fence life isn't for me.' I asked how your mother reacted. Dora said, 'Same as always. Colette just shrugged it off, said everything happens for a reason, and how lucky Jase was that Lillie's problems prevented the picket-fence life.'"

Whitney sipped her tea. "I think maybe your mother was right."

"Really." Jase stiffened. He didn't like being the focus of a conversation like that. Didn't like the way Whitney appeared to enjoy his mother's feelings toward Lillie either.

"It's easy to see why she feels that way. She probably knows how tough it would have been for you, raising a child alone, while Lillie was off...well, you know..."

Jase did his best to reel in the resentment

broiling in his gut. Whitney had no right, making assumptions about her! Yeah, he did know Lillie. Probably better than she knew herself. If they *had* married and had a baby before the accident, she never would have grown dependent on drugs, no matter how bad the pain got. Devotion to her child would have assured it. It hurt more than he cared to admit that her devotion to *him* hadn't been enough to keep Lillie from—

"When I saw you with her today," Whitney said, picking at her burlap place mat before turning her gaze to him, "I realized I needed to let you know… I'd never hurt you that way. *Never.*"

Jase bristled slightly under her intense scrutiny. Was she gearing up to say she loved him? He hoped not. They'd been seeing each other for nearly three months, and while he cared for Whitney, he wasn't anywhere ready to say those words.

Jase blanketed her hands with his own. "You look really pretty today. Did I tell you that?"

A myriad of emotions flickered across her face. Confusion. Disappointment. Hurt. To her credit, Whitney got hold of herself quickly.

"Only four or five times," she said. "But what girl doesn't like hearing her guy thinks she looks good!"

Lillie didn't. She'd waved off every word of praise that came her way, whether about her good looks or her vocal and artistic talents. "I can't take credit for any of that," she'd say. "It's built into my DNA. My parents and grandparents should be hearing the compliments, not me!"

"You sure you don't want to go to Sabatino's? We still have the reservation."

"Yeah, okay," she said, echoing his earlier words. "I'd like that."

He squeezed her hands, then let go as she stood.

"Just give me a few minutes to freshen up."

While she was gone, he walked from the kitchen to the living room, where she'd arranged sleek, modern furnishings on a white shag rug. Tall narrow black figurines stood on the marble mantel, and heavy swirled-glass bowls decorated the teak coffee table. He could see storm clouds through the sheer white curtains.

"You about ready, Whit? Looks like we're in for some rain…"

"Just two more minutes, hon," he heard her say from the bathroom doorway.

Hon. If anyone else had said it, Jase would have chalked it up to a "Baltimore-ism." But Whitney had never been one to imitate others.

Unlike Lillie, who loved colloquialisms and spouted them every chance she got.

He caught himself smiling, and didn't like it one bit. Jase ground a fist into a palm. He'd worked hard to get her out of his system, to get on with life, without her. And he'd succeeded. He couldn't—*wouldn't*—let her destroy that!

"IT'S ABOUT TIME you got here." Jase's sister-in-law leaned in and lowered her voice. "Your mom is looking a mite peaked today."

"Is that right." He hadn't planned on stopping by to visit his mother this evening, so her snappish comment didn't make sense. "She looked fine when I was here the day before yesterday."

Dora huffed. "Well, she doesn't look fine now. She's in her office." She made a shooing motion with her hand. "Go. I'll bring you both some iced tea."

"Okay, thanks. That sounds great." He paused in the kitchen doorway. "Where's Drew?"

Dora rolled her eyes. "Working. Naturally."

Perhaps that explained her surly mood. "You and that brother of mine put in way too many hours." He would have added, *It's probably a good thing that you two don't have kids*, but his dad had made that mistake once, years back, and immediately regretted it. "He's joining us for supper though, right?"

"Your guess is as good as mine."

"He's nuts if he doesn't show up. Something smells delicious."

"Stuffed shells. My grandmother's recipe."

"Now I'm glad my dinner date was canceled."

"Oh? Trouble in paradise, huh?"

In place of an answer, Jase raised his eyebrows.

"Let me be more precise. Are you and Whitney fighting?"

"No." Times like these, he didn't need to remind himself that Dora was a lawyer. "Why do you ask?"

"You look a little down."

"It's been a long, weird day." Weird, and exhausting. The on-then-off-then-on-again restaurant date had killed his appetite, and he'd been relieved when Whitney called it off…again. When she'd come out of the bathroom, the bad weather seemed to have shifted her mood again, and she'd asked for a raincheck.

Dora shrugged. "This is out of line, so I'll apologize ahead of time for saying, right up front, that I'll never understand what you see in her."

Jase stepped back into the kitchen.

"She seems nice enough, and there's no denying she's smart. Everyone at the firm thinks so. But I get the feeling you're not very comfortable with her. Whenever she's around, you seem like you're walking on eggshells."

Women's intuition? Or more proof that she was a good attorney? Jase had always worked hard to keep things like that to himself.

Dora held up a hand and continued with, "I know you didn't ask, but if you had, I'd say you just don't seem happy with her. Not like you were with Lillie, anyway. I loved watching you two together, the way you'd go back and forth, cracking jokes, laughing, so at ease with one another."

Jase had never put much stock in metaphysical stuff, but it sure did seem like the universe was conspiring against him today. First, he'd run into Lillie and her dad. Then, Whitney got all bent out of shape over the meeting. And now, here was Dora, telling him that he'd seemed more content with Lillie than with Whitney. Had she forgotten everything Lillie had put him through, everything she'd cost him? Did she think *he'd* forgotten?

Dora pressed a tumbler against the ice dispenser. "I know what you're thinking," she said as cubes clinked into the glass. "You think I've forgotten everything that happened after her accident. To be more precise, everything she *did* after the accident." She filled a second glass with ice and all but slammed it onto the counter. "You know we were friends. I remember how quickly she went downhill. Was I hurt by it? Of course. Was I disappointed in her? You bet! But addiction is a sickness, Jase. If her doctors hadn't overprescribed those meds in the first place, then cut her off just like *that*..." She snapped her fingers. "Suffice it to say we could all have been there for her. We were supposed to love and support her."

He *had* loved Lillie, more than he'd loved any

woman before or since. Loved her still, despite his best efforts to smother it. As for being supportive, how many chances was he supposed to give her?

"Look, Dora, I know you mean well, but trust me, there were a lot of things you didn't see or hear, things I've never talked about." Like the times Lillie had overdosed, and if he hadn't been around to rush her to the ER…

He knuckled his eyes, hoping to rub away the painful images. "Anyway, I appreciate your concern, but you can relax. Whitney and I aren't fighting."

She stared at him for a few seconds before saying, "That's good, because you're the closest thing I have to a brother, and I want you to be happy."

"I have everything a guy could want—good job as CEO of a thriving company, nice condo, enough money to keep the wolf from the door, loving family, gorgeous, successful girlfriend—who just hinted that she loves me, for your information—so why on earth *wouldn't* I be happy."

"Oh, Jase…she did?"

Unless he'd lost all people-reading skills, Dora looked pained.

"How did you handle that?"

"If she actually says it, well, I'll cross that bridge when we get to it."

Months ago, he'd decided to give up on dating.

He'd had it with well-intentioned friends trying to set him up with the perfect woman, one who'd help him get over Lillie. And then, at one of Drew and Dora's shindigs, he'd met Whitney. She wasn't *perfect*, but then, neither was he. Besides, perfection was overrated. A satisfying existence could be just as fulfilling as a happy one, right? And he sure didn't appreciate the *cosmos*, or whatever it was, interfering with his almost perfect life.

Jase picked up the glasses, and as he turned to leave the kitchen, he grazed Dora's cheek with a brotherly kiss.

"Thanks for caring, *sis*. And just so you know, I love you, too."

He could still see her tiny grin as he rounded the corner into his mother's office.

Colette was lounging in her favorite chair—a flowery, overstuffed thing that was wide enough to accommodate a linebacker—a romance novel in her lap. She'd kicked off her shoes and propped both stockinged feet on the matching ottoman.

"You're early," she said, glancing up from her book.

"Early? You didn't even know I was coming over tonight." He put the iced tea glasses on coasters, then sat on the end of the sofa nearest her chair.

She used her thumb to mark her place in the paperback. "I thought maybe since that little set-to with Whitney caused you to miss dinner at Sabatino's…"

"Set-to?" He hadn't seen it that way at all. But wait… "How'd you hear about that? I only left her place half an hour ago."

She fluffed chin-length white hair. "Dora got a phone call not long after she got here. Guess who it was."

Yet again, he was reminded of the Drew-Dora-Whitney connection down at the law office.

"She's such a lovely young woman. So soft-spoken and ladylike. She'll make someone a wonderful wife, and be a great mother someday. That someone could be you…if you don't blow it, pining over Lillie. That girl put you through the wringer."

Once upon a time, his mom had cared for Lillie as if she'd been one of her own, often making excuses for her erratic behavior. Until she caught Lillie slipping a hundred dollars from her wallet. Colette had been furious when she'd told him about it. "Not because I need the money," she'd said, "but because Lillie has made fools of all of us." She'd gone on to say that unless the craziness with the drugs stopped, Lillie would break his heart. Deep down, he'd known his mother was right but had held out for a miracle. And a week later…

Jase pressed fingertips together, and like a spider doing pushups on a mirror, flexed and relaxed, flexed and relaxed his hands. He knew his mom had received a check a month or so ago. Lillie hadn't succeeded in getting money from Colette, and yet she'd paid back every dollar she'd *almost* stolen. In private moments, Jase admitted the sincere words in the note Lillie had included for Colette had touched him, too.

"So how are you feeling, Mom?"

Blue eyes narrowed to mere slits, and her left brow rose high on her forehead. It was the look she'd branded him and Drew with as boys, when she suspected they'd broken a household item or violated a rule.

"Why do you ask? What did Dora tell you?"

"Only that you looked a little pale today."

"I love her to pieces, but that girl can be such a fussbudget."

Jase grinned. "I have to admit, it's hard to believe that just a month ago, you were rushed to the hospital."

"Oh, that." She waved a pink-taloned hand. "Just a little TIA. I'm following doctor's orders to the letter, so all's well."

"Just a little TIA," he echoed. The symptoms of a transient ischemic attack included weakness, double vision, dizziness, numbness on the left side of her face…all of which she'd exhibited before he'd dialed 911. And all of which could lead to another, more serious stroke.

"It was just a ministroke, honey. Don't make more of it than there was."

"Is."

"Semantics. All you need to know is that I'm fine now. And as long as I keep doing what Doctor Ginnan says, I'll stay that way." She leaned forward to pat his hand. "Besides, I have the best business partner this side of the Rockies." Colette winked. "And don't give me that look. You love running the company almost as much as you love being on TV."

He couldn't deny it. What had started as Jase helping out with bookkeeping and ordering supplies for his mom's little craft shop had developed into Jase subbing for her on cable TV's most prominent shopping network. He'd felt silly at first, standing beside the show hosts, describing his mom's handcrafted wooden and ceramic birdhouses, wall decorations, lawn ornaments and colorful bakeware. Before long, though, her products grew so popular that she'd had to sign on with a manufacturing company to mass-produce her can't-get-them-elsewhere items. Even before the money started rolling in, Jase looked forward to monthly flights to Florida to do live shows during which audience members, mostly women, called in to ooh and aah over Colette's Crafts...and flirt with him.

"You've been a huge help to me, honey. If not for you, I'd still be operating out of this office-slash-parlor-slash-library-slash-craft room." She hesitated. "You know, if you need a break, we're doing well enough to afford to hire an actor to take your place on the show."

"Why would we do that?"

"So you can get back to your music, part-time, of course, because I need you as CEO. And maybe even tell Whitney that you love her, too, settle down and start a family." She sniffed. "At the rate you and Drew are going, I'll be a decrepit old woman before I become a grandmother."

"Wait. *Too?*"

"Don't look so surprised. We've sort of become friends. And friends confide in one another."

Things like *I love your son*?

"For one thing, the subject of *love* has never come up." He wished he hadn't just told Dora that it might. "For another, I don't much appreciate finding out that my mother and the woman I'm dating are talking about stuff like that behind my back." He cringed. "It's creepy."

"She's more than just the woman you're dating."

He could only stare in disbelief.

"She's your girlfriend."

"Mom..."

"Well? Do you?"

"Do I what?" *As if you didn't know...*

"Good grief, Jase, don't be so obtuse. Do you love Whitney, or not?"

Jase could admit that he enjoyed spending

time with her. And that it felt pretty good, seeing a twinge of envy on other guys' faces when he entered a room with the gorgeous blonde on his arm. But love?

"Mom, I—"

"Are you hesitating because you're still in love with Lillie?"

"No way." He tried to sound like he meant it. "You're right. She messed up my head, bad. I have no desire to go through that again."

"Not even now that she's home again, supposedly cured of her addiction?"

Whitney couldn't have told her about *that*, because to his knowledge, Whitney knew almost nothing about Lillie's drug history. Unless…

"Please tell me you didn't discuss Lillie's past with Whitney."

"What difference would it make if I did…if you're over Lillie?"

"Whitney told you we ran into her and Liam today, didn't she."

"Yes. So?"

"So I don't appreciate having my personal business broadcast all over town."

She and Dora had both accused him of having trust issues. Was it any wonder!

Colette clucked her tongue. "First of all, I realize I've gained a few pounds, recovering from the TIA, but I'm certainly not big enough to be referred to as a whole town. And second, you were with Whitney when you ran into Lillie. I'd say that makes it her business, too. And if she wants to share a thing like that with me..." She shrugged. "Jase. Honey. I just want you to be happy."

Almost word for word what Dora had said. Seemed a pretty feeble way to excuse their intrusion into his personal business.

"I pray every night that Whitney is the woman who'll make your heart skip a beat, who'll take your breath away. That she'll make you smile just by walking into a room. Your father made me feel like that, right up until the end."

And that, Jase believed, was part of the problem. As Lillie disappeared down the rabbit hole, over and over, he'd lost faith in her. Lost his confidence in his ability to tell the truth from a lie. How was he supposed to connect with a woman—or trust one for that matter—when he couldn't trust his own judgment?

He was in too deep to change the subject now, so he said, "I don't mind admitting, I'm a little envious of what you and dad had."

"There's something to be said for old-shoe comfort, for that spark that makes you...well, you know." She giggled. "I tell you, that father of yours had the power to make me go weak in the knees with nothing more than a look. And when he kissed me?" She rested a hand over her heart, then finished with a mischievous wink.

She threw back her head and laughed. Then, as suddenly as it began, her laughter subsided. "I have a question for you, son."

"Uh-oh," Jase said. "I'm almost afraid to hear it."

She went on as though he hadn't spoken. "When you kiss Whitney, does your heart skip a beat? Does the breath catch in your throat? Do *your* knees go weak?"

"That was three questions."

"Despite my advancing age and allegedly frail condition, I'm not that easily distracted."

Jase could answer all of her questions with a single word: *no.*

Because he'd felt that way only with Lillie.

He'd loved her, maybe too much, and it galled him that she'd chosen drugs over him.

Seeing her today proved two things. First, despite his denials, he still felt something for her. And second, self-preservation told him that he needed to smother it, fast.

Love without trust was a recipe for agony.

And he didn't believe he had the mettle to lose her again.

CHAPTER THREE

"THERE SHE GOES AGAIN," Molly said, "with her 'back in the old days' reference."

Since returning home, that was how Lillie referred to her life before the accident. The phrase inspired relentless teasing from her siblings—a whole lot easier to bear than the standoffish behavior they'd displayed prior to the repayment of every dollar borrowed and stolen—and her heartfelt apologies.

In response to her sister's latest dig, Lillie said, "At least I didn't commit marital alliteration. Matt and Molly, I mean really."

"Marital alliteration?" Her brother reared back with mock surprise. "She dragged the dictionary out for that one, and much as I hate to admit it, she's right!"

Arms crossed, Molly huffed. "You're a fine one to talk, *Sam*, marrying a girl with the same name."

Liam's laughter filled the sunny yard as his wife said, "All right you guys, if you want to eat later, get back to work!"

The construction crew had completed the exterior work and moved inside to put the finishing touches on the kitchen addition. That left the outside clear for Lillie's family to work on. Plants that had grown in beds around the old porch now stood in lopsided plastic pots along the back fence.

"Lillie, would you mind going around front to tend the rose garden? I know the crew tried to be careful, but they made a huge mess out there. You have the magic touch, maybe you can save them."

Lillie grabbed a shovel, a trowel and her garden gloves. "Happy to, Mom." And she meant it. Working out front would allow her to contribute to the cleanup project while ignoring the occasional sidelong glance or raised eyebrow, proof the family wasn't entirely convinced of her trustworthiness.

After fertilizing and replanting several rose shrubs, Lillie decided to form a border around the bed by moving dozens of marigolds and zinnias from the side yard. Standing back, she gave her work an admiring nod. "Not bad if I do say so myself," she said.

"Self-confidence looks good on you."

Startled, she spun quickly around, nearly losing her balance. If Jase hadn't grabbed both biceps, Lillie would have landed on the spade's sharp blade. She couldn't remember the last time they'd stood so close.

Blue eyes boring into hers, he said, "Didn't mean to scare you."

He turned her loose and took a step back, and she saw she'd left muddy handprints on his white shirt.

She removed her right glove and made a half-baked attempt to brush away the dirt. Sadly, it only made the mess worse. "Omigarsh. Look what I've done. I'm so sorry. And this looks like a freshly pressed shirt, too." And his jeans were dark, making him appear taller and slimmer than she remembered.

"It's okay. Couple squirts with some stain remover and it'll be good as new."

He pointed at the flowers. "Nice job. You always did have an artistic eye. And a gift for stuff like this."

"Thanks." Just as she had weeks ago outside the Flower Basket, Lillie struggled for the right words. But what could she say? She'd promised to call him and hadn't. Would he see that as proof she was still untrustworthy?

"Guess your dad doesn't have my number after all."

So, his mindreading talents hadn't faltered while she'd been in New York.

"He probably does, but to tell the truth, I never asked for it. I've been working a lot of extra hours, waiting tables and clerking at the hotel up the street. Unfortunately, I'm still a couple hundred dollars short of what I owe you."

His Orioles cap shaded the upper half of his handsome face, but not enough to hide his furrowed brow.

"You don't owe me anything, Lill. Really."

"Are you kidding? Of course I do. If you'd like, I can write you a check right now, and pay the rest just as soon as I've earned it."

Feet planted shoulder-width apart and arms crossed over his broad chest, he studied her. Because he hadn't answered any of his questions? Or because of what she still owed him?

"Two jobs. In addition to helping out around here. When do you sleep?"

In fits and starts, she thought. *A guilty conscience will do that to a gal.*

She considered joking her way through a response, when he asked, "You have wheels?"

"I borrow Mom's car when I need to drive someplace."

"That's gotta be tough on somebody like you."

Somebody like her? This whole conversation felt forced. Stilted. Uncomfortable. Good as it was to see him again, she wished he'd just leave.

"What I mean is, you used to be so independent."

Used to be, as in, *before you became an out-of-control, thieving drug addict.*

"So you're walking to and from your jobs?"

"Unless it's pouring rain. I'd walk then, too, if Mom didn't insist that I drive."

"Uh-huh."

She wished he'd yell at her. Curse at her. Give her a stern talking-to. Anything was preferable to this oh-so-calm stoic demeanor that told her he didn't care enough to let anything she did rile him. Right now, Lillie wished she'd spent a lot more time talking with her therapist about her feelings for Jase. Seeing him at the flower shop had rocked her, but not nearly as much as standing mere feet from him.

"So, which restaurant?"

"The Sip & Bite."

"And I'm guessing since you're hoofing it, you're clerking at the inn at Henderson's Wharf?"

"Mmm-hmm."

Why did he care? He didn't love her anymore. *The way you still—*

"Why not wait tables in their restaurant?"

"There weren't any openings when I applied. Besides, I can pretty much choose my schedule at the Sip & Bite. And the tips are great."

Jase's brows drew together. "Do you ever miss being onstage, singing?"

"I'll say. It's one of the reasons I started volunteering at Hopkins' Children's Oncology. Some days I sing to the kids, other days I paint faces."

He thumbed his cap back, causing some of his shining black hair to fall forward, hiding one eyebrow. Skeptical was as close as she could come to describing his expression. Had she hurt him so badly that he couldn't believe it possible for her to spend time with sick children? That shamed her. Hurt her, too. But, she had no right to feel anything but sorry for all she'd put him through.

"I hate to sound redundant, but with two jobs, helping out around here, and putting in time at the hospital, when *do* you sleep?"

Now that he knew she couldn't repay him—*yet*—why was he still here? To make her regret losing him even more than she already did?

Maybe a change of subject would put them both at ease. "Saw you on TV the other day." He'd looked so handsome. So at ease, smiling for the camera, making small talk with the show's host. Thankfully, she'd been alone in the family room, so no one had seen her drop onto the couch cushions and blubber into a throw pillow. "You're a natural."

"It's a different way to make a living, I'll admit, but since Mom's stroke—"

"What! Stroke? When did that happen? How bad was it? Is she all right?"

He held up a hand. "Whoa. Easy, girl." Grinning, he said, "She's fine. Happened a couple months back. Doc says she should be fine as long as she takes her meds, exercises, eats smart."

She felt selfish. Self-centered. Childish. Because in all the time she'd been away, her only contact with Colette had been when she placed a check into a carefully chosen greeting card that featured lilacs, Colette's favorite flowers. According to her bank statement, the check had been cashed almost immediately, eliminating the need to call and make sure Jase's mom had received the payment. It had been a relief, but sad, too, because she and Colette had once been almost as close as mother and daughter. One more loss to chalk up to the addiction…

"You'll be happy to know that Mom is as spry and spunky as ever."

Lillie inhaled a deep breath and let it out slowly. "Thank goodness. I suppose I should give her a call. Or better still, stop by with a little get-well gift."

As soon as the words were out, she regretted them. Some people, her counselor had stressed, would never fully get over what she'd done to them.

Yet again, she wondered why he'd stopped by. He didn't have a mean bone in his body, so it surely hadn't really been to torment her…

"Mom and Dad are out back, cleaning up after the construction crew. The Sams and Matt and

Molly and the twins are back there, too. I'm sure they'd—"

"I didn't come here to see them."

Despite the heat of the day, a chill snaked up her spine. She'd already made it clear that, unless he was willing to take a partial payment, she couldn't reimburse him.

"Your..." Lillie couldn't bring herself to say *girlfriend.* "Whitney seems nice." *She's pretty, too. And tall.*

Lips narrowed, Jase stared at the ground between his feet. Lillie had seen that grim look only once before, on the night he'd listed every way and every time she'd let him down. It took months to figure out why, in addition to anger and disappointment, guilt had flashed in his eyes that night: exercising tough love had been hard on him. But why did he look that way now, at the mention of Whitney?

His right hand shot out, startling her.

"Sorry. Didn't mean to scare you again. Just didn't want this guy getting all tangled up in your curls."

Oh, he scared her, all right. But not because he held a daddy longlegs by one spindly appendage.

A tense snicker popped from her lips. "Yeah, well, maybe getting stuck would have been a good lesson for him. Hard to tell how long he would have been trapped in there!"

One corner of his mouth lifted in a slight grin. "A lesson. For a spider."

"Then *he'd* know how helpless it feels." She tucked a wayward wave behind her ear. "Being trapped, like the flies and moths he catches in his web, I mean."

If she had to guess, Lillie would say he shared her next thought: *I know exactly how* that *feels.* She'd been trapped by addiction, and so had Jase because he'd loved someone in the trap.

"Are you thirsty? I made iced tea and lemonade this morning. We could drink it on the porch, out of the hot sun."

Jase shot a quick glance at the porch and the row of rocking chairs that flanked the big double doors. Was he remembering, too, the way they'd whiled away the hours, counting stars, strumming guitars and finessing harmonies of new songs, or designing their future as crickets chirped and night birds peeped?

"No thanks, can't stay. Just stopped by to say hi, and see how you're adjusting to being home again."

Home again. Not long after she joined the band, he'd written a song with that title, saying when he introduced it that he hoped it would inspire her to stay in Baltimore, rather than going back to touring the country.

Lillie shook off the bittersweet memory. "It's all good." It wasn't. Not when she remembered the reactions of everyone she'd repaid. Not when she admitted they might remain leery of her. "I haven't *used* in a long, long time, so I'm healthy, too, physically and emotionally." She sighed. "Much to the surprise of just about everyone."

"Who's everyone?"

"Family, friends, the guys in the band." *And you...* "Not that I blame them." She tugged off the other work glove. "A lot of water passed under the bridge."

"More like a flood."

Lillie couldn't very well disagree. Face the discomfort, she told herself. Face it head-on.

"Yeah," she said. "It's only natural that people doubt a full recovery. Even after talking with the rehab staff..." She shook her head. "I don't expect most of the people in my life will forgive and forget easily. I realize that I still have a lot to prove." Should she say it? Lillie went for broke: "To everyone."

She braced herself, waiting for Jase to agree that he, too, was still wary.

"I can't be a hundred percent certain," she went on, "but it seems at least Mom and Dad have confidence in me again."

"But not the Sams, or Molly and Matt."

"Oh, they're all being really nice. I think they know how hard I'm trying, but—"

"A case of 'do or do not, there *is* no try,' huh?"

If she'd had her way, their first real conversation wouldn't have been anything like this. For starters, she'd have called him, arranged a time and place to deliver the money she owed, and in place of muddy sneakers, holey jeans and a paint-spattered cap, she would have shown up in something feminine and colorful. Lillie had never minded his take-charge personality. It was how he'd stayed on top of things as manager of the pub, what helped him turn his mother's business into a thriving corporation. Without that trait, he wouldn't have looked and sounded so professional on TV.

Right now, though, Lillie wouldn't have complained if Jase was a bit less competent.

In all fairness, Jase wasn't responsible for how bleak she felt. Her addiction was. One of the toughest things about coming home had been seeing and hearing for herself that everything they'd said at Rising Sun had been true: *you may never win back their trust, so remember, you're doing this for yourself.* Lillie felt strong enough to cope with that for now, but what if her loved ones felt the same way in six months or a year? Would she be strong enough *then*?

"Aw, quit looking so glum, Lill. I watched you tough it out through those awful exercises during physical therapy. And you wouldn't be here if you hadn't toughed out rehab, too. You've got that going for you, plus, you're stubborn. More stubborn than anyone I know. *If* you really want to beat this thing—permanently this time—you will."

If? Why the extra emphasis on the word?

"So how long have you and Whitney been dating?" Lillie hoped he wouldn't tell her there was more to the relationship than that.

"Not long. Couple months, give or take."

Her dad implied that Jase had seen other women, too, since their breakup. Any rational person would agree that he had every right to move on. At the moment, Lillie wasn't feeling very rational.

She started to ask how they'd met when he stopped her with "I, uh, I guess I'd better head out. Need to get dog food, pick up some groceries and stuff."

"When did you get a dog? What breed is it?"

This time his quiet laughter sounded halfway sincere. "It isn't mine, it's Mom's. He's a mutt. German shepherd–Doberman–Irish setter mix, near as the vet can tell. Good-lookin' pup, but big. And sheds enough to make a whole other dog. Ronald showed up at her door one day, and stayed."

Lillie smiled at that. "Ronald, huh?" She remembered the full-color autographed photo of the former president on Colette's office wall, right beside the letter he'd dictated, detailing the country's appreciation for Jase's dad's years of military service.

Jase only nodded.

"I'm sure she's grateful for the companionship, especially since you and Drew and Dora travel so much."

A look of disbelief crossed his face, and he took a half step back.

"I didn't mean for that to sound like I think you aren't doing enough for Colette. I'm sure you're there every chance you get. Drew and Dora, too. I haven't exactly earned any daughter-of-the-year points, so I have *no* room to talk."

Jase's eyes narrowed just enough to tell her he wasn't sure whether to believe her.

"Anyway," he said, replacing his cap, "I'm outta here. It's good to see you're doing well, Lill."

"Good to see you, too, Jase." Saying his name brought forth the memory of Whitney, calling him Jason. "You *are* still going by Jase, right?"

"Of course. You know how I feel about being called Jason."

"I only asked because the other day, Whitney—"

The muscles in his jaw tensed. "Yeah, she's the only person who calls me that. I've kinda learned to live with it."

He sounded as annoyed as he looked. Difficult as it was to take Whitney's side, Lillie said, "She probably just wants to make sure everyone knows that her relationship with you is different—more special—than any other."

"I guess that might explain it."

Although he followed up with a dry chuckle, Lillie sensed that he wasn't happy. She tried a different tack.

"Have you told her that you prefer Jase?"

"Not in so many words." Jase removed the cap again, ran a hand through his dark hair. "Well, I have to go."

A strange twinge pinched at her heart: What if…what if he'd stopped by to tell her he'd proposed to Whitney, but decided she wasn't strong enough yet to hear the news?

"Didn't mean to take you away from your work."

"You didn't."

Lillie held her breath, hoping he'd say, *When can I see you again?* or better still, *I've missed you, Lill.* He nodded and made a thin line of his mouth. His "I don't know what to say, so I won't say anything" face, she remembered. "You're welcome here anytime, Jase."

Just then, his cell phone dinged. A worry line creased his forehead as he read the caller ID screen. Whitney. Lillie would have bet her wheelbarrow on it.

Jase slid wraparound sunglasses from his shirt pocket.

"See you around, Lill," he said, and made his way down the driveway.

It wasn't what she'd hoped to hear, but it beat "goodbye."

Lillie faced the rows of marigolds and zinnias she'd planted in front of the roses. Funny, but they looked even brighter through the sheen of tears.

The counselors had cautioned her against expecting anything more than an arm's-length friendship with Jase, and yet, somewhere deep in her heart, she'd hidden a glimmer of hope that when he realized how much she'd changed…

"Oh my, Lillie," her mother said, leaning over the railing. "You've done a beautiful job! Are you almost finished?"

Turning so her mom wouldn't see her tears, Lillie said, "I just need to give everything a good soaking and put away the tools."

"Well, well, well. Will you look at this," Liam said, coming to stand beside Amelia. "Looks like a professional landscaper did the work."

Lillie couldn't thank him for the compliment, because a sob ached in her throat.

"Hot dogs and hamburgers are ready, kitten, and your mom made her famous potato salad."

Her mother took a step forward. "Are you all right, honey?"

"Just a little tired. Not used to being on my hands and knees," she croaked out. It was only a half lie. The ache in her leg—so familiar since her accident—had flared up during all the yardwork. She'd be limping tomorrow.

"You must be famished. A good thing, because Sam is about to take the meat off the grill."

"Are we eating out back?"

Liam said, "Yup. Red-checkered tablecloth, the whole nine yards." Her dad started down the steps. "Let me help you clean up."

Lillie twisted the hose nozzle and gasped when water spritzed the upper half of her body.

Another good thing, as it turned out, because the droplets camouflaged her tears.

CHAPTER FOUR

"I WISH YOU didn't have to go." Whitney leaned her head on his shoulder. "I was so looking forward to introducing you to the new partner."

Jase grabbed a handful of popcorn and stared at the preview on the movie screen. "He'll be with the firm for years. I'm sure we'll get together some other time."

She snuggled closer. "Are you sure you can't get out of it? Just this once?"

"I think I know why your parents spoiled you."

"I'm *not* spoiled."

Said the girl who drove a Mercedes at sixteen. Attended Vanderbilt, despite so-so grades. Owned a town house in an upscale neighborhood—a graduation gift from her folks.

"You're right. Sorry," Jase said, meaning it. Since signing on with the law firm, Whitney had earned everything she called hers.

"Because I'd hate to think you feel that way about me."

Even pouting, Jase thought, she was a knock-out. Not as pretty as Lillie, but gorgeous nonetheless.

"Sorry," he said again. Not because he'd almost called her a nag, but because he couldn't stop thinking about Lillie, or comparing her to Whitney. It wasn't fair to either woman.

Jase needed space, and time to clear his head. Standing in the aisle beside his seat, he leaned in to say, "How about some candy? I'm in the mood for Milk Duds."

"The lines will be long, Jason. I hate to ask you to put yourself through that."

"You aren't asking. I offered, remember? So what'll it be? Peanut butter cups? Chocolate-covered raisins?"

"How about a salted pretzel?"

Jase winked and made the thumbs-up sign. "Consider it done."

Whitney had been right; the lines were twenty deep at every cash register. Most nights, he would have walked right back into the theater. Tonight, he considered it therapy. He had to figure out exactly how he felt about Lillie. He knew he still loved her. He'd probably always love her. Enough to set aside his suspicion? Therein, as the bard might have said, lies the rub.

A family of four left the counter, and Jase moved forward a few spaces.

A new thought occurred to him. What if part

of her therapy was to make amends and repayments...and then sever ties with everyone who'd been a part of her life as an addict?

The kid at the counter said, "Can I help you, sir?" And from the look on his face—and the faces of the people to his right and left—Jase realized the boy had said it more than once.

"Salted pretzel, please. And some of those." He pointed, and the cashier grabbed a yellow box. "Two waters, too."

He paid for his order and somehow managed to make it back to the theater without dropping anything. Halfway between the entrance and their seats, Jase wondered if Whitney liked mustard on her pretzel. *If she does*, his Lillie-addled brain answered, *she'll have to eat this one plain.*

By the time he reached her, the movie's opening credits filled the screen. Fortunately, this was a screening of a classic movie he'd seen before, so if Whitney wanted to talk about it during the ride to her place, he wouldn't sound like a complete idiot.

Even though you are *a complete idiot.*

The whole what-if question echoed in his head, even as the story unfolded, even as he took Whitney's elbow and led her across the parking lot, even as he helped her into the cab of his pickup. It would solve all of his problems if Lillie's counselors had told her to leave him in the dust.

Right?

"You're awfully quiet," Whitney said. "Thinking about your trip to Florida?"

Jase nodded as he backed out of the parking space.

"Have you packed?"

"Not yet."

"You'll get it done in no time. As many times as you've made this trip, I'll bet you can prepare for it in your sleep. Besides, you'll only be gone for a few days."

"I guess." Maybe he needed to have a talk with Lillie, face-to-face, find out where she stood on the subject of *them*.

"You're not angry with me are you, for making you take me out tonight, when you could have been home, getting things ready?"

"No, Whitney. I'm not angry. And you didn't make me take you out tonight. I'm here willingly."

"You're sure?"

"I'm sure." Why couldn't she be a little more like Lillie, comfortable with companionable silences?

Whitney fiddled with the radio, stopping when a rap song filled the cab. If it had been Lillie sitting over there, he'd be listening to country right now. Oldies but goodies. Jazz or blues. Anything but rap. Again, a familiar annoyance simmered in his gut. He wasn't irritated with Whitney *or* Lillie. He was mad at himself for behaving like a spineless goofball, incapable of making up his mind *or* controlling his emotions.

Reaching across the console, he grasped Whitney's hand. "I know I wasn't the best company tonight, and when I get back, you can arrange dinner with the new partner and his wife. Someplace nice. My treat." He gave her hand a light squeeze. "Sound good?"

She returned the squeeze. "I can't very well turn down a deal like that, can I?" Grinning, she added, "Not without sounding spoiled, anyway."

"Very funny," he said, winking again.

It wasn't in her wheelhouse to crack jokes, and he appreciated her effort to lighten the mood.

"Did the show send your schedule?"

The producers from the shopping network had always made sure he knew well in advance what time he'd be on-air. And Whitney was aware of this, too.

"Yup."

"When you get a minute, will you take a screenshot of it, so I'll know when it's okay to call? I'd hate to interrupt you while you're in the middle of describing one of your mom's crafts."

During his trip a few weeks earlier, she'd called and texted a dozen times a day. Called at night, too. And once, his cell phone had buzzed while he was on-air during the Father's Day specials—loudly enough that the mic picked it up. His own fault. He should have left it in the dressing room.

"'Course."

"You'll call every day?"

"Sure."

An odd thought popped into his head. She hadn't been clingy or possessive before meeting Lillie. She'd even started referring to his past as "the Lillie years." He'd assure her that things had ended between him and Lillie a long time ago…except, he wasn't sure that was the truth. Or that he wanted it to be the truth.

"Good. Because I'll miss you."

"Me, too."

"I don't know why, but it always seems you're gone for weeks, instead of a few days."

Always? He'd gone to Florida only two other times since they'd met. But he'd been quiet and standoffish all night. What could it hurt to say something nice?

"Since you're like a human World Clock, maybe you can be my wake-up call every morning."

"Give me a minute to collect myself," she said. "I don't want to appear overeager. What would my fellow feminists say if they heard me gushing like a schoolgirl at the chance to rouse her *boyfriend* while he's on a business trip?"

Boyfriend. Jase didn't know how he felt about that.

"Fellow feminists," he said. "Is that an oxymoron?"

She laughed. His mother may just have been right when she'd said that Whitney could be good for him…if he'd let her.

Jase nodded and smiled, smiled and nodded as she talked about the movie's plot, the weather, the legal brief she needed to finesse for a pretrial hearing in the morning.

"Are you sure you can't come in?" she asked, leaning into him.

"I'm sure. I need to get home, throw a few things in a bag. Besides, you have that brief to work on."

Hands on his shoulders, Whitney kissed him, slowly, longingly. He waited for the weak-in-the-knees, heart-pounding reaction his mother had described. When it didn't happen, Jase blamed himself. Maybe if he put a little more into it…

Still nothing.

"Drive safely," she said when it ended, "and pack some immune boosters. You don't want to catch a cold, breathing that recirculated air on the plane. Not a good idea to drink coffee or tea, or let the flight attendant put ice in your drink. I read an article that said there are swarms of bacteria in the water system and the ice maker."

Jase chuckled quietly. "Swarms, huh?"

"Hordes, even!"

"It's sweet of you to be so concerned about my health."

"Completely self-centered," she said, smiling

prettily. "I want you coming back to me hale and hearty."

She cared about him, and he'd done nothing to earn it. It was time to leave Lillie in the past, and let this relationship take its course. Whitney deserved that, at the very least.

"MR. YEAGER," THE flight attendant said, "it's good to see you again so soon!"

"Good to see you, too, Gloria." He'd made this same flight between Baltimore and Miami and back again dozens of times, and knew the flight crew by name.

The woman in line ahead of him turned and said to her husband, "Oh my goodness, Fred, it's Jase Yeager, from the TV shopping club!"

Fred gave a half-hearted smile. "Thanks to you, the UPS truck pulls into our driveway out of habit, even on the rare day when Vera *hasn't* ordered something."

"We appreciate your support, Vera." One hand on Fred's shoulder, he added, "And yours, too."

Vera dug around in her purse and came up with a pen, then slid her boarding pass out of her husband's pocket. "Give him yours, too, Fred, so he can sign them for us."

Jase didn't think he'd ever get used to being recognized, at the gas station, in the grocery store, on airplanes. "Happy travels," he wrote on each, then scribbled his signature.

Delighted, the couple moved into the cabin and Gloria said, "You know, Mr. Yeager, with those long legs of yours, you'd be much more comfortable in first class."

He'd considered it. Colette's Crafts was doing well. So well in fact that the company could certainly afford the upgrade. But he couldn't in good conscience spend money on his own creature comforts when his mother and their employees might need it down the road. Besides, he'd gone the first-class route a time or two, for pleasure trips, and didn't see the point for such a short flight.

"It's only a two-hour flight. But thanks for the suggestion. If I ever book a transcontinental flight, I'll keep that in mind."

She waited until he was situated, then bent at the waist and, smiling wider still, whispered, "Maybe I can rustle you up an extra bag of peanuts."

The woman to his right snickered. "Who does she think *she's* fooling? We'll *all* get a second bag of peanuts."

Jase smiled and nodded, then slid a paperback from his briefcase and hoped she'd take the hint: he'd rather not chitchat all the way to Miami. He had a lot of thinking to do.

His mom's health scare had inspired her to move "become a grandmother" to the top of her bucket list. Which put pressure on him. He needed to figure out why he didn't love Whitney. She was as close to perfect as a woman could get. She'd even put up with his bad temper lately.

Yup, he needed to make a decision, for her sake, not his. A woman like that deserved a man who'd give her his whole heart. He couldn't do that. Not until he'd resolved things with Lillie. It simply wasn't fair to string Whitney along while he made up his mind.

Any time he or Drew put things off, his dad liked to say, "What're you waiting for, an engraved invitation?"

The question provoked the image of a white trifold card inviting everyone to his and Whitney's wedding…

He gritted his teeth. This had to stop, and soon, but for the life of him, he didn't know *how.*

Too much time on your hands, that's what. It was time, he decided, to drag out his guitar, tune it up and get his voice back into shape. Going to Miami once a month, serving as CEO of his mom's company, attending family functions and spending time with Whitney didn't leave much time for performing, but rehearsals and the occasional weekend with the band, he hoped, might keep his mind off Lillie.

Who was he kidding? All of that would center his focus directly *on* her.

Somewhere between the captain's seat belt announcement and arriving at MIA, Jase dozed off. When the landing startled him awake, his seatmate said, "My, my, you're certainly a sound sleeper. I'm a lifelong insomniac. You don't know how envious I am of people like you!"

Jase knuckled his eyes. He'd been out for most of the two-hour flight.

"Gloria," the woman said, "tried several times to serve you cookies and peanuts, but you were dead to the world."

His body might have been out of it, but his brain had swirled with images of Lillie. Being wheeled into surgery. Looking small and vulnerable in the ICU. Working harder and longer than necessary to put physical therapy behind her, all without a word of complaint. He remembered something his sister-in-law had said, about the doctors being partly to blame for the addiction.

His seatmate rose, her head barely grazing the ceiling, and hefted her bulky carry-on over one shoulder. He guessed her age at fifty, maybe fifty-five. Lillie would probably be a lot like her when she reached that age…spry, spunky, intelligent, friendly…

Lillie. Again! *What's* wrong *with you, man!* Jase could hardly wait to get home. He'd need to buy all new sheet music, though, because he and Lillie had harmonized to every song in his files. Files he'd stored in his mom's basement because they reminded him too much of what they'd shared…and lost.

He stepped into the aisle and let his neighbor go ahead of him.

As he made his way to the front of the plane, Gloria said, "What time will you be on the show, so I can tune in?"

She knew as well as he did that they usually scheduled him for the hours right before and after supper, then again around the time the late-night news came on.

"Soon as I know something more specific, I'll let you know."

"What is it the actors say? Break a leg!"

Grinning, Jase thanked her and headed straight for the rental car counter. The kid said, pointing into the lot, "Sorry, but that's all we have right now."

Jase had three choices: an enormous red luxury car that reminded him of the one Lillie's parents traded for the Jeep, a boxy, sport-utility vehicle, and a bright blue minivan, almost exactly like her brother and his wife carted their twins around in.

"I'll take the minivan." He'd meant to say SUV. So why hadn't he! Jase blamed it on all the Lillie-thoughts.

The agent's fingers click-clacked across his computer's keyboard. "Family's joining you later, huh?" And before Jase had a chance to answer, he added, "They'll love Miami's Seaquarium. Guess you lucked out. The minivan seats go way back, so if the wife and kids get tired, they can snooze on the way back to the hotel."

How was he supposed to stop thinking about Lillie if everything and everyone reminded him of her!

"No family," he barked. And when the kid's eyes widened in response to his tone, Jase added, "I'm only in town for a few days. On business."

A young couple with three children in tow stepped up behind him.

The older boy tried, and failed, to whisper, "Hey, Mom. Isn't that guy from the show you like to watch?"

Jase pretended he hadn't heard.

"Why, yes, I think it is."

"Hey, mister," the youngest said. "Are you the man that sells birdhouses on TV?"

He'd bet anything that as a girl, Lillie had looked a lot like this kid, with a mop of reddish curls and freckles scattered across his nose.

"Yup. That's me."

"Cool," he said, facing his big brother, "somebody famous, and we've only been here ten minutes!" He stood beside Jase. "Are you rich?"

That produced a genuine laugh. "I wish!"

"Do you live in a mansion and drive a Ferrari?"

"Sorry," the dad interrupted, guiding the boy closer to his wife. "Kids. They can be nosy, can't they."

"We're not nosy!" the little guy said.

"Are too," his sister shot back.

The little guy shoved her into his brother, who bumped into Jase.

"You three stop that right now!" the mother scolded. She led them away from the counter.

He couldn't help but smile to himself as he finished with the desk clerk. He made sure to offer a grin and a "Have a good one!" to the family as he passed them on his way to the minivan. And felt pretty good about leaving them with the sleek and spacious SUV.

During the fifteen-minute drive to the hotel, Jase thumped the small pine tree hanging from the rearview mirror. Hard to tell what its scent was supposed to mask. Something told him he was better off not knowing.

As soon as he got into his hotel room, his cell phone beeped. Whitney. He considered letting it go to voicemail, but she'd only call back. And keep calling back until he picked up.

"Hi, Jason. What's new?"

He'd seen her less than five hours ago. What could possibly be new?

"Not much. Just checked in. I drove a minivan from the airport. Light blue. Can you picture it? Me, in a soccer mom vehicle!"

"Oh now, that isn't so far-fetched, is it?"

He didn't like the sound of that, and decided to reroute the discussion, fast.

"So did you finish your brief?"

"Of course."

She sounded peeved. If his brain wasn't already thumping with Lillie thoughts, he might have asked why.

"What time's court tomorrow?"

"Ten o'clock. But this judge is never on time. If we were late, she'd probably whack us with her gavel, yet she gets to waltz in anytime she pleases. It isn't fair."

Life isn't fair, he almost said. "Keep a good thought. Maybe tomorrow she'll be on time."

"That'll be a nice surprise." She paused. "What did you have for dinner?"

"Haven't eaten yet. Thought I'd get to my room, shower and order something from room service."

"Aw, poor Jason. Eating all alone in a nasty old hotel room."

"Actually, the room is great. I have a view of the water and everything. Better still, it's a five-minute drive from here to the station."

She giggled.

"What?"

"I'm still picturing you behind the wheel of a powder blue minivan."

He remembered Lillie's paint palette, and the dozens of half-empty tubes in her kit. It had been relaxing, watching her turn a blank canvas into a flowery meadow or a wine bottle surrounded by a variety of cheeses. She had a habit of talking to herself while she worked, choosing one color over another, this brush over that, so he'd learned a thing or two about the process by osmosis.

"It's more cyan than powder blue."

For some reason, that made her giggle. "Still, it matches your eyes, right?" Then, "Wish I could be there with you, Jason. I miss you. Already."

"Yeah, me, too." Better to tell her what she wanted to hear than admit that he enjoyed being alone.

"So what time is your show tomorrow?"

He'd texted her a screenshot of his schedule, just as she'd asked him to. Jase gave her the benefit of the doubt. Maybe, with the legal brief on her mind, she hadn't checked her phone yet. He unfolded the page he'd tucked into his pocket and read, "Ten until noon, three until five, and nine to midnight."

"That isn't very smart of them, wearing you out when you still have three more days to go."

She knew as well as he did that these hours were the same for most guests. He'd also told her that the producers provided him with a well-appointed dressing room, and had food brought in.

"I'll be fine, Whit. This isn't my first rodeo."

"You're used to it, I know, but I still worry about you."

"No need. It's all good." Lillie had said that in her parents' front yard…

"Did you get a chance to start that book I gave you?"

"No. I fell asleep not long after takeoff." He pictured his seatmate, who'd reminded him of an older version of Lillie. He shook off the image. *You're losin' it, dude...* "Thought at first I'd get stuck with a chatterbox. Luckily, I didn't."

"That's good. I'm glad," she said around a yawn. "Well, it's nearly midnight and you sound tired. You'd better get to bed. Still want me to give you a wake-up call?"

"Sure."

"And after that?"

Jase stifled a groan. "I'll call you first chance I get. Probably around suppertime, if that works for you."

"I'll tell you what. Why don't we talk while we eat? It'll be like having dinner together."

"Sure. Why not."

"I'm going to run through my notes one more time before I go to bed. If I handle things well, we can avoid a trial. This is my first case with this client. She'll bring big bucks to the firm, so there's a lot riding on how well I do."

For the next fifteen minutes, Whitney told him, step by step, how she hoped to force the defense attorney to beg for a deal.

"You're so quiet," she said, laughing. "Did I bore you to sleep?"

"Of course not. Your work is interesting. It's

just that I'm tired and hungry. If it won't bore *you*, maybe you can tell me all about it tomorrow during dinner."

"You know what they say, careful what you wish for." Whitney laughed. "I'll let you grab a bite to eat and get some sleep." She paused, then added, "If I was there, I'd call room service for you."

"If you were here, you wouldn't need to. I'd take you someplace nice to eat."

"You're so sweet. And so good to me."

Yeah. Right. Sweet. He felt like a jerk, giving her the bum's rush, but all he wanted right now was to hit the hay. And hope like crazy he wouldn't dream about Lillie.

"G'night, Whitney."

Her sigh drifted into his ear. He recognized it as a stall tactic, and if he didn't hang up, she'd start talking again. Lillie hadn't been like that. Any time he needed to be away for a night or two on pub business, she'd always sensed when he needed to hang up. It wasn't so bad, was it, wishing Whitney could be a *little* more like her?

Yes, it was bad. And yes, he was a jerk. A jerk who needed to figure things out before he hurt a perfectly nice woman.

"G'night, Jase."

"Good luck tomorrow, Whit. I'm hanging up now." And he did.

He'd probably pay for it tomorrow, but at least he'd have a good night's sleep first.

Yet again he hoped his Lillie-stuffed brain wouldn't conjure dreams of her…

CHAPTER FIVE

TODAY MARKED LILLIE'S sixth visit to Children's Oncology, and she'd settled into an efficient routine that made the most of her allotted hours. Adjusting to the sight of gaunt, hollow-eyed kids attached to tubes and monitors hadn't been nearly as easy. The children faced fear and sadness all day, every day—from their parents, friends and relatives, when looking at one another—so she worked hard to stay bubbly and upbeat. She'd become a volunteer to atone for her sins, and it wouldn't count if her demeanor added to their suffering.

"Daisies are my favorite flowers," Sally said.

"Mine, too." Lillie dipped her brush into a dab of yellow tempera and painted tiny random circles on the girl's forearm. Switching brushes, she surrounded each with bright white petals.

The child-sized plastic playroom chair squeaked when the girl giggled.

"It's tough to sit still when someone is tickling you with a paintbrush, isn't it?"

Sally squinted in her attempt to exercise self-control. "Just a little." Then, "But you know what? I think you're *so* smart, painting on kids' arms instead of their faces. We don't need a mirror to see the artwork!"

"Yeah, every now and then I have a pretty good idea!"

"You're better than most of the face painters who come in here."

Lillie smiled. "Well," she began, "it's still nice when people come to visit and try to make you happy, right? Besides, we can't all be van Gogh, y'know."

Sally gave it a moment's thought as, from across the room, Jason said, "Who's that?"

Lillie faked shock. "Who's van Gogh! Why, he's only my most favorite painter, ever!" Lillie wiped her brush and dipped it in a blob of green. "Tell you what, when it's your turn, I'll find a couple of his paintings on the internet so you can see how beautiful they are."

"Does this Go guy live in Baltimore?" he wanted to know.

"It's *van Gogh*, you big silly!" Sally groaned and slapped a hand over her eyes. "No, he doesn't live in Baltimore. He was born in Holland. In 1853. I know, because I wrote a report on him, and got an A+."

"*Pa-ar-don* me." Jason sniffed. "So Lillie, can you paint Spider-Man?"

"You bet your Legos I can!"

What kind of crazy luck was it that there were *two* boys on the ward named Jason? More curious still, one that had asked her to call him Jase. Would she ever escape the memory of what she and her Jase had shared?

"I love my daisy chain! I can't wait until my dad gets here so I can show him." Sally held up her arm—the one without the IV board attached to it—and admired the flowers connected by curlicues Lillie had painted from Sally's wrist to the bend in her elbow. "Isn't Lillie a great artist, Jason?"

The boy smirked again. "We'll see after she finishes my Spider-Man."

Lillie carried her supplies to the table where he'd built a tiny fort out of Lego bricks, then unpocketed her phone. "Want me to look up some of van Gogh's works?"

"That's okay. It'll give me something to do tonight when I can't sleep."

He said it so matter-of-factly that the casual observer would have overlooked its true meaning. Lillie's heart ached for these kids, here because of cancer, heart or lung disease, accidents, burns, even parental abuse. Earlier, she'd painted a Pokémon character on a three-year-old who'd swallowed drain cleaner. Her limited knowledge of the game made it tough to figure out which character he wanted, but the way his eyes lit up when he saw Pikachu in her notebook of illustrations made it worth every painstaking hour it had taken to create the samples.

Young Jason rolled up his sleeve as Sally scooted her IV pole up to the table. "Can I watch?"

"You have eyes, don't ya?" he said.

She looked at Lillie and sighed. "Boys. Why must they always be so difficult?"

"I have a brother, so I know what you mean," Lillie agreed.

"Yeah, well, I have two sisters, so I know that boys are nowhere near as difficult as *girls*." Jason leaned forward as Lillie opened her paint kit. "Why do you keep your stuff in a tackle box?"

"I had a regular paint kit once, but it was too small. This one holds everything I need. Brushes in this cubby," she explained, pointing, "nice deep bottom for tubes and bottles of paint, a place for cotton swabs and paper towels and even plastic cups to hold the rinse water. There's even a space for my palette." She lifted a tray and showed them.

"Pretty cool," he said with a nod of approval.

Her mouth went dry, remembering that it was a gift from *her* Jase, who'd told her that if she intended to keep walking to the end of the dock to paint seascapes and sunsets, she needed something more sensible than a backpack to transport her supplies.

"Thanks, a friend gave it to me." She felt a bit

dishonest saying it. Yes, Jase had been a friend. The best she'd ever had. But he'd been so far more than that. Though she hoped she could revive all they'd shared, Lillie suspected she'd have to teach herself to settle for his friendship—if he even wanted that much contact with her.

She squirted dollops of red, blue, black and white on her palette, and using a thin line brush, proceeded to draw the superhero's outline on little Jason's forearm.

Sally, elbows on the table and chin resting on her fists, said, "How many kids do you have, Lillie?"

"None." It hurt to admit it. Back in college, while her friends were spouting the "I don't need a man to complete me" mantra, she'd dreamed of a Victorian-style farmhouse filled with the sounds of exuberant children. She'd wondered then why couldn't a modern woman have both. These days, as she watched those same friends struggle to find a happy medium between motherhood and their careers, Lillie still clung to the belief that, with the right man, she could balance the white-picket-fence life with a fulfilling job.

"Aw, don't look so sad," Sally said. "My mother was thirty when I was born. You still have time to be a mom."

Jason said, "How 'bout a husband? Got one of those?"

She could have, if she hadn't allowed *pills* to rule her life. "No, I'm afraid not."

His pale face crinkled in a frown. "I don't get it. You're pretty and smart and funny, and you can sing and paint. Are you crazy or something? Is that what scares men off?"

"Jason!" Sally scolded. "That wasn't a very nice thing to say." She sighed heavily. "Not everybody wants to be married, you know."

"I didn't mean anything by it," he said. "My mom is always saying that my aunt Charlie is crazy, and that's why she isn't married. I love my aunt Charlie! *She's* fun and pretty, too!"

One of the hardest lessons she'd learned, working with these children, was how mature and intuitive they were. Not surprising, she supposed, considering everything they coped with on a daily basis, from surgeries to treatments to trips to the imaging center.

Jason looked at Sally and blushed. "*You* know how much I want to get married." Facing Lillie, he added, "My mom wants grandchildren. It's practically all she talks about these days. It's like she forgets that I'm not her only kid."

Sally gave that a moment's thought. "Maybe she thinks if she finds a good enough reason, you'll keep fighting until you're cured."

"Maybe." He blew a stream of air through his teeth. "But what if Doctor Kay told her something he didn't tell me?"

Sally got up, rolled her IV poll to the other side of the table and, placing a hand on his shoulder said, “You’ll be fine. It’s hard for parents to watch all the stuff they do to us in here. They want it to be over for us, fast.”

“Then I think we should tell them we want it even more than they do.”

Sally returned to her seat, the wheels of the tall aluminum pole squealing in protest. “Oh, I think they know.”

The children sat in pensive silence, watching Lillie put the finishing touches on Jason’s Spider-Man. She started humming quietly, more to keep from bursting into tears than to comfort or entertain them. It never ceased to amaze her how caring and intelligent these kids were. With maturity came empathy that allowed them to better understand others’ reactions to their illnesses. And it shamed her, because if she’d possessed a fraction of their courage, she never would have grown dependent on—

“You paint so fast,” Jason said, displaying his forearm. “This other volunteer paints ugly roses and he’s *so slow.*”

Lillie repeated what she’d said to Sally, earlier. “But still, it was nice of him to come here, right? I mean, he could have stayed home and played cards with his wife or something, you know?”

“Oh, yeah? Well, if he’s so nice, why didn’t he come back?”

In the short while she'd been volunteering, three of the kids she'd done painting for had died. Despite the best efforts of the staff, their futures had been unpredictable, at best. Not an easy thing to accept, even for seasoned doctors and nurses.

"People like him," Jason went on, frowning, "are here to get high fives from their friends. They might fool those people, but they can't fool me. It's *mean*, using sick kids to make other people think they're *good*."

The longer he talked, the more agitated the boy became. Lillie searched her mind for the words that would ease his distress.

"Sometimes, grown-ups let others down. It isn't easy admitting that, but it's true."

He fell silent for several minutes, and she used the time to add a few embellishments to his painting.

"Can you do Batman?" he said, pulling up his other sleeve.

"Sure."

Lillie wasted no time starting the superhero's outline. Jason's ire opened Lillie's eyes to something she hadn't considered before: Did her siblings, the guys in the band, even her parents, think that her coming here was a show of some sort, acted out so that she'd look better in their eyes? Was that what *Jase* thought?

Sally's voice broke into her thoughts.

"Don't mind him, Lillie. Even his mom says he's too intense."

"Only about fake people," he defended. "I don't like 'em. That guy was the biggest faker ever."

"But we like you a lot, Lillie," Sally said. "'Cause you're not fake."

Or was she? Lillie's heart hammered as she said, "I like you guys a lot, too."

There were plenty of reasons to admire them. While fighting tirelessly to get healthy, they rarely cried or complained, even when the nurses administered shots, changed bandages and inserted fresh IV lines into exhausted veins.

"You forgot Batman's emblem," Jason pointed out.

"Oh, my gosh! What was I thinking?" Lillie added the gold oval to the superhero's chest, then painted a bat silhouette inside it. "There. How's that?"

"It's perfect." Beaming, he studied the painting. "Just like you."

He couldn't have been more wrong. In Lillie's mind, she was about as far from perfect as a human could get.

JASE HELD UP a bright red, shoebox-sized birdhouse. When he saw the spotlight's glare reflected in the lacquered coating, he tilted it slightly.

Trina, the show host, ran a fingertip across the top of it, designed to look like the thatched roof of an Irish cottage. "Aren't these just lovely! I have the green and yellow in my backyard."

The camera panned the row of birdhouses on the shelf below the display counter as she added, "Today only, we'll send you one for the special low price of $29.99."

Now, as the camera zeroed in on Jase's smiling face, he said, "Order two and the shipping and handling is free."

Half an hour later, alone in his dressing room, he pulled up the latest stats on his laptop. It had been a good morning, real good, as evidenced by the show's sales chart. He clicked another link and displayed the numbers from Burton's Manufacturing.

"Oh, great. Just great," he grumbled, pacing as he pecked the manager's number into his cell phone.

"Dan. It's Jase. What's up with the stock on the birdhouses? I'm stuck here in Florida another two days, and the computer says you only have 200 left on the shelves."

"Let me check."

He listened as Dan's keyboard clicked. "We have 250, actually. And we've got a line set up to crank out another thousand first thing tomorrow."

Jase noticed that the producer had placed a basket of fruit beside a reproduction of Andrews's

Field of Daisies. Great. Just what he needed. Another reminder of Lillie. He plucked a grape from the bunch.

"How soon will they be ready?" he said around it.

"Day after tomorrow, if we're lucky."

He turned his back to the painting. "If you're lucky? Look, Dan, we sold a couple thousand during the morning show alone. I go on again in two hours to hawk serving platters, but the birdhouses are on again at eight. How soon can you deliver…once you get the numbers, that is?"

"We'll double the numbers, run some overtime if we have to. But you know what Rich is gonna say…"

That Colette's Crafts wasn't the only company on the Burton books, for starters. Jase saw no reason to point out that their work orders had come along just in time to save Rich from Chapter 11 proceedings. Yet.

He didn't mind the corporate stuff. Contracts, negotiations, new contacts. The on-air stuff? It was a necessary evil. The best he could say about it was that it reminded him a little of being onstage, doing what he loved best, singing with Lillie.

With Lillie? Where had *that* come from? He slapped a palm to the back of his neck.

"Tell Rich not to sweat it," he all but barked. "He'll get paid, same as always." He hit another tab on the computer screen. "Tell me about the casserole dishes. We're showcasing those day after tomorrow, and you only have 500 in stock."

"I'll fire up a second line."

"Okay. Good. Let's set up a day next week to talk. I can't come back down here unless I'm sure we have plenty of inventory."

"Right. I'll have Daisy fiddle with the calendar and shoot you an email with a couple of choices."

His head was pounding by the time the call ended. No surprise there. He'd skipped breakfast, and nothing on the food cart had looked particularly appetizing. Jase snapped a banana from the bunch in the basket, taking care not to look at the picture.

"You're ridiculous," he muttered, peeling the fruit as he made his way to the parking lot. All the way to the hotel, he thought about the print. It was a copy of a masterpiece, of water lilies of all things. Why had it reminded him of her!

He didn't want to think about Lillie anymore. What he wanted was a burger. Fries, smothered in catsup. A hot shower and eight hours of sleep.

Once at the hotel, he pushed the key card into its slot. Jase could almost taste the cold beer he'd ask room service to send up with the food.

He opened the door, and there in the middle of the room stood Whitney, looking like she'd stepped out of a fashion magazine in her form-fitting black dress, strappy heels and earrings that nearly touched her shoulders.

"Surprise," she said, gesturing toward the candlelit table beside her. "I know how you are when you're working, skipping meals and whatnot, so I ordered you a steak and a baked potato." She lifted a silvery lid from one of the plates. "And a Caesar salad, your favorite."

His favorite beer, too, he noticed as the candle flame flickered behind the golden liquid.

"Happy to see me?"

She hadn't moved, unless he counted the broadening of her smile.

"Sure." He closed the door, tossed the key card onto the dresser. "You look real nice."

Whitney took several steps closer, stopping just out of arm's reach. And then she frowned.

"Are you okay?"

"Sure," he said again, and loosened his tie. "Just tired. And hungry." He draped the tie over the doorknob, crossed the room and gave her a hug. "You didn't get anything for yourself?"

"I ate earlier." She pulled out his chair. "You should eat before everything is ice cold."

Jase sat, and she did, too.

"So how'd things go today?"

While he devoured the meal, Jase told her how many birdhouse units he'd sold. Added that he'd had to call the warehouse, put the screws to them about getting more stock on the shelves. And that he'd come *this close* to reminding the manager who'd saved the company's bacon.

"What stopped you?"

"If I'm going to bite somebody's head off, it oughta be Rich's."

Elbows on the table, she stared at her hands. And rubbed her ring finger.

"I get it. One of those 'choose your battles well' kind of things."

Jase had a pretty good idea what had prompted her subconscious gesture. Why did it seem that the more he tried to focus on Whitney, the more he thought of Lillie?

"Something like that." He pushed back from the table and patted his stomach. "That was good. Just what the doctor ordered. Thanks, Whit."

"I enjoy doing things for you."

And it showed. He appreciated every thoughtful thing she'd ever done for him…helping him choose shirts and ties to wear on the show, making sure he had a meal, worrying that he was spending too much time alone…

"Can I ask you a question?"

"Of course," she said. "Anything."

"Why are you here?"

The wide-eyed look of surprise made it clear she hadn't been expecting him to say *that*.

"Why, I, um, it's… I wanted to see you. Because I missed you. And I was awake half the night, thinking about how lonesome you sounded on the phone…"

If she'd heard anything, it had been frustration—at himself—for not being able to get Lillie out of his head.

"…so I thought I'd make sure you had a good meal tonight, and tomorrow while you're working, I'll do some shopping. All my crazy work hours added up, so believe me, I can afford some time off and a spree! When you're finished at the studio, we can have dinner, maybe take a walk on the beach."

He'd never experienced this much closeness. Well, that wasn't true. When he and Lillie were a thing, they'd spent ten or twelve hours a day together, sometimes more, if an out-of-town gig required a long drive. With her, he'd never felt smothered, hadn't looked for excuses to spend time away from her.

Why did he feel the opposite with Whitney?

"I know how you treasure your privacy, so I reserved my own room." Standing again, Whitney walked to the desk and returned with a pale blue box, tied with a black ribbon. "I spent hours online last night," she said, untying it, "and discovered this fabulous bakery." Lifting the lid, she showed him the cheesecake inside.

His favorite. She'd known that, too, and she knew it because she'd paid attention. If someone asked about her favorite dessert, he wouldn't have been able to answer. It wasn't fair. He had to do something, something for *her*.

Something his mother had said echoed in his mind: *I pray every night that Whitney is the woman who'll make your heart skip a beat, who'll take your breath away. That she'll make you smile, just by walking into a room.*

Lillie had left him long before she boarded the train to New York. She'd made her choice, and it hadn't been him. If he blocked her from his mind, from his heart, maybe he had a chance at a happy future with Whitney.

Jase went to her side of the table and brought her to her feet. "You're pretty amazing, you know?"

"So are you."

He kissed her and waited for that weak-in-the-knees sensation his mom had described. When it didn't happen, he kissed her again, and as he had before, put everything he had into it, hoping it would ignite a spark that would even come close to what he'd shared with Lillie.

Again, nothing, and Whitney must have sensed it.

"I should get to my room," she said, stepping back. "You have an early morning."

"What about the cheesecake?"

Turning, she replaced the lid, crossed the room and put the box into the minifridge. "It'll keep until tomorrow. We'll skip dessert at the restaurant."

"Sounds good." Jase pocketed his hands. "What about breakfast?"

"I'm on vacation. You have to get up at six to make your eight o'clock show, but I don't!"

His heart wasn't in it when he laughed. "Where's your room?"

"Three down and across the hall."

He grabbed the key card from the dresser. "I'll walk you."

"Jason, I'm perfectly capable of getting there on my own."

There it was, that independent streak. Just like Lillie's. "Of course you can. Just humor me."

"Okay, if you insist."

She'd always been easy to get along with, too. Just like Lillie.

Arm in arm, Jase and Whitney made their way down the hall.

"Call me after you finish up tomorrow," she said, standing in the open doorway.

"Will do."

No more than twelve inches separated them, so why did it feel like a mile?

She bussed his cheek. "Get some sleep. The way you're behaving, I think you need it," Whitney said as the door clicked shut.

He waited until the bolt slid into place before making his way back to his room, where the table setting reminded him how far she was willing to go to please him.

What was wrong with him? He wanted to love her. So why couldn't he do something about it!

His mother's suspicions had been on-target, that despite the way things had ended between him and Lillie, despite all she'd done to him, despite his efforts to put what they'd had behind him, he still loved her.

Was he holding on to Whitney as insurance in case Lillie had decided that the only way to stay clean was to distance herself from him?

Jase didn't want to be that guy, the one who thought only of himself, who thought only of his own needs. That guy was worse than a heel. Worse than a jerk.

It was time to make some changes. Big changes.

Because Whitney deserved better than that guy.

CHAPTER SIX

"We should frame your arm!" Sally's dad said. "That's as good as anything I've seen at the Walters!"

Baltimore's famed art museum had exhibited all of the greats. His words were flattering, but really, what else could he say with Lillie standing beside his happy little girl?

"She brought her guitar this time," Sally said, climbing into her dad's lap. "She already sang, though."

The man towered over Lillie. "My girl went on and on about you last time you visited, so I'm sorry I missed your performance." Extending a hand, he said, "I'm Brant Perry, and it's a genuine pleasure to meet you."

She felt the heat of a blush. "Oh, it was hardly a performance. I just went from bed to bed for the children who couldn't come to the playroom, then sang in here for the kids who could."

"She likes it when we sing along," Sally said. "It's so fun!"

Brant sent Lillie an apologetic smile. "I'd

planned to be here but got stuck in traffic. I'm really disappointed."

"Me, too," Jason said. "I had to leave so the nurse could flush my IV."

It seemed there was an echo in the room as one after another, the children and parents in the playroom agreed.

"Could you stay a little longer, Lillie," Brant asked, "for those of us who weren't here to hear you?"

"I've already overstayed my time limit by nearly half an hour, and the rec director made it clear on my first day that I need to stick to the schedule so the kids won't miss medications, meals and rest."

"Don't you worry about that," Jason's mom said. "If the director says anything, we'll make sure she knows we insisted."

Sally hopped down from her dad's lap and squeezed Lillie's hand. "Please, Lillie? Just a couple of songs?"

The rest of the kids joined the chorus: "Please, please, *please*?"

They reminded her a bit of her twin nieces who, when she'd tucked them in just the other night, had begged and cajoled to squeak an additional fifteen minutes before turning out the lights. She'd been volunteering for only a little more than a month…long enough to know that the children felt caged in by their hospital rooms and beds. If she could buy them a little more time here in the playroom, Lillie would happily risk the director's reprimand.

"Okay, but some of you are looking kinda peaked, so only a couple of songs..."

Brant and several other parents gave a nod of approval, and while she uncased her guitar, young Jason took control, guiding those in the playroom to sit in a circle, and dragged an adult-sized chair to the top of the big O.

During the fifteen minutes of her mini concert, Lillie felt more like her old self than she had before rehab. Singing to the group while accompanying herself on the guitar was only half the fun. The best feelings came from seeing the light of enjoyment in their eyes. Several nurses, a doctor and two interns had lined up against the back wall, heads bobbing and toes tapping in time to the music. She'd entertained far larger audiences, but these intimate performances were far more gratifying. Only one thing could make it more perfect: having Jase here to harmonize with her.

Afterward, she packed up and said her goodbyes, and made her way to the elevator. If she went straight home, there'd be plenty of time to make her parents a good old-fashioned spaghetti dinner. Her stomach growled, reminding her that she'd skipped lunch. Frosted toaster tarts, she admitted, didn't stick with a body very long.

"Lillie, do you have a minute to talk?"

"Mr. Perry! I didn't see you there!"

"Sorry if I surprised you. And please, call me Brant." He handed her a glossy black business card that looked and felt quilted. Beneath bold raised gold letters that spelled out Perry Creative Talent, smaller text said Representing Athletes, Voice-over Artists & Musicians.

"You're just a bundle of talent, aren't you? Voice, guitar, art..."

She'd never learned how to respond to such compliments, so Lillie said a polite thank-you and let it go. Turning the card over, she read his contact information.

"You're based here in Baltimore?"

One shoulder lifted. "Too much competition in New York, Chicago and LA. There's more than enough talent—and plenty of work—right here in Charm City." He rattled off a list of car dealerships, hospitals, banks, and real estate and law firms that needed actors and musicians to perform in their TV ads. He named several Orioles and Ravens team members and college athletes who'd signed with his agency.

"I'm not really in the market for an agent," she began. Should she tell him that she'd been in rehab as little as a year and a half ago. "It's been years since I've performed solo, so if you're thinking of hiring me for a company function or family party—"

He laughed, a warm, jovial sound. "No, nothing like that. But my job does put me in close contact with people in the recording industry… people who've turned a handful of my clients into household names."

Brant cited a few examples, and Lillie recognized every name.

"You're too good to be stuck here, alone."

"I'm not stuck. I love it here." Compared to rehab—even a place as ritzy as Rising Sun—Baltimore was paradise.

"Don't get me wrong," he went on. "Last thing I'd suggest is that you stop visiting Hopkins. As you've probably guessed, I spend a lot of time at the hospital. Trust me. I can say with some authority that what you did here today…" He sighed. "Lillie, believe me, it's nothing short of miraculous." He paused. "But you can work this into your schedule, even if you're on the road."

"I spent a few years singing in hotel lounges and pubs all over the country. In Canada, too. I loved the work but hated getting to and from each job. And I wasn't exactly crazy about spending so many hours alone in hotel rooms either."

The elevator doors opened at last, and a nurse nodded as she passed them on her way up the hall.

"Besides," Lillie continued, "to quote my dad, aren't we putting the cart before the horse?"

"Not at all. I'll set up a meeting, but trust me, that'll just be a formality. I know this guy and I know what he likes. He's gonna *love* you. You're the whole package—talent, personality, looks… oh, yeah, he'll love you, all right."

She knew just enough about the recording industry to understand that everything was a gamble. Even megastars were only as good as their last release. She had worked hard in rehab and wasn't willing to put it all on the line for a maybe.

"Who is this guy?"

"A producer-manager by the name of Rusty McCoy. He takes new artists, helps them build a platform, introduces them to labels… I have a daughter, too, so trust me when I say I wouldn't put you together with him if I didn't think he was a standup guy. Wouldn't throw you out there all alone on the road either."

Lillie had been home for only a few months. How could she leave now, just when the people she'd hurt were finally beginning to show signs of believing in her? If she left now, all the hard work she'd put into rehab, into rebuilding relationships… Would it all go by the wayside? Would everyone throw up their hands, thinking "It's just a matter of time before she starts using again"? Besides, what had she done to deserve a break like this?

"I know it's a lot to absorb. Tell you what. Take a few days. Take a week, even, to mull things over. What can it hurt? You have my card. Call anytime, and I'll set something up. But keep in mind that Rusty comes to town every couple of months."

"He isn't Baltimore-based?"

"Nashville."

From the time she was a little girl, Lillie had dreamed of performing in Music City… She glanced at the card again. Brant was right. It couldn't hurt to think things over.

"Thanks, Mr.—I mean, Brant." She tucked the card into the front pocket of her purse. "Your idea is very…intriguing."

"So you'll give it some thought?"

"Not to be rude, but…what's in for you?"

As she stepped into the elevator, he said, "The knowledge that I've put someone with real talent on the road to stardom."

The doors closed before she could respond. A good thing, too, because Lillie had no idea what she might have said.

Nonsense, she thought, climbing in behind the wheel of her mother's car, *you know exactly what you'll tell him...*

"It's all very flattering," she said to herself, "but I can't leave Baltimore right now. Maybe never. So thanks, Brant, but no thanks."

Just in case, though, it couldn't hurt to buy some new sheet music and learn a few new tunes…

"CAN I HELP you find anything, sir?"

Jase smiled at the young clerk. "Not really. I don't know what I'm looking for, but I'll know it when I see it."

"Well, let me know if you need anything."

Jase thanked the kid and went back to finger-walking through the standing stacks of sheet music.

He'd heard some great Phil Phillips songs, and decided they'd make a good addition to his repertoire. Moving down the stand, he flipped the P tab and read each title. Smiling, Jase plucked five songs from the rack. He was about to carry the sheets to the cash register when movement on the other side of the display caught his attention.

Lillie, in a bright yellow sundress. The matching headband held her hair back, emphasizing her widow's peak, and the new off-the-face hairdo made her big eyes stand out even more. A thin veil of moss green shadow glowed from her eyelids, and as she looked down, studying song titles, long dark lashes dusted her sun-pinkened, freckled cheeks.

She must have sensed that someone was watching her, because she glanced up. His heart thudded as she met his eyes.

"Jase…"

"Hey. What're you doing here?"

Dumb question, he thought, taking note of the

sheet music in her hand. This store was where they'd always shopped for new material.

"Just adding to my collection."

He'd thought the conversation at her folks' inn had gone pretty well, all things considered. Based on her wavering smile, he guessed he'd been wrong.

Jase held up the sheets he intended to buy. "Same here."

They both moved toward the cashier's stand.

"You got to the store first, so go ahead," she said.

"Yeah, but ladies first."

The stilted conversation only reminded him how compatible they'd once been.

Disregarding the gloomy thought, Jase peered over her shoulder and read the title on the top of her stack: *One Hundred Sing-Along Songs for Kids*. Her nieces had loved it when she serenaded them. Had she promised to sing for their upcoming birthday party? He'd been invited to three of those gatherings, and ought to remember if the twins were turning ten or eleven.

The kid who'd offered to help him earlier now pecked keys on the register. "This one's on sale," he said, running the book across the scanner screen. "Are you a kindergarten teacher or something?"

Lillie grinned. "No, nothing like that. I volunteer at Hopkins Children's Oncology every couple of weeks, and my material is getting stale. Those kids are going through enough without me adding boredom to their lives. Not that they complain. They're the bravest little souls I've ever met."

Lillie tended to ramble when nervous, and he felt bad that his nearness made her feel that way. Truth be told, he wasn't exactly feeling comfortable either, especially given his decision to give things with Whitney a real chance.

"My cousin was in there a few years ago," the kid said, sliding another songbook over the screen. "Leukemia won."

Jase watched as Lillie, ever the caring comforter, lay a hand atop his.

"I'm so sorry," she said. "How old was he?"

"Fourteen."

How many times had he told her that her heart was bigger than her head? Too many to count.

The cashier bagged her music and hit the register button to ring up her total. "It's really nice, what you're doing," he said, handing her the receipt. "The thing he hated most about that place was how long the days were with nothing to do but watch TV and listen to his monitor beep."

Jase had to agree… It was a good thing she was doing.

She thanked the kid and turned to face Jase. "Well, it was a nice surprise, seeing you again."

"Can you hang around a minute, just until I pay for this stuff?"

She looked surprised, and in truth, he'd surprised himself. But he couldn't just let her leave. Not without finding out more about her work at the hospital. And what, if anything, rehab had inspired her to do about *him.*

"Okay," she said. "I'll wait for you over by the door."

The kid made small talk with him, too, but Jase barely heard a word as he watched her from the corner of his eye. Silhouetted against the bright sunshine coming through the window, he couldn't help noticing the way her chin-length hair curled above her shoulders. She used to dress like a tomboy. Sneakers and jeans with comfy T-shirts, like she'd worn to plant flowers that day in her parents' yard. But that little dress—

"All set," the kid said, holding up Jase's bag.

He thanked the boy and wasted no time joining Lillie.

"You want to grab a cup of coffee?" He held open the door, hoping that slight frown didn't mean she'd say no. "It's only a short walk to Café Latte-Da..."

"On Aliceanna Street. I remember."

Of course she did, because they used to go there at least once a week to decide the order of the songs they'd sing at Three-Eyed Joe's.

"So what do you say? I'll treat you to a sandwich. Or pie. Or both." Recalling how little it took to fill her up, he added, "We could share..."

Her sweet, sad smile told him she, too, remembered all the meals they'd shared. And again, it made his heart beat a bit harder.

"I don't have to be at work until six, so okay, pie and coffee it is."

They were waiting for the light to change at Fleet and Aliceanna when she said, "This won't upset Whitney, will it?"

"She won't mind if I have coffee with an old friend."

"I, well, that day at the Flower Basket, I got the impression she knows that we were a couple."

"Were," he repeated, "past tense. And like I said, it's just two pals, catching up over coffee."

The image of that candlelit table in his hotel room flashed in his mind, reminding him that Whitney might not see it that way. "So how long have you had this Hopkins gig?"

"Couple months now."

The light changed, and he pressed a hand to her lower back and guided her across the street. Not that she needed his assistance. Still, it felt good, felt right, being this close to her, shielding her from potential harm.

Inside Café Latte-Da, Jase admitted that he'd skipped breakfast.

"The guy who's forever reminding people

it's the most important meal of the day?" Lillie laughed.

"Just got back from Florida and didn't have time to make a grocery run. My cupboards are as bare as Mother Hubbard's."

"I caught the last few minutes of the casserole demonstration. You were born to be a TV host."

He and Lillie had performed at a couple charity functions that aired on local television. While watching the tapes with her afterward, Jase had remarked how well they worked together. "No need to sound so surprised," she'd said then. "That's how it is when people are meant to be together."

"I think I'll get the chicken wrap. What about you?" he asked. "In the mood for something more substantial than pie?"

"Just coffee, thanks."

"Thought I heard your belly growl earlier…"

"I'll whip up a sandwich or something before I clock in at the hotel."

When she'd paid for the sheet music, Jase saw a lone ten-dollar bill in her wallet. He knew her well enough to understand why she'd said no: Lillie had decided that until she'd repaid every dime she owed, she wouldn't take anything more from him. Unnecessary as that was, Jase respected her decision.

And wondered if it went hand in hand with

some goateed therapist's advice: "If you want to stay clean, kick that guy to the curb."

They found an empty table near the door—a rare occurrence on a Saturday afternoon—and settled in.

"Tell me about this volunteer work. When did you sign on for that?"

"A week or so after I got home, I gave in to a moment of self-pity." She stared out the window. "It made me realize it was time to stop focusing on me and start focusing on others." Gaze locked on his, she added, "Best—and worst—thing I have ever done."

He didn't get it, and said so.

"Life has put those kids through the wringer. Some of them are barely hanging on, but they're hanging on tight. A person can't help but admire the *fight* in them." She sipped her espresso. "Hard to feel sorry for yourself after spending time with them."

It made sense, considering how she'd always said that self-pity was the most dangerous emotion.

"Must be tough, though, working that closely with them."

"Only during the drive home."

"Why?"

Her eyes shimmered with unshed tears. "Because I never know which of them won't be there when I go back."

And not because they'd gone home, healthy, he surmised.

She started talking about individual kids, their diseases and conditions, the parents and siblings that supported them and the staff that cared for and comforted them. Hands folded on the table, Lillie said, "And then there's little Jason, the sweetest, cutest ten-year-old boy you'll ever meet. He told me the other day that he wants to marry one of the girls—Sally—because his mom's biggest regret is that she'll never see him walk down the aisle with the girl of his dreams."

Swiping at a wayward tear, she added, "Then he asked me if I'd sing at their wedding and help him make arrangements. Flowers. Streamers. Punch. Cake."

Even before she said so, Jase knew that she'd agreed to everything. He wanted to take her in his arms, tell her what a terrific person she was. Admit how proud he was of the way she'd come through rehab. And that he'd missed her.

But he'd made a promise to himself, a promised that included Whitney, not Lillie. And it wouldn't be fair to any of them if he went back on it. Still…

"How can I help?"

"Help?" Her eyes widened. "You?"

"Hey. Quit looking so shocked. I do nice stuff once in a while."

"I know that better than almost anyone," was her quiet reply.

Jase hoped she wouldn't recite a list: Money he'd loaned her. Times he'd driven her to the ER. All the ways she'd betrayed him. And how everything had hurt him, deeply.

"Maybe we can work up a couple of tunes, two or three of the things we'd sing at Three-Eyed Joe's when people were celebrating anniversaries, and perform them at this little wedding."

Helping out at the hospital wasn't really the same as breaking his promise to Whitney. Or was it? What kind of man was he turning into?

"I think the kids might like that."

She *thought* the kids *might* like it? Why the hesitation? And then it hit him: she was just as afraid of being close, of reliving warm and wonderful moments, as he was.

"Then let's put our heads together, figure it out… When is this ceremony, anyway?"

"In two weeks." There wasn't a trace of a smile on her face when she added, "Unless…"

"Keep a good thought, Lill. If the kid is determined to do this for his mom, he'll make it. And who knows? Maybe it's just what he needs to push him closer to recovering."

She brought the espresso cup to her lips and, nodding, met his eyes.

He cleared his throat and downed a gulp of his iced tea. "So where do you think we should get together? My place? We'd have plenty of quiet and privacy there."

Too much, too soon, he realized when her eyes grew big.

"The acoustics are great in the inn's turret. I'm sure Mom and Dad won't mind. In fact, they were just asking about you the other day. I'm sure they'd love seeing you."

"Sounds good. I don't go back to Florida for a month, so my schedule is pretty flexible. You're the one who's clocking 200 hours a week, so..."

"Seems you haven't changed much," she said, smiling. "Still exaggerating to make a point... one of the things that made me crazy about you."

She gasped a little when that last line came out and, hands over her mouth, Lillie said, "Good grief. I'm sorry, Jase. That was really inappropriate. And bad timing."

"It's neither, and it's okay. Nothing wrong with remembering the good times. We had plenty of those before..."

Lillie shoved the espresso cup into the center of the table, her way of saying their meeting was over. She gathered her things and stood, and he did, too.

"So should I call you?" she asked. "Or would you rather call me? About a time when we can get together. To rehearse, I mean."

Rambling again. And again, he felt bad for raising her stress level. "Do you have a pen?"

Like magic, she produced one from her purse.

Leaning over the table, he scribbled three phone numbers on a napkin. "Home, cell and office," he said, "in that order. You can always get me on my cell. Call anytime."

Call soon, he thought. As he pressed the napkin into her hand, their fingers touched. Not for long—a blink in time, if that—but long enough to send an ache straight to his heart.

He'd been behaving like some guilt-ridden goofball who'd dumped his best girl, when in reality, *Lillie* had ended them by choosing booze and pills over what they'd had.

It hit him like a punch to the gut: suggesting that they get together, for any reason, had been a bad idea. Mostly because it would hurt Whitney. Suddenly, Jase was sorry he'd invited Lillie here. Sorry he'd given her his numbers. Sorry he'd suggested working up a couple of numbers for the fake wedding.

Jase added *idiot* to the list of things he'd been calling himself. Feeling miserable and confused, Jase held open the café door.

A tiny frown furrowed her brow. "Are you okay?"

"Yeah. Just remembered something I forgot to do." *Like...calling Whitney.*

"Oh. Because you look...different."

"Don't mind me," he said, leading the way

across the street. "I'm a little annoyed with myself, is all. I hate forgetting things."

"I remember what a perfectionist you are, and how frustrated you get with yourself when you let something slip through the cracks."

Yeah, she knew him, all right. Their closeness was what allowed her to use him, time and again, to suit her addiction.

Traffic had picked up considerably, thanks to the Orioles' win. Between the noise of passing traffic, honking horns and the exuberant shouts of fans, Jase could barely hear himself think. It seemed to take forever to get back to the music shop.

"Where are you parked?" he asked.

"Right behind the store."

"Me, too. Guess we're stuck with each other for a few more minutes."

He hadn't intended to sound short-tempered. And the way she looked at him—as if she'd just seen his face on a wanted poster—told him it surprised her even more. It wasn't fair, taking things out on Lillie, even if she had waltzed into his life just when he'd finally pulled himself together.

Or thought he had…

"When are you scheduled to go back to Hopkins?"

By now, she'd fished her keys from her purse and, standing behind her dad's red Jeep, Lillie leveled him with a what's-your-problem? gaze. "Next week. Tuesday."

"And when's this wedding supposed to happen?"

"The following week. On Saturday. I know this must seem like a lot of time and effort. But I have to do it. I gave my word. The only glitch might be talking my bosses into giving me the day and night off. Saturdays are busy."

"If they give you any grief, they're heartless."

"Not really. I was totally honest about my past, so it's only natural that they watch me like a hawk, and count every penny in the cash drawer. If I ask for the day off, I know exactly what they'll think."

That she wants to cash her paycheck and spend it on drugs or booze. Or both. And maybe, just maybe, she would.

"When I managed the pub, it drove me nuts when people called in at the last minute—or didn't call in at all—and forced me to scramble to fill their hours. You're giving them more than enough time to switch the schedule up a bit. And I'm willing to bet your replacements will be glad about the extra hours."

"True. And worst-case scenario, I'll have a slightly longer walk getting to and from a *new* job."

He fished out his keys from his pocket. "Well,

I'd better get to the office. Couple of things I need to check on…" *Before you call Whitney.*

"And I need to get busy on supper." Lillie smiled. "One of the best things about being home again is having access to a full kitchen."

"I thought you had an apartment above Pete's?"

She shrugged. "Just a minifridge, microwave and hotplate. And a sink the size of a shoebox. Not that I'm complaining, mind you. You know the old saying."

"There are a lot of old sayings…"

"'Beggars can't be choosers.' Pete let me stay in the apartment, rent free. He said I was doing him and Betty a favor, keeping the doors from squeaking and the appliances from getting moldy. But they weren't fooling me. They paid me nearly double what they paid everyone else." She leaned in and cupped a hand beside her mouth. "Which would have started a mutiny if the others found out." She straightened to add, "So when I wasn't waiting tables, I did their bookkeeping and cleaned the pub *and* their condo."

Talking about her history couldn't be easy. Admitting the price she'd paid to get back on track had to be tougher still. But Jase remembered other times she'd claimed to have stopped using; he had no desire to travel that rocky road again.

"Good seeing you," she said, sliding in behind the steering wheel.

"You, too." And despite the hard memories, it *had* been good spending time with her again.

He made his way to the pickup, watching from the corner of his eye as she turned right. In minutes, she'd arrive at her parents' inn on South Amelia Street, where the people and surroundings made him feel like family. He missed the place. Missed the people, too, and bit back the urge to blame Lillie's addiction for taking it all away from him.

Jase maneuvered the truck onto the minuscule parking pad behind his row home. As soon as he settled in for the evening, he'd call Whitney. It was long past time for an honest, open exchange.

CHAPTER SEVEN

"GUESS WHAT," LILLIE announced over supper, "I've saved up enough to get my own car and insurance, *and* repay Jase."

Amelia frowned. "I thought he told you not to worry about that. Why put pressure on yourself if you don't have to, honey?"

"Hon, stay out of it," Liam said. "If Lillie wants to clear the board, let her do it." He met Lillie's eyes. "This sauce is terrific, kitten!"

She thanked him, not only for the compliment, but for understanding that she *needed* to clear the board. Everyone who'd helped her had done so at great personal and financial cost. Settling up with them would add credence to her apologies, while making it easier for them to believe that drugs were firmly in her past. Oh, how good it would feel to step out from under the guilt and shame she'd been shouldering all these months!

"You guys have been terrific. There isn't enough money in all the world to repay you for what you've done." Tears burned behind her eyelids, so Lillie rushed to get the rest out. "You took me at my word, gave me another chance when I needed it most and welcomed me home with open arms."

"Honey, we're only too happy to do it."

"You mom's right," Liam said.

"I know." She got up, went to their side of the kitchen island and draped an arm around each of their shoulders. "It seems such a pathetic, paltry thing to say, but thank you." Lillie kissed their cheeks, then returned to her seat. "I'm thinking that by spring," she said, spearing a meatball, "I should have enough for a deposit and first month's rent on a place of my own."

"Oh, don't be in such a hurry," Amelia said. "We love having you here. And you're a big help!"

"When all this construction ends and the grand reopening is behind you, the guest rooms will fill up. And won't it be nice to have that extra bedroom for nights and weekends when Kassie and Kate want to sleep over?"

Her parents exchanged a quick glance.

"We've always made room for them," Amelia said. "No need for you to rush into things before you're ready."

"Your mother is right. Why saddle yourself with the stress of car and rent payments?"

In other words, why risk the chance that the added pressure might cause a relapse?

Lillie could hardly blame them for feeling that

way. She'd put them through a lot. As her grandfather used to say, "Talk is cheap. You want to prove something? Then just do it."

And that was just what Lillie aimed to do.

As she had prepared to leave Rising Sun, and during every follow-up session since leaving, the counselors hammered home the difficult fact that yes, some of the people in her life would come around, eventually…but some of them would never believe in her again. When all was said and done, only one opinion would keep her on the straight and narrow: her own.

"What does your contractor say about wrapping up the renovations?"

Liam groaned and Amelia sighed.

"Every week, he tells us it'll just be one more week. I had a dream the other night," her dad said. "Your mom and I were silver-haired, shuffling along behind walkers. Kirk had a mop of white hair and a walker, too, when he said, 'Patience, Liam. Just a few more days and the boys an' me will be outta here.'"

"That's not a dream, Dad. That's a nightmare!"

"Tell me about it!" he said, joining in her laughter.

"For your sake, I hope he means it this time. How great will it feel when you don't have to duck through those grimy sheets of plastic covering all the doorways or tiptoe around coils of extension cords?"

Amelia quirked a brow, then looked at Liam and shook her head.

"What," Lillie said. "I have spinach between my teeth?"

"You aren't fooling us, kitten. Ever since you got home, you've talked about everything *but* Jase. You can't avoid him forever, especially since you're bound and determined to pay what you think you owe him."

"I'm not avoiding him. Why, I saw him today, as a matter of fact. Bumped into him in the music store and he asked if he could buy me a cup of coffee. And when he found out about my work at Hopkins and little Jason's mock wedding, he offered to sing a couple of duets with me."

Her mom's eyes lit up, and it had been a while since Lillie had seen her dad smile like that, too.

"Oh, honey," Amelia said, "I'm so happy to hear it. Your dad and I have always thought he was perfect for you, haven't we, Liam."

"He's a good guy, all right. But a lot of water has passed under that bridge since you broke up."

When she'd cited the adage to Jase, he'd suggested *flood* might be more accurate.

"Don't get me wrong," Liam continued, "we think the world of him. But you've both changed a lot since then, and things might not work out like you hope they will."

"I'm not hoping for anything." Not the whole truth, but not a lie either. "The only thing I hope is that you won't mind if we practice in the turret, if we decide to go ahead with the duet thing."

"Mind!" her mom said. "We'll love it! It'll be so lovely, hearing you two sing together again. Such perfect, close harmony!"

He'd provided her all the information she needed to call him. Lillie wanted to, more than she cared to admit. But the way his disposition had changed from warm to aloof made her wish she hadn't said yes to his coffee invitation *or* his offer to help with the ceremony.

"I'm stuffed," she said, hoping to change the subject. "Shouldn't have taken that second meatball."

"Wouldn't have been a problem if you made 'em smaller," Liam pointed out.

Amelia gave his forearm a playful slap. "Bite your tongue! My family never makes tiny meatballs!"

Leaning closer, he placed a sweet kiss on her cheek. "After forty-five years together, you'd think I'd know that, wouldn't you?"

Lillie could count on one hand the number of times she'd seen them angry with one another. All her life, she'd dreamed of finding a love like that. She'd found it in Jase. But…

Far better, Lillie decided, to adopt a Scarlett O'Hara mindset, and think about it tomorrow. Or the next day.

She began gathering plates and flatware.

"Oh, no you don't," Amelia said. "You cooked. I'll clean up."

"It won't take long. I really don't mind."

"But *we* do," Liam chimed in. "You haven't stopped working since you got home."

Lillie laughed. "I only worked the breakfast rush this morning."

"I don't mean today," he countered. "I mean since you got *home*."

"Two months ago," Amelia said.

"Nearly three," Liam interjected, "but who's counting!"

Her parents now stood side by side at the sink, Liam rinsing the plates, Amelia stacking them in the dishwasher.

"She's still here," Liam said from the corner of his mouth.

Amelia echoed his phony irritation, "I know. The kid can't take a hint!"

Laughing, Lillie held up her hands. "All right, okay, I'm going up to take a shower and get into my pajamas. And when I'm finished, I might just tote my guitar into the turret and put some of the sheet music I bought today through a test run."

Her parents gave her approving smiles, then sobered, as if remembering that they'd been pretending to be annoyed.

"She's *still* here!" Amelia whispered.

"Stop making eye contact and maybe she'll go away..."

"Okay, all right," she said again. "I'm going!"

Just outside the kitchen door, Lillie stooped to tidy the old rug her mom had placed in the entryway to capture drywall debris and sawdust from the workers' boots.

"Does she seem happy to you?" she heard her mother say.

"That's a relative term."

"I'm serious, hon. She's trying really hard to put on a good front for us, but she isn't fooling me. I can see it in her eyes…"

Lillie froze, because if she went upstairs now, the half-dozen creaks in the wide-planked foyer would let her parents know she was eavesdropping.

"…she misses Jase. And if you ask me, she wants him back in her life."

"I agree, but much as I'd like to see those two get back together again, let's not push it, okay? In fact, let's just stay out of it altogether. Lillie is hell-bent to prove herself. We need to let her see that we believe she can do it this time."

This time. With just two words, Liam had reminded her how many times she'd hurt and disappointed them. She had so much to make up for. To them. To her siblings and their spouses, her nieces. The guys in the band, who'd once been treasured friends. And Jase…

She shook off the self-pity and tried to remember which boards squeaked. Sam had taught her and Molly how to avoid them when they were teenagers. Now how did his little rhyme go? "Two steps forward, one to the side, left foot, right foot, or prepare to hide." Thankfully, it worked, and Lillie hurried up the double-wide dark oak staircase.

Her room was strewn with notepads, sketches and pens across the bed and desk. She'd almost forgotten her work on the flyers and pamphlets that would make as many people as possible aware of the inn's reopening. She'd written drafts of the media press release, plus a newsletter-type invitation for friends, family and neighbors. With some minor tweaking, the text would be soon be ready for the print shop.

Next, she'd make a trip to the attic in search of old photographs that told the inn's story, from its 1799 brewery days to her folks' most recent addition, and every change in between.

Lillie changed into old jeans and a T-shirt, traded her flip-flops for sneakers, and tucked her hair into a baseball cap. On the way to the narrow curved staircase, she grabbed a flashlight and hoped the batteries were fresh.

An hour later, crawling across the dusty wood floor, Lillie counted the boxes she'd gone through. Just one more, she thought, lifting a fifth box. Her mother had printed "Kids" on its lid. Chances were slim that she'd find photos of improvements her folks had made to the inn, but Lillie opened it anyway.

Sam, Molly and Lillie, romping through the sprinkler.

The three of them tearing into their gifts on Christmas morning.

Her folks' long dining room table—extended by two card tables—decked out for a family Thanksgiving feast.

The Sams' wedding. Molly and Matt's, too.

Her prom. The eight-by-ten black-and-white head shot her first agent had insisted on sending to pub owners and lounge managers from New York to LA.

An envelope plopped into her lap. She saw in her mother's handwriting "Lillie and Jase/Three-Eyed Joe's."

On top of the stack, a picture of her and Jase, sharing a mic and looking into each other's eyes in the halo of a single spotlight.

Beneath it, another picture of her and Jase, this time sitting side by side on the inn's top porch step, her head resting on his shoulder, his head resting atop her curls.

Next, Jase and Liam, laughing at something. And one of him with her dad, brother, and brother-in-law, cheering over something on the blurry color TV in the background.

Jase, by himself, sneaking a brownie from the kitchen table.

And Jase, arms wrapped tight around her as they admired the nine-foot-tall snowman they'd built using stepladders and stools and gardening tools. He'd stolen her scarf to wrap around its neck, and while he was busy jamming stick-arms into place, Lillie had grabbed his Orioles cap and climbed the ladder to put it in place.

Tears stung her eyes as she slipped the pictures back into their envelope. She'd chosen eight photos to use on the flyers, and standing, tucked them into the back pocket of her jeans.

Halfway down the stairs, the flashlight began flickering. Lillie might have credited herself with good timing…if she hadn't mistimed so many things in the last two years.

Sitting crouched on the grubby attic floor, leaning on beams to dig through boxes, had left her feeling achy from neck to knees. *That's what you get for skipping your exercises three days in a row.* Every injury sustained in the accident had healed. The surgical scars had faded.

She found aspirin and ibuprofen in the medicine cabinet, and behind them, a bottle of Percocet, prescribed by her dad's doctor following a tooth implant several months earlier. Lillie clutched it so tightly, her fingers ached. Had her father left the prescription here to see whether she'd developed the willpower to avoid temptation?

You're being paranoid, Lill. Dad isn't like that.

He'd forgotten, was all.

The pills inside click-clacked against the plastic as she read the label. *Liam Rourke*, it said. On one side, *325 mg. Take one tablet every six hours as needed for pain*. And on the other, *This medicine is a blue, round, scored tablet imprinted with "ALV 196" and is manufactured by ABC Pharmaceuticals, Inc*. She unscrewed the childproof cap. Sure enough, there were round blue pills inside.

Lillie's mouth went dry and her hands began to shake as every muscle tensed, adding to her discomfort. She held her breath and squeezed her eyes shut and summoned self-control. If this wasn't a supreme test, she didn't know what was.

"You'll face temptation," her counselors had warned. "Devise a plan for how you'll smother it." Several people in the circle said they'd picture themselves, staggering, stuttering and hollow-eyed. A few more decided to visualize the disappointed looks on the faces of their loved ones. When it was Lillie's turn, she'd simply said "Jase." She'd never forget the way he'd looked at her, his beautiful, expressive face a mix of sorrow and pain, anger and regret. Lillie's mom had been only half right. It would be a dream come true if she could reunite with Jase. But what she wanted even more was to see the look of approval in his eyes.

You're supposed to stay clean for yourself. "Think of it this way," one counselor had said.

"It's like you're in an airplane that's going down, fast. You can't help others if you're a mess. That's why you put your oxygen mask on first."

You're supposed to take care of you *so the rest can fall into place.*

Lillie opened her eyes, put the cap back on the bottle, and returned it to its shelf. It wasn't until she closed the mirrored door that she realized she'd been crying.

Weakness had been the root of all her problems. But she'd worked hard to leave that behind.

Grabbing a tissue, she dried her eyes and blew her nose, then threw back her shoulders.

On the heels of a cleansing breath, she looked into the mirror again.

"You did it," she whispered. "You *did* it."

It hadn't been the first time she'd passed such a test, and it wouldn't be the last. Temptations would occur less frequently, the counselors had assured, and each victory would help bring about triumph over the next.

One day at a time...

Something Jase had recently told her came to mind.

After pointing out that drive and determination had seen her through months of punishing physical therapy, he'd reminded her that she had worked through several months of grueling psychotherapy at Rising Sun, as well. He'd called her tough. And stubborn. "You've got that going for you," he'd said. "*If* you really want to beat this thing, you will." At the time, Lillie hadn't liked the way he'd emphasized *if*, but now the word helped her raise the bar. She'd show him. She'd show them *all* that she was no longer weak.

She limped to her room and quietly closed the door behind her. A good night's sleep promised a fresh start in the morning. Despite the pain, it felt good knowing that the ugliest facets of her character were in the past. But if she didn't focus on them, they'd become part of her present. Of her future. She'd focus on better, happier times, too, to help her reach for what had seemed an unreachable goal.

Jase had been a big part of those better, happier times. No matter how many *ifs* and *buts* peppered his dialogue, Lillie would continue working to prove that she'd changed, permanently. They'd probably never revive the love they'd once shared—he was with Whitney now—but they could be friends, couldn't they?

Tomorrow, she'd call him to set up a rehearsal. Hour by hour and day by day, she'd show him that she could be trusted, that she hoped his life would be full and rich and happy…even if he shared it with someone else.

Exposure to the kids would be good for him, and Jase would definitely be good for them.

He'd be good for her, too.

CHAPTER EIGHT

JASE CHUGGED DOWN the last of his coffee and put the mug into the dishwasher, trying to decide where to call for takeout.

Whitney had called first thing this morning and invited him to lunch. He'd agreed, but suggested they meet at her place. He decided on pizza. Easy. Cheap. No muss, no fuss.

During the drive from the pizzeria to her place, he admitted that he had no appetite—for food *or* the dialogue he intended to open.

Whitney wasn't home when he arrived. He knew, because her car wasn't parked in front of the garage-turned-storage unit. So Jase sat in the pickup, inhaling the pizza scent, hoping she wouldn't keep him waiting too long. Despite the thick cardboard, it wouldn't stay hot for very long. And the ice was already melting in the drink cups.

Jase climbed out of the truck and pocketed his keys. Grabbing the drinks tray handle with one hand and balancing the pizza box on the other palm, he used his rear to slam the driver's door.

Though it was eighty-five degrees, he was almost comfortable on her shaded porch step.

Another five minutes passed, and still no Whitney. On the phone this morning, she'd told him how much she hated days like these, with no client appointments or court appearances to help the time pass more quickly. Lunch with him, she'd said, would break up the day nicely.

He could hardly wait to hear her explanation for being late *this time.*

Jase imagined himself writing a note that he'd tuck into her screen door: "I waited for nearly half an hour. Sorry, but I ate all the pizza." Shaking his head, Jase resisted the urge to help himself to a slice from the sausage side and concentrated on neighborhood activity, instead. An elderly woman nearly mowing down an already dented aluminum trash can as she backed out of her driveway. A middle-aged guy walking his Great Dane. A rabbit devouring an entire petunia blossom.

"Scram," he said. It froze and stared at Jase for all of a minute before returning to its snack. Obviously, it didn't identify him as a threat. "Fine. Insult my machismo. See if I care."

It hopped away, but only because Whitney had pulled up.

She parked her boxy red hybrid beside his pickup, and approaching the porch, smiled. "Have you been here long?"

"Not really."

Whitney skipped her usual "why I'm late" excuses—heavy traffic, an accident blocking highway lanes, running low on gas—and climbed the brick steps that led to her door.

Once inside, she stood at the sink and lathered her hands. "Why don't you grab us a couple of paper plates," she said, nodding toward the cabinet above the toaster. "The napkins are—"

"On the table," he finished.

He decided to let her eat before he introduced the subject of *them*. She devoured two slices of pizza, talking nonstop about the cute young intern the firm had brought on for the summer.

"He couldn't be more than eighteen," Whitney said, "and has no idea how to behave in an office setting." Laughing, she added, "All I can say is, he's lucky *I'm* not in charge of hiring and firing."

"You'd fire a kid?" he asked, feigning surprise. "A kid who works for free?"

"I would. And speaking of which, let me tell you about my big news!"

Whitney got up and put the pizza box on the kitchen island. "The partners called me in for a private meeting last night," she said, returning to her chair. "They opened another office, this one in San Francisco."

The firm already had branch offices in every major US city, including LA. But Jase failed to see why they'd assemble a private meeting to announce this one.

"They want me to manage it," she continued. "They'd pay all relocation costs, including two round trips to look for a place to live. And if my house doesn't sell within thirty days, they'll buy it."

She hadn't been exaggerating. This *was* big news.

"What did you tell them?"

"Why, I said yes, of course!"

Of course? She'd made a decision that significant without even running it past him? Clearly she hadn't been putting as much importance on their relationship as he'd thought.

Whitney grabbed his hand, gave it a squeeze. "You can do your job anywhere, as long as you have internet access and a Wi-Fi connection. Everything you do for your mom's company here, you can do remotely. And the trip between SFO to MIA airports is only a couple of extra hours..."

It appeared that she'd given the matter a lot of thought. So why hadn't she talked to him first?

"My whole family is here." He slipped his hand from between hers. "So's yours."

Her laughter was nervous. "It's not a long flight. We'd come home often, and they can visit us there."

"We?"

"Of course," she said again, her smile fading.

Jase leaned back in his chair, trying to make sense of the situation. Had she really accepted a transfer to the other side of the country based on the belief that he'd follow along like a well-trained pup?

He wouldn't. Period. *Stop acting like a just-dumped teenager.* She'd saved him from delivering his "why you deserve better than a jerk like me" speech.

Jase didn't want things to end on a sour note, though, so he said, "Sorry, Whit. But I'm afraid I have to stay put. A lot of people are counting on me here."

Eyes narrowed, she said, "Which people?"

"My mother, for starters. You know she isn't in the best of health."

Whitney brightened. "Here's an idea: we'll get a place with an in-law suite. That way, all of us will have our own space, and you'll be nearby if she needs you."

That might work, if he and Whitney had a future together. But since they didn't…

"She'd never go for that."

"How do you know?"

"Because I know my mother. She'd be leaving Drew and Dora to go there."

Frowning, she tugged at the straw in her soda. "Will you at least think about it?"

Elbows resting on the table, Jase said, "I wish

you all the best. You'll do great out there." And with her long-legged, blond, buxom good looks, she'd fit right in with the California crowd.

"If I didn't know better, I'd say you were breaking up with me."

He considered pointing out that she was leaving him, not the other way around. But since her announcement of the job transfer had come at a perfect time, he decided against it. Their splitting up was a good thing. For both of them.

She grabbed his hand again. "We can still *be* together though, right?"

"You mean, have a long-distance relationship?" Jase shook his head. "I've never heard of a couple who could make that work, long-term."

"Then…then you just *have* to come with me!"

"Look, Whitney, let's be practical. We've only been dating for a couple of months."

"More than *six* months. My parents were married two months after they met, and they're still together after nearly forty years."

That comparison made him tense up. How had the conversation turned from her promotion to marriage?

"I'm happy for you, Whit. Proud of you, too. The partners must have a lot of confidence in you to make an offer this great. And I know you'll be a terrific manager."

She let go of his hand and hugged herself. "So it's like that, is it?"

Jase raised his eyebrows. “Like what?”

“You’re issuing an ultimatum. Either I stay, or we’re over.”

He wouldn’t have put it that bluntly, but yeah, she’d pretty much described how he felt.

“Tell me why, Jason. *Why* don’t you think this could work?”

Because to commit to a thing like that, I’d have to love you like crazy.

Jase owed her a kinder answer than that.

“You’re a great gal, and you deserve nothing but the best. That isn’t me.”

She got a little misty-eyed, then she surprised him by saying “You’re right.” Laughing, she quickly added, “Not the part about how I’m so great and deserve the best, but that we’re just… this just wasn’t meant to be.”

Relief flooded him. Gratitude, too.

Whitney got to her feet, collected their paper plates and soda cups and dumped them into the trash.

Jase stood, too. “When do you leave?”

“First thing next week, I’ll go out to have a look at the office space, order furniture and electronics, interview job candidates. And look for a house, of course. I’ve already put this one on the market. The agent will be here this evening with the contract.”

She’d done all that since last night’s meeting?

Jase almost laughed out loud. No wonder she'd been late!

And to think he'd been up half the night, worried that his decision to end things might hurt her. *That'll teach you to walk around, all big-headed and full of yourself, Yeager!*

"Wow. Things are happening fast." He smiled. "The partners chose well. Why don't we have dinner tonight. No…tomorrow, since the agent will be here tonight. We can celebrate your promotion."

She waved his words away. "Well, I'd better start thinking about what I want to pack. And get back to work. I need to meet with HR, to look over the résumés they've been collecting." She pushed her chair under the table.

She stepped up close, close enough to kiss if he had a mind to.

He didn't have a mind to.

"I just want you to know, Jason, how sorry I am that we can't work things out." She tidied his shirt collar. "I think we would have made a pretty good team."

His dad had a favorite saying, one he'd repeat any time Jase performed at less than his best: "good enough never is." He couldn't see himself settling into a life of *pretty good.*

She walked with him to the foyer. "If you want me to, I'll call you once I'm settled in. Just to let you know how things are going. And give you my new address, of course."

"Of course I want you to."

"My cell number won't change," she said. "Will you call me from time to time, to let me know how things are going for you?"

"You bet."

"Because there's no reason we can't be friends, right?"

Jase threw her favorite line back at her: "Of course." At the moment, a white lie seemed gentler than the truth.

And the closing door described the situation well.

CHAPTER NINE

JASE SAT IN his recliner, a slice of cold pizza in one hand, the TV remote in the other. When Robert Duvall's mustachioed face filled the screen, he stopped scrolling. He'd seen the Western twice but would never tired of it.

It wasn't easy, paying attention to the exchange between Duvall and Kevin Costner. Not with the whole scene between Whitney and himself still so fresh in his mind. He hadn't exactly reacted to her good news with unbridled enthusiasm, so with any luck, at least his congratulations had sounded sincere.

Feeling edgy—and not knowing why—Jase turned the TV off and carried his dinner dishes from the family room to the kitchen. He decided to take a drive, maybe even surprise his mom, or Drew and Dora, with a visit.

Taking his keys from the glass bowl on the table in the foyer, Jase stepped onto the small back porch. His cell phone rang as he reached inside to pull the door shut. He didn't recognize the number, but noncritical updates on business-related matters usually came by way of text message. He prepared himself for bad news. *Easier to put out a small fire*, he decided, hitting the accept icon, *than wait for trouble to spread.*

"Yeager," he said.

"Hi, it's Lillie."

It hadn't been necessary for her to identify herself. He'd been hearing that voice in his dreams for years. Jase almost wished it had been Dan, calling to report that the materials he'd need for the next show were still in short supply.

"Hey. Lill. How goes it?"

"It goes."

They'd started hundreds, maybe thousands of conversations this way before her stint in rehab.

"So what's up?" he asked, though he knew the answer.

"I'm just calling to see when you're available to run through a few songs. For the Hopkins' kids' wedding, remember?"

Of course he remembered. It'd been less than a week, yet he'd thought of little else since driving away from the parking lot. But wait…she hadn't asked if he was still interested. Did it mean his sudden mood swing hadn't been so prickly after all? He hadn't exactly behaved like a candidate for the Positive Attitude Award during that visit to her folks' front yard, or at the coffee shop. In their heyday, Lillie would have held his feet to the fire for succumbing to "grumpy old man" conduct. Why not this time? If accepting people at face value was part of her recovery, Jase needed to add it to his mental list of changes in her. Positive changes.

"I'll open up my calendar."

There were no meetings this week, and he had ten days to prepare for his next trip to Florida. He didn't need to look at his calendar. What he needed was time to formulate a response.

"I have to work tonight and tomorrow night," she told him, "and the lunch rush tomorrow. But I'm free the next day, and the day after that."

"Tell you what. How 'bout if you choose a couple of days and times that work for you, and get back to me?"

The pause was lengthy enough that Jase pulled the phone away from his ear, to see if the call had dropped.

"We can get together day after next," she said, "anytime."

"How's ten o'clock? Too early?"

Lillie laughed. "Have you *met* me? I'm up with the birds, remember?"

Yeah, he remembered all right. Not long after she'd joined the band, they'd all gone camping with a plan to work out some new tunes. Jase and the guys had turned in a good two hours before Lillie, yet when the sun came up, she'd greeted them with coffee, toast and bacon on the grill, and a chirpy "Good morning!" While the guys grumbled, Lillie had whipped up a panful of scrambled eggs, and served up the meal with a smile. Every time that memory surfaced, Jase compared the scene to the changes caused by the pills. But cheerfulness was in Lillie's DNA.

"If you like, we can get together in the afternoon. Or the evening, for that matter."

"No, ten's fine. In your folks' turret?"

"Yep. You're gonna love the sound quality in there."

"Okay. It's a date, then."

A second, perhaps two ticked by, and she filled the prickly silence with, "I'm looking forward to it."

"Me, too." And he meant it.

Repocketing the phone, he shut the door behind him. He decided against visiting his brother, or his mom. What he needed was noise and activity to divert his thoughts. He'd find both—in spades—at his old bandmate Spence's house.

On the way to Ellicott City, he stopped at a big box store and picked up an assortment of toys and puzzles. He hadn't even rung the front bell when the band's bass player flung open the door and wrapped Jase in a brotherly hug.

"Dude! What brings you to this side of town?"

"It's been a while since I saw those rug rats of yours." He held up the big plastic bag. "Thought I'd bribe 'em into telling their ol' uncle Jase a few knock-knock jokes."

"You start that ball rollin'," Spence said, giving Jase a playful shove, "and you're on your own. Those kids don't know the meaning of the word *enough*."

"What I want to know is how in the world they memorized that many jokes!"

Spence tapped his temple. "They take after their dad." He cupped a palm beside his mouth, bellowed, "Fiona, hon! C'mere!"

Drying her hands on a dish towel as she rounded the corner, Spence's wife did her best to look and sound like a stern mother. "For heaven's sake, Spencer, must you shout *all* the time?"

"Only when the cat drags in stuff like this." He stepped aside, and when she saw Jase standing near the door, she grabbed his elbow and pulled him inside.

"How long has it been since you stopped by?" she asked, guiding him toward the kitchen.

"Too long." By his count, it had been nearly six months. The Muzikalees were still the house band at Three-Eyed Joe's. And since Deke, the owner, counted on Jase to keep the books straight, he'd seen the band members weekly. Their wives and kids were another matter.

She linked her arm through his and led him into the kitchen. "What have you been up to?"

"Working, mostly."

Eyes narrowed, she rested both fists on her hips. "Mostly?"

He didn't dare say "Breaking up with one girl, spending a little time with Lillie," because a) she would read him the riot act for both, and b) what she didn't know couldn't hurt him.

"Where are the kids?"

"We're running late with dinner today, thanks to homework, drum lessons…stuff. They're out back, kicking a soccer ball around," Spence said.

"Go on out there," Fiona said. "They'll be over the moon when they see you!"

Jase flung the big bag over one shoulder and, as he stepped onto the deck, watched the Smith kids jockeying for control of the ball. Their happy laughter and taunts floated around the tidy yard, and as Glen, the youngest, kicked it toward the tall hedge that formed the property line, Jase hollered, "Ho-ho-ho!"

The ball landed in the shrubs as all three boys raced toward him.

"Uncle Jase!" they shouted, hugging his knees.

"What's in the bag?" Glen, the seven-year-old asked.

"Just a couple of surprises for you guys."

Greg, the nine-year-old, said, "Can we see 'em?"

He put the bag on the deck and sat at the table. "Better check with your mom first. I don't want to get in trouble for making you guys even later having your supper."

"Mom!" Grant bellowed. *"Mom!"*

Fiona parted the curtains of the window above the sink. "Unless somebody's bleeding, I don't want to hear noise like that!"

"Uncle Jase won't give us our surprises until after we eat," Grant said.

"I've already set him a place at the table. Supper's in ten minutes, so go wash up, right now, you hear?"

Now he faced the prospect of stuffing his face with a second dinner meal. When he'd decided to drop by, he didn't think he'd be interrupting suppertime…

"Aw, does that mean we can't see our surprises yet?"

"'Fraid so," Jase said. "Don't want to rile your mom, now do we?"

Jase led the way inside, and the boys dogged his heels.

"We saw you on TV," Grant said. "You did a really good job!"

He ruffled the boy's hair. "Thanks, kiddo."

The foursome formed a line at the powder room door, each waiting his turn to clean up. By the time Jase stepped up to the sink, the towel bore gray streaks. Laughing, he found a clean dry corner and blotted his damp hands.

"So what can I do to help?" Jase asked, finding Fiona in the kitchen.

She handed him a bag of salad fixings and a

stack of small bowls. "You can put this on the table. The dressing is in the fridge."

While he worked, she said, "So how are things going with you and Whitney?"

"They aren't. She pulled the plug today."

"No way."

"The firm made her an offer she couldn't refuse, so she's moving to San Francisco."

"No way!"

Nodding, Jase said, "She leaves next week for Phase One."

"I always suspected she was an idiot. Now I'm sure of it."

He grabbed four bottles of salad dressing and lined them up on the table as she continued.

"Goofy girl doesn't know a good catch when she sees one." Then, "When did she break it off with you?"

"She didn't. Exactly." He told her how things had gone. "Believe it or not, she did me a favor. I'd been about to tell her that I think we should see other people."

"No. *Way!*"

Jase nodded. "She couldn't have timed it better if she tried."

She pulled out a kitchen chair and pointed at the seat. "Park it, mister, and tell me all about the reasons you were about to say goodbye."

Jase looked left, then right, and satisfied they were alone, said, "It sounds stupid, I know, but we just didn't connect. There just wasn't any..." At a loss for words, he shrugged.

"No spark, huh?" Fiona sat across from him, and tidied the flatware beside her plate. "Like there was with Lillie."

He didn't know what she might say, but Jase hadn't expected *that*.

"You can drop the act, m'friend. I remember how it was between you two. I've never seen a couple more in love than you and Lillie."

Jase couldn't very well argue. They *had* been great together before the accident.

"Okay, fine, it's a touchy subject. I get that." She looked left and right, too. "So...I hear she's back in town..."

"Yeah. She's been home for a couple months now."

"Is that what prompted the breakup with Whitney?"

Now it was his turn to say "no way."

"Why not? She did her time in rehab and, from what I hear, worked hard to pay all her debts." She regarded him with a wary eye. "Ah, I get it. She's using again, huh?" Fiona shook her head. "That's a shame."

"Far as I know, Lillie is still clean. But I'm not with her all that much, so how would I know, y'know?"

"Yeah, I know. You haven't trusted her in a long, long time. It's why you broke up, and if you ask me, *that's* why you guys haven't hooked up again, now that she's back."

Jase winced. "Boy, when you hit the old nail on the head, you don't fool around, do you?"

"I don't have time for drivel. I believe in going straight to the heart of matters."

It reminded him of something Lillie used to say: "Beating around the bush is a waste of time and unnecessarily hard on the shrubbery." He supposed that explained why she and Fiona had always gotten along so well.

"You still care about her. Don't bother denying it. It's written all over your face."

"Sure I do. We were…we were really close. So yeah, I care, but only in an 'I want her to be happy' way."

"Baloney." Fiona got up and went to the stove.

"Salami," he kidded, and when she rolled her eyes, Jase said, "Seriously, Fi, I've only spent *maybe* an hour, total, with her since she got back. And none of those old feelings resurfaced." That wasn't entirely true, but he chose not to dwell on it.

"Jase Yeager, you might be able to fool your other friends, but you can't fool me. I'm raising three boys. I know a fib when I hear one." She tossed a hot pad into the center of the table, then placed the big stew pot on top of it. "Do me a favor and round up the monkeys before they need to wash up all over again. You'll probably find Spence in his office, tuning his guitars. I'd bet my diamond ring that he'll want you to jam with him and the boys after supper."

Spence had bought the kids a piano, guitars and a drum set, and even while they were still in diapers, they could produce almost tolerable music. A jam session sounded good to Jase. A little more time with the rowdy Smith clan was sure to keep his mind off Whitney. And Lillie.

CHAPTER TEN

"WHERE IS EVERYBODY?" Jase asked, putting down his guitar case in the foyer.

"The construction crew is gone, for now, anyway," Lillie said. "Mom and Dad are shopping. It's been a while since they've been able to properly stock the pantry."

"That's what I need to do. Between flying back and forth to Florida and running the day-to-day stuff at the company, I haven't had time to hit the grocery store."

"But let me guess… There are at least three boxes of breakfast cereal in the cabinet above your stove…"

Jase smiled at that. "Four, actually, but you get bonus points for remembering where I keep them."

She'd cooked dozens of meals for him, had made lasagna in his kitchen the day before the breakup. Did he think her addiction had addled her brain to the point she wouldn't remember something like that?

Lillie bit back her annoyance. She'd been

warned that people would question just about everything about her. *And who do you have to blame for that?*

"I want to show you something," she said, changing the subject on the way to the kitchen. She threw open the French doors and led the way onto the back porch. "I wish I had more time to spend out there, reading, sipping sweet tea, enjoying the breeze… Isn't that the most gorgeous gazebo, ever?"

"Yeah. Gorgeous."

He'd been looking at her, not the gazebo when he said it. Lillie decided she'd better not read too much into that. She tidied the flowery cushions on the wicker glider, and from the corner of her eye, noticed that he wasn't standing up as straight as usual. A sign, she recalled, that he'd been pushing himself too hard. Faint dark circles under his eyes told her he'd probably been up all hours, making mental to-do lists instead of sleeping. He'd probably been skipping meals… and not just because he hadn't taken time to shop.

"I didn't have breakfast," she fibbed. "Do you mind if I fix something before we get started?"

He shoved his hands in his pockets. "Don't mind a bit."

"Over easy?" She cracked two eggs in the skillet.

"You remembered?"

"That you're always hungry, or how you like your eggs?"

It had been that adorable slanted smile—the one that exposed a deep, oblong dimple in his left cheek—that had captivated her during her audition at Three-Eyed Joe's. Lillie used to tease him that if not for that dimple, she wouldn't have fallen in love with him. And he made her pay for the statement by charging a fee: a kiss, placed smack dab in the middle of that dimple.

She opened the refrigerator door. "I remember a lot of things about you."

The smile diminished as she stacked the egg carton, a package of link sausage and butter in her arms. "There's coffee over there. Help yourself."

Her heart swelled when he went right to the spot where her mom had always kept the mugs. No surprise, really, since he'd joined her family dozens of times. Affection pulsed in her heart.

Stop behaving like a love-struck ninny, she scolded. *He's* with *someone.*

"Can I pour you some?" he asked, still holding the pot.

"That'd be nice. Thanks."

After arranging the sausage links in a cast iron skillet, Lillie set the table. "There's OJ and tomato juice in the fridge," she said, placing squatty glasses near the plates. "I'll have tomato."

He seemed relieved to have something to do.

When he finished, Jase leaned against the counter beside the stove and crossed his arms over his chest. “I like your hair like that.”

“Thanks. I cut it as part of my ‘start over, start fresh’ campaign.” When he didn’t respond, Lillie said, “I like yours, too.”

Jase ran his fingers through his dark bangs and, laughing, said, “Haven’t had time to get to the barber’s either. It’s a hair longer than normal—pardon the pun—but otherwise, it’s the way I’ve worn it for years.”

She dumped several pats of butter into a Teflon frying pan. “I liked it then, I like it now.”

“I, uh, thanks.”

Was his sudden silence the result of remembering the way they’d always watched movies… his head in her lap, her fingers gently massaging his scalp? Oh, what she’d give to touch his hair right now!

Jase peered into the dining room, where stacks of folded plastic sheeting and coils of electric cords lined the far wall, the only remaining signs of the remodel. “So the crew is pretty much finished, then. Bet your mom is relieved.”

“No question about it.” She turned on the flame under the pan. “This stove was special ordered from a culinary school in France. Beautiful, isn’t it?”

“Yeah. It’s really something, all right.” This

time as he spoke, Jase actually looked at the stove.

"Mind if I have a look around, see what else has changed since I was here last?"

"Make yourself at home." Lillie cracked four eggs into the skillet. "But wait a minute." She waved the spatula in the air. "Didn't you come inside when you stopped by?"

"When I stopped by..."

"Dad told me that you popped over every few months," she began, hiding a grin, "usually with a different woman on your arm?"

Jase took a step away from the counter and put his hands in his pockets. It was what he'd always done when at a loss for words. Lillie wished she could rephrase the question, with no special emphasis on the word *woman*. It made her sound like a jealous wife, and they both knew she'd never be anything of the kind.

"Lill, you know as well as I do that I like your mom and dad. Your brother and sister, too. Heck. All of them made me feel like family, even the twins. I didn't think you'd have a problem with it if I stopped by now and then, to see how they were doing."

After flipping the eggs, she lined up the sausages on a plate. "So how are Drew and Dora? Still working too much?"

His expression had gone from friendly to borderline annoyed. And who could blame him?

"Yeah. Some things never change."

His tone had changed, too, from warm to coolly detached.

"That's too bad. Life is short. All work and no play…"

"…makes Jack a dull boy," they said together.

At least he was smiling again.

His ability to read her mind had always amazed her. But now? After all this time apart? It stirred the embers she'd hidden deep inside her heart, and the dim glow gave her hope that there might be a chance for them. Emotionally, Lillie felt stronger than ever. She truly believed she had beaten the monster Addiction into submission. She'd learned in rehab that any crazy thing—disappointment, hurt feelings, the judgment of others—could hurtle an addict straight back into the abyss. Despite the drugs' ability to deliver temporary respite from pain, she'd hated that dark, lonely place and never wanted to go back there again.

"Did you sing much while you were…away?"

Was he having trouble dealing with the fact that she'd been in rehab? Or maybe, instead, he thought she didn't like reminders of her time at Rising Sun.

"Not a note."

He stared at her for a long, silent moment, then topped off his coffee. "Why not, if you don't mind my asking?"

"Pete asked me to, dozens of times, but the association between music and…" *And you*, she thought, *made it unbearable.*

She pretended to be distracted, getting breakfast on the table, and once they were seated, Lillie turned the conversation to Jase's work.

"You seem really comfortable, being on TV."

"I wasn't at first. Got so nervous during the first airing that I had to take a break halfway through it to change my shirt."

The only time she'd seen him sweat had been the night he spelled things out in no uncertain terms. *It's me or the drugs.* Lillie shook off the awful memory.

"But you were always so great onstage."

"Yeah, in front of a couple hundred people, tops. Big difference between that and a couple *million.*"

"I hadn't considered that."

"Plus, onstage, I had the guys covering my back."

Interesting, Lillie thought, that he hadn't said *you* and the guys. She'd let him down in a lot of ways, but never when it came to the performance.

"Don't get me wrong," he continued, "the show hosts jump in a lot, which relieves some of the pressure. Trouble is, some of 'em don't know when to jump *out.*" He held up his right hand, made it say "Blah-blah-blah-*blah.*" Then,

"And as often as not, they get the product details wrong. Drives me nuts, having to correct them on-air."

"I can understand that." She sipped her tomato juice. "Does your mom ever appear on the show?"

"No, she wants to stay as far from the cameras as possible."

"I suppose that makes sense. With her recent health scare, why risk the added stress?"

"She acts like that's no big deal. Shrugs it off as a ministroke."

"Still, she had a TIA, right? It might not be as grim as the real deal, but it's still serious, since it warns what might happen without proper medications and care."

"How'd you learn so much about it?"

"You remember my dad's heart attack, years ago. It was fairly mild, as heart attacks go, but his cardiologist made it pretty clear that it could lead to another more destructive one—or a stroke."

"Yeah, I do remember." He studied her face again. "And knowing you, you studied up on both."

"Well yes, so I could help Mom keep him on a diet and..."

When Lillie saw his admiring expression, she stopped talking. She hadn't earned that from him. Not yet. But she decided to ignore the feelings. Giving them more significance than they warranted would only lead to trouble.

"How's Deke these days?"

Jase drained his coffee mug. "He's great. Saw him a couple days ago. Every time I stop by, I expect to see some signs that he's actually in his sixties. You know, gray hair, wrinkles, an arthritic knuckle or two. The guy is ageless."

"Still holding the Sloppiest Office in America title?"

The question invited a chuckle. "Yeah. And y'know? Maybe that's what keeps him young. Deke never sweats the small stuff..."

"...and it's all small stuff," they said at the same time.

Laughing, Jase shoved back from the table and patted his stomach. She couldn't help noticing how flat it was. "Whew. I'm stuffed. Thanks, Lill. Breakfast was great."

She wished he'd stop looking at her that way—eyes beaming with affection, a smile that warmed her to the soles of her feet—because it reminded her of better times and raised her hopes even more. Lillie broke the intense eye contact and got to her feet to clear the table. Lillie's hands trembled as she put a thumb into her own juice glass, a forefinger into his. They clinked together as she lifted them, shattering both rims...and leaving an inch-long gash in the bend of her thumb.

"Oh, good grief," she said, quickly depositing both into the sink. "I'm such a klutz."

Jase was beside her in an eye blink and, gently cupping her hand in his, turned on the faucet. Brow furrowed with concentration, he leaned in for a closer look.

"It's barely a scratch," she said, willing her voice to stop shaking. "I'll be fine."

Without letting go, he turned, eyes flicking from her lips to her cheeks before meeting her gaze. "While I appreciate the consult, Doctor Rourke, I think we should wait a few minutes before deciding that it's fine." He looked back at the cut. "If it hasn't stopped bleeding in ten minutes, I'll drive you to the ER."

For a moment, neither of them spoke as they stood, shoulders touching, his hand under hers. She dreaded the possibility of stitches. Then, an idea came to her…

"Have you ever made a butterfly bandage?"

Bright blue eyes met hers—eyes that gleamed with concern—and sent her heart into overdrive.

"Can't say that I have."

"I can teach you. I learned how at Rising Sun, a class in emergency first aid."

His left eyebrow disappeared behind his bangs. "Someday, I hope you'll tell me all about what you learned—and what you went through—up there."

Lillie held her breath and hoped Jase couldn't

hear her hard-beating heart. Jase had always been a caring man who rarely said things he didn't mean. That alone made what he'd said that night so hard to hear.

Lillie had two choices: start listing life lessons learned in rebab, or change the subject.

"Just so happens I aced all my craft classes. In fact, my basket weaving was so perfect, the counselor called dibs on mine." Peripheral vision drew her attention to the sink. Watching her blood swirl down the drain made her lightheaded. Jase had been right. The cut *was* deep, and showed no signs of clotting.

"There's medical tape in the powder room."

"Don't move. I'll get it."

Jase jogged down the hall, muttering something unintelligible as he searched for the tape. He was back in no time with the tape, a small pair of scissors, peroxide and a clean towel.

Standing beside her again, he scrubbed his hands. "You really think this special bandage idea of yours will stop the bleeding?"

"Worst-case scenario, it'll slow it down."

"Well then," he said, pulling out a kitchen chair, "let's get this operation underway."

The instant she sat down, Jase took a knee.

"Okay, what do I do first?"

"Tear off five strips of the tape, and stick one end of each to the edge of the table."

Jase followed instructions to the letter. "And now?"

"Uncap the peroxide for me," she said, draping the towel over her knees.

He did, and when she splashed it over the cut and onto the floor, Jase winced. "Sheesh. I could have done that!"

She grinned and dabbed blood from around the gash. "Don't worry about it."

"Hey, it's your folks' new hickory floor, not mine."

"Soon as we're finished here, I'll wipe it up. They'll never even notice."

He harrumphed. "If you say so. What's next?"

"Put a twist into one of the tape strips. Put it right in the middle." When he did, she added, "Now twist it again, so that both sticky sides are face down."

"Okay..."

Using her free hand, Lillie pinched both sides of the wound together until it formed a thin line. "Put the twist over the cut, to hold the cut closed. That's it. Perfect. Now stick another to the right of it, and one to the left."

He admired the X shape he'd made. "Hey. That's pretty cool. It's hardly bleeding at all anymore."

His approval shouldn't have meant so much, but it did. She hid her feelings behind a grin.

"Stick with me, Yeager. You might just learn *another* thing or two."

Leaning a hand on each of the chair's arms, he said, "So that's it? We're done?"

He was close enough to kiss. Part of her wanted to give in to it. And part of her knew what a mistake that would be. There was another person to consider. Whitney.

"Not quite. You need to tape over the edges, to hold all the strips in place."

"But…how do you protect the cut? There's barely anything covering it."

"Oh. Right. I'd almost forgotten about that. There should be some gauze in the medicine cabinet, along with some antibiotic ointment."

Grazing her cheek with a fingertip, Jase smiled. "No problem." When he got back this time, he didn't wait for instructions. Didn't ask questions. Didn't make comments. Instead, he squeezed a pea-sized blob of the ointment onto a fingertip and spread it onto the gauze. After placing it greasy-side-down over the cut, he secured all four sides with more tape.

Lillie wanted to throw her arms around his neck. The fact that she couldn't—that she probably *never* could—put tears in her eyes.

He scooted a chair closer to hers and sat, facing her. "Hey. What's wrong?" Again, Jase cradled her injured hand. "Was I too rough? Did I press too hard getting the gauze in place?"

Lillie shook her head. "No, no, nothing like that."

"Then what's with this?" he asked, catching a tear with the pad of his thumb.

She'd always loved the thick dark lashes that framed his eyes—eyes the same shade of blue as the periwinkle acrylic in her paint kit—but never more than right now, when despite everything she'd put him through, he looked upset. Not the worried expression he'd worn all those times he'd rushed her to the hospital, but a look that said he cared about her, still.

"Well, I, thanks for this," she said, easing her hand from his. "Guess I should get the dishes done..."

She started to get up, but his big hand on her shoulder prevented it.

"Are you crazy?"

"The yolks will harden if I don't—"

"The dishwasher isn't even hooked up yet." He pointed at the machine, sitting at an odd angle against the wall, and the black hoses dangling from one side. "I worked hard on that enormous, crazy-looking bandage. No way am I letting you get it all wet." Jase rolled up his sleeves. "*I'll* do the dishes." He refilled her mug. "You just sit there and look pretty."

Lillie had been miserable without him, but at least she'd known where she stood. Now, after he'd been so sweet, after those tender looks and thoughtful words, she wasn't sure how to feel. Or how *he* felt, for that matter. Over the years, Jase had done a good job of making others think he was rough and tough, but she'd witnessed far too many examples of his sensitive side to believe it: pulling a baby duck out of the sewer; leaping into the murky harbor waters to save a wharf kitten from drowning; getting teary-eyed while watching the conclusion of the movie *Sommersby.* For all Lillie knew, today's acts of kindness had more to do with his innate goodness than what she'd needed.

"Is your coffee hot enough?"

"It's perfect," Lillie said. *Just like you.* Then she noticed his tattoo. "When did you get that?"

He followed her gaze to the deep blue anchor on the inside of his forearm. "Got it about a year and a half ago, give or take a few weeks."

She'd been gone about a year...

"Why not a guitar or a microphone? A treble clef? A semiquaver? Something that represents music?"

"Music. Gimme a break." He rinsed a plate and stood it in the dish rack. "The anchor symbolizes stability. And putting down an anchor represents the end of a journey."

Lillie surprised herself by saying, "That last year with *me* was the journey, right—a not-so-pleasant one—and the anchor is to remind you to stop drifting aimlessly, waiting for the day when I'll finally keep a promise."

Jase froze in place for a second or two.

"How's the hand?" He put more energy than necessary into scrubbing the black skillet. "Throbbing by now, I'll bet."

"My hand is fine." *It's my* heart *that's aching.* Lillie added this moment to her list of regrets. "I'm sorry, Jase. I know you've heard that before, too many times to count, but it's true. I never meant to drag you into my—"

"You have any acetaminophen?" He added the pan to the dish rack.

So that was how it was, huh? Evading any discussion of their past was enough to give him a headache? That hurt far more than the cut!

"I'm sure Mom has a bottle in the powder room." She got up, collected the tape and other supplies. "I'll bring it for you after I put this stuff away."

Finally, Jase faced her. "It isn't for me. I just figured you might need it." He nodded at her hand. "For that."

She met his gaze, blink for blink. Moments ago, they'd glowed with warmth and affection. Now, they sparked with brittle mistrust, just as they had on the night she returned his ring.

"I don't take painkillers anymore."

"Never? Not even aspirin?"

His expression softened, just enough that it

inspired her to add, "I've learned it's easier to live with some physical discomfort."

Jase dried his hands and draped the blue-checked towel over the clean dishes.

"After all this time, you're still hurting?"

Never more than at this moment. But that wasn't true. The heartache that began that awful night was the worst she'd ever experienced. And time hadn't dulled it.

"Where? What hurts?"

She clutched the supplies closer to her aching heart. "My leg, mostly." Turning, she took a few steps toward the hall. "Soon as I get these put away, we'll get busy on those songs. You have better things to do than stand around talking about my aches and pains."

Lillie didn't wait for him to agree. It took effort to make her way back down the hall without limping. Once everything was back inside the medicine cabinet, she quietly closed its door. "Fool," she told her reflection, fighting back tears. How would she get through their rehearsal without blubbering like a baby? Losing him had hurt far more than any injury sustained in the accident. Being so near him, talking to him, looking into those remarkable, concerned eyes had awakened every sentiment she'd worked so hard to bury. He'd been her friend. Her confidant. Her first real love. She'd had a good, happy life before meeting him, but Jase had made it better. And she'd traded all that…for *what*?

Lillie looked at her white-bandaged hand. In a week, maybe less, it'd be good as new. If only the injuries she'd caused Jase could be mended as easily.

"Lillie…?"

She jumped at the unexpected sound of his voice.

"You're crying again."

Lillie swiped at her traitorous tears. What right did she have to feel sorry for herself? Her disappointments had been self-inflicted, unlike those she'd thrust onto him.

Eyes closed, she willed him to go away. She didn't want to sing with him. Didn't want him helping out with the Hopkins' kids' pretend wedding. Right now, all she wanted was—

Before she knew what was happening, he'd drawn her into a loose hug, and she let him.

"I know how hard you've been trying, Lill."

She felt his warm breath on her temple…right before his lips made contact with it.

"You're different somehow, so yeah, it's clear that you're working hard to stay clean. This time."

Who knew that two little words could sting as much as a cold slap?

Lillie tried to back away, but the powder room was small, and she had nowhere to go.

"Like I said before, you're stubborn. You can beat this thing…if you want it badly enough."

Lillie felt like shouting "If? This time? I've already beat it! I've been clean for more than a year, and I'm going to stay that way!"

She tried pushing him away, but he only tightened his hold. It wasn't until he lifted her chin on a bent forefinger that she realized she'd said it all, out loud.

"I know that, and I'm proud of you. I shouldn't have tacked on that *this time* nonsense. That was…insensitive."

Lillie studied his face, searching for signs of sincerity. Or doubt. Relief flooded through her when a slow smile lit his face. Not enough to display that endearing dimple in his cheek, but a smile nonetheless. She inhaled a deep breath and let it out slowly, summoning every ounce of willpower in her.

Because if he kept looking at her that way—the way he had before she destroyed them—Lillie feared she might say something to mess up the little bit of *good* she'd just earned in his eyes.

CHAPTER ELEVEN

"HARD TO BELIEVE you haven't picked up a guitar that you haven't sung—except for the kids at Hopkins—in a year." Jase shook his head. "Have I told you how great you sound?"

Lillie blushed. "Only half a dozen times. Have I said thanks?"

"Only half a dozen times." He opened the screen door. "You'll call me? When the kids get all the details figured out?"

"Of course."

He noticed the slight hesitation, and wouldn't blame her if she didn't call. Although he'd tried hard to regulate his words, he'd upset her to the point of tears. Twice. What made him feel worse was the fact that Lillie had never been the type who cried easily. Not when the nurses forced her to walk the halls following every surgery, not when she pushed herself past her limits during physical therapy.

Jase said, "Okay then, you have a good day."

"You, too."

"Say hi to your folks for me."

"Will do."

Should he hug her goodbye? Drop a quick kiss on her cheek? It didn't seem right, considering everything they'd just shared, to leave without a gesture of some sort.

So he winked. *Winked!*

You're a conceited jerk, he told himself.

He considered asking her what a guy should wear to a make-believe wedding for children. If gifts were required. How many guests might attend the ceremony. But those were all things he'd find out later. Having run out of stall tactics, Jase turned and made a beeline for his truck. While sliding the guitar case onto the back seat, he caught a glimpse of her, still standing in the open doorway, uninjured hand raised in silent farewell.

She looked like an angel, wavy hair glowing like a halo in a shaft of early-afternoon sunlight. He liked the physical changes in her…a little more meat on her bones, shorter hair, dresses and sandals instead of jeans and sneakers…

Jase returned the wave and climbed into the pickup's cab. As he drove away, it took effort to look straight ahead instead of catching a last glance at her.

She'd made inward changes, too, things that a casual friend probably wouldn't notice. Her serene bearing, for starters, contrasted with her former hate-to-sit-still demeanor. And while her quick-witted sense of humor remained firmly intact, maturity had tamed her tendency to turn just about anything into a joke. A facade, he wondered, donned to prove how hard she'd worked to kick her habit?

Waiting for the traffic light at Broadway and Fleet to turn green, Jase remembered the way she'd defended herself when his attempt at a show of support failed, miserably. "If?" she'd all but shouted. *I've been clean for more than a year!*

For her sake, he hoped that was true. Hoped, too, that Lillie would still be clean a year—ten years from now.

Jase had driven all of three blocks when his cell phone rang. He hit the Bluetooth answer button on his steering wheel.

"Yeager..."

"Jase, hi. It's Lillie. I can't believe I forgot to tell you about the inn's grand reopening..."

As they'd gone over the list of song titles she'd chosen, Jase had noticed a green folder on the turret's oak coffee table. *Invoices*, its tab said, with a slash that added *Reopening*.

"I'm sure Mom and Dad would love to see you there."

But you wouldn't? "When is it?"

"Two weeks from Saturday, between two and eight. Bring your appetite, because we'll have a ton to eat."

"Wouldn't be a Rourke get-together if there wasn't. Your mom doesn't know the meaning of 'just a little food.'"

He could almost hear her smile, and wished she *had* remembered to tell him about the opening, so he could see it in person.

"Feel free to bring Whitney and your mom."

Whitney. He hadn't told her about Whitney. But…but he'd held Lillie, consoled her. Did that mean anything to her?

Jase's grip on the steering wheel tightened. "Thanks. I'll let you know."

"Well…enjoy the rest of your day."

The kind of thing you said to an acquaintance, not someone who had come *this* close to becoming your spouse.

"You, too. And thanks again for breakfast. It was great."

You're reaching, dude... But repeating himself was the only thing he could think of to keep her on the line. Although why he wanted that so badly, Jase didn't know.

Silence told him that Lillie had ended the call. It didn't hit anywhere near as hard as when she'd pressed the engagement ring into his hand, but it didn't feel good either. He searched his memory for the litany of phrases he'd recited to keep putting one foot in front of the other once the reality of the breakup had set in:

Get over yourself.

This is for the best.

You didn't deserve that.

Stay busy.

There was paperwork at the office, and he hadn't been kidding about restocking his kitchen. Jase pictured his unmade bed. The magazines stacked lackadaisically and newspapers strewn across his sofa. He'd stop at the store, and once the groceries were put away, he'd tackle the mess and do some much-needed housekeeping. After that, he'd shower and pay a quick visit to Three-Eyed Joe's. With any luck, the tasks would take up enough space in his head to crowd out thoughts of Lillie.

How he'd push her out of his heart was another matter entirely.

THE DOOR HADN'T even closed behind him when someone shouted, "There he is, America's newest TV star!"

Every head in the pub turned toward the door. A few patrons waved, several more said, "Hey, Jase!" The rest quickly turned their attention back to the O's game on the widescreen behind the bar.

Deke tossed a towel over one shoulder and said, "What brings you here on this bright, sunshiny afternoon?"

"Needed a Three-Eyed fix." He winced at himself. *Talk about insensitive.* Especially after spending time with Lillie that morning, and witnessing firsthand how hard she was working to leave addiction in her past.

"Beer?"

"Nah, it's a little early for booze. But it's like an oven out there, so I'll take a soda, lotsa ice..."

After filling a tall curved glass, Deke came around the bar and settled on the stool beside Jase's.

"Okay, out with it, kid. What's eatin' you?"

He'd never been able to hide anything from his old friend and saw no reason to start now.

"Work has been crazy busy," he began. "Whitney accepted a transfer to California. Mom refuses to accept that she needs to take better care of herself. And Lillie's home."

"Man. You don't believe in burying the lede or anything, do ya?"

Jase took a long slow drink of soda.

"Have you seen her? Is she doing okay?"

"Saw her just this morning." Jase explained how he'd offered to help out at the make-believe wedding at Hopkins, and about the practice session. "She sounds great. Looks great." *Really great*, he didn't add. "And unless she's just telling me what she thinks I want to hear, she's been clean for a year and a half."

"Well, good for her. Always liked that li'l sweetheart. Not only could she outsing any gal who's got a label, but she's got a heart of gold, too."

Jase nodded, remembering her rich, throaty notes...powerful, yet smooth and warm, like thick, sweet honey.

"She's matured in a lot of ways," he told Deke.

"Yeah?"

"Not the mostly elbows and knees kid who left Baltimore for New York anymore, for one thing. She cut her hair. Doesn't fidget like she used to. And she's quieter."

Deke drummed his fingers on the lacquered surface of the dark wooden bar. "So when's this fake wedding? Can anybody attend, or is it a closed ceremony?"

"I'll have to ask. But if I know Lillie, she'd love to see you again. She asked about you today."

Deke smiled. "Well, when you talk to her, tell her hey for me." He leaned both beefy forearms on the bar and, looking directly at Jase, said, "So?"

"So what?"

"Don't give me that, smart-mouth. So now that Whitney's history, are you and Lill gonna pick up where you left off?"

Jase stared at the intricate eagle-on-globe tattoo that decorated Deke's forearm. *Semper Fidelis* said the ribbon that wrapped around it. *Always faithful*. Ironic, on multiple levels. But staring at the marine tattoo did nothing to distract him from the question.

"Doubt it," he answered.

"Why?"

"You want a numerical or alphabetical list of reasons?"

"Aw, knock it off. You two were made for each other. So she got a little off track. She's back on the straight and narrow now. Isn't that what really counts?"

His brain shuffled through all the lies, the broken promises, those scary trips to the ER when he thought for sure he'd lose her permanently.

This time, Jase answered with a shrug.

"What makes you think she'll backslide?" Deke asked.

Yet again, his mind raced with fears. And disappointments. "I don't *know* that. I hope she's kicked the addiction, for good this time."

Deke snorted. "Never knew you to be a coward."

Jase did a double take.

Deke shrugged. "What's the worst that could happen? If you start over with her, I mean."

The big guy grabbed a thick pretzel stick from the tumbler on the bar, snapped it in two and bit off one end. Maybe his old pal was right. Maybe Jase *was* a coward. But Lillie held all the cards, held all the power, and she could break him just as surely as Deke had broken that pretzel. He'd survived it once. If there was a next time, would he be so lucky?

"New tat?" he asked, pointing at the *USMC* inked across Deke's knuckles.

"Purty, ain't it?" he said, flexing his fingers. "Reunion comin' up in September. Got one more tat in mind, and just enough time to get it beforehand. *Helo*," he said, and using a fingertip, drew E/2/5 on the bar.

"E-two-five?"

"Echo Company, 2nd Battalion, 5th Marine Regiment."

He recalled stories Deke had told—after downing a few after the customers had left and the pub was dark and quiet. The man had survived the horrors of war, lost his wife to a younger man, sidestepped bankruptcy—twice—yet never once thought of giving up. Jase felt a mix of shame and sorrow for his fear of another Lillie-related heartache.

Sitting up straight, he snapped off a quick salute. "Thank you for your service, sir."

Deke returned the gesture, and grinning, added, "Don't call me sir."

He'd heard the what-not-to-call-a-sergeant story before, but since Deke seemed in the mood to talk, Jase said, "Let me buy you a beer and you can remind me *why*."

Back on his side of the bar, Deke filled two glasses and slid one to Jase. "Because I *worked* for a living, that's why." He downed a mouthful of summer ale and used the back of one hand to wipe suds from his upper lip. "I'm an old man, so show me some respect, whippersnapper. Answer my question. And make it short and sweet. The joint will be jumpin' soon."

"Which question?"

Deke groaned, then repeated, "What's the worst that could happen if you and Lillie got back together?"

Only honesty, Jase believed, would bring this unpleasant subject to a close. "Life is unpredictable. Something could happen to make her turn to drugs again."

"Y'think? Like what?"

"Her dad has a heart condition. What if—God forbid—it takes him from her?"

Deke shook his head. "Call me obtuse, but didn't she get *into* drugs in the first place to cut the pain from all the stuff she went through after the accident?"

He answered with a one-shouldered shrug.

"Whole different kind of pain than the loss of a parent." He scowled and stared into his glass. "Or a spouse."

Jase wasn't so sure of that, but let the comment pass.

"How's she doing in that regard, anyway? PT a thing of the past?"

"Yeah, she finished up with her physical therapy

before leaving for New York. But she's still favoring the bad leg. Says it hurts pretty much nonstop."

"What's she taking for it?"

"Nothing. Lillie told me this morning that she hasn't taken so much as an aspirin in more than a year."

Deke gave a slow, thoughtful nod. "Nothing for the pain, even though she hurts every day…" He stared at Jase, as if his stony expression would provide food for thought.

"Okay. Fine. I get it. But like I said, life can be hard. How long before she can't put up with it anymore and decides to take something?"

"Here's an idea, genius. Why don't you *ask* her?"

Not a bad idea. Jase wondered why he hadn't considered that himself. It made perfect sense to find out if she had a plan for handling those tough times life would throw at her. If she did, and the plan seemed plausible, it might just be safe to test the Lillie waters.

CHAPTER TWELVE

"LILLIE ROURKE, PLEASE."

"Speaking..."

"Lillie. Hi. It's Brant Perry, Sally's dad?"

She hoped he wasn't calling to set up an interview between her and his producer friend. She hadn't had time to give his offer the serious consideration it deserved. And as she'd admitted to Jase, it had been a long time since she'd *really* put her voice into action.

"I'm afraid I have bad news."

She'd heard that tone before. She'd asked the hospital's volunteer coordinator to let her know whenever one of the kids had died, so she could prepare herself before going in to see the others. Sinking onto the foot cushion of the gazebo's chaise lounge, she held her breath. *Not Sally*, she thought. *Please, not Sally...*

"It's about Jason."

"Oh, no..."

"Not sure what happened, really. While I was visiting Sally this afternoon, they rushed him to the OR. Overheard a couple docs and a nurse discussing his case. Seems this operation is his last hope…if he survives it."

"I—I don't know what to say."

"I understand. Believe me. Sally's a mess. This isn't the first time another kid has, well, you know…but Jason and Sally have a special bond. More like siblings than fellow patients. For the life of me, I can't figure out what to tell her."

"Poor little thing," Lillie said. "Is there anything I can do?"

"As a matter of fact, yes. Can you come down here? No need to bring your guitar or paints. She thinks a lot of you, so I'm guessing a short visit will snap her out of her funk."

"I've been working in the yard. Give me half an hour to clean up, and I'll be there."

"Thanks, Lillie. I appreciate it more than words can say."

As she got ready, Lillie considered things she could bring to cheer up a very sick, very sad little girl. Candy was out of the question, thanks to her treatments, and at her age, flowers didn't seem appropriate. Besides, the staff prohibited plants of any kind, since they exposed the vulnerable kids to mold, bacteria or fungus. A book, or better still, one of those adult coloring books that had a lot of complexity. Colored pencils, too. She'd noticed during her last visit that most of those donated to the playroom were broken.

"Mom? Is it okay if I borrow your car?"

Amelia looked away from her latest painting. “Sure, honey. Where are you going?”

“To Hopkins. Little Jason is in bad shape, and Sally isn’t taking it very well.”

“Oh, dear. What’s wrong?”

Lillie gave her mother a quick rundown of what Brant had said. “I hope he’ll rally. He was counting on making that wedding happen for his mom.”

“I love your big caring heart, honey, but please don’t get all worked up over this, okay?”

Worked up. In other words, *don’t backslide.* She’d done everything in her power to show how she’d changed. If the big smiles, the always happy demeanor, the continual upbeat outlook hadn’t convinced them, what would?

“Don’t worry, Mom. Even if—God forbid—the worst happens, I’m not going to sink back into the addiction pit. I promise.”

“Oh, sweetie, *that* was the furthest thing from my mind! It’s just, well, I can see how upset you are.”

“Thank you for caring.” She stood beside her mother and admired the colorful vista leaning on the easel. “Wow, that might just be one of your best works, ever.”

Amelia chewed the end of her brush. “I don’t know…it needs something. More blue?”

“Maybe just a touch, right there.” She pointed to an area between wispy cirrus clouds. “Not too much, though, because they look real enough to develop into rainmakers." Pressing a kiss to Amelia's cheek, Lillie said, "I shouldn't be long, but don't hold supper for me."

With that, she hurried out the door. If she didn't waste time, the gift shop would still be open.

She'd just paid for two coloring books, a sharpener, a big box of crayons and another of colored pencils when her cell phone rang.

"Hello?" Lillie said, talking as she made her way to the elevators.

"Lill…it's me."

Jase? Good as it was to hear his voice, she couldn't imagine why he'd called.

"Just spent some time with Deke and—"

"Is he all right?"

"Sure. Of course. Better than all right, in fact."

In reaction to an announcement that floated down from the overhead speakers, he said, "You're at Hopkins? I thought you weren't due back there until next week."

Lillie told him about the call from Sally's dad.

"Aw, jeez. Sorry to hear that. Anything I can do?"

"Nothing I can think of, but thanks for offering. I'm heading to Sally's room. Don't know if I'll get a signal in the elevator."

"It's okay. I just called to tell you that Deke sends his best. And…"

Why the hesitation? she wondered.

"And to see if we can get together later."

"Why?"

"It can wait. How's the hand?"

"Fine. A little stiff, but no bleeding."

"Told you it wasn't a good idea to bang on that old Yamaha so soon after—"

"Elevator's here," she said. And just as she'd suspected, her cell signal disappeared the instant the doors hissed shut. Lillie didn't have time to wonder about Jase's call, because in an instant, the doors opened again, and there stood Brant Perry.

"At the risk of being cliché," he said, "you're a sight for sore eyes."

One hand on her elbow, he guided her toward Sally's room.

"She stopped crying the instant I told her you were coming. So thanks for showing up."

Why wouldn't she show up? Had he somehow heard about her history?

"I'm happy to help, any way I can." And she meant it, too, because with everything else life was throwing at these kids, being disappointed by a friend shouldn't be among them.

"What's in the bag?"

"Oh, I just thought it might be easier for Sally to loosen up, get a few things off her chest if she was distracted, coloring."

"What a great idea." He gave her an admiring smile. "You're something else, you know that?"

Standing just outside his daughter's door, Brant added, "She really misses her mom at times like these."

She'd heard from some of the nurses that his ex-wife moved to Paris with her new beau, a tenor with the Bordeaux Opera House in Paris. According to those same disapproving nurses, the woman had visited Sally only once during her many months in and out of Hopkins. That had to be difficult, Lillie thought, for Sally *and* her single dad.

She slowed her pace as they neared Sally's door. "Just as soon as she hears Jason is out of surgery and doing fine, Sally will be her usual happy self again. You'll see."

"I hope you're right."

"What's the operation for, anyway?"

"Near as I can tell," he said, "it's what they call palliative care. They *said* they're removing his port, to improve his mobility. But the way they raced out of here?" Brant raised his shoulders in a gesture of helplessness. "It isn't like he needs it anymore, because, well, you know." He exhaled a shaky breath.

"I hear you out there, Dad," Sally called.

He chuckled. "Can't put anything past that kid," he said, and entered the room.

Lillie stood back while they exchanged a hello

hug. He waved her forward. "Look what the Elevator Fairy just delivered!"

"Lillie! Dad said you were going to try and get here," she said, administering a fierce hug from her spot in bed. "I'm so, so, *so* happy to see you!"

"I'm happy to see you, too, sweetie," Lillie said, unbagging the coloring books. "I hope you don't have these already."

"This coloring book looks amazing!" She patted her mattress, then picked up a coloring book. "Choose a picture, Lillie, and we'll color it together."

After dropping her purse on the windowsill, Lillie sat cross-legged at the foot of Sally's bed. "How about if *you* choose a picture. I've made so many decisions today, I'm positively dizzy."

The girl flipped through the book, stopping when she came to a complicated garden. Removing a blue colored pencil from the box, she said, "What kind of decisions?"

"Well, my mom and dad own a little bed-and-breakfast in Fells Point, see..." Sally began filling in some flowers, Lillie realized it was the same shade of blue as Jase's eyes. "Anyway, my folks did some remodeling, and in a couple weeks, they're having a party to show it off. I've been working on some ads and stuff, to make sure lots of people know about it. People who might reserve rooms at the inn, or recommend it to their friends."

"So you're kinda like the party planner, aren't you?"

Lillie pictured the to-do list that included invitations and mailers, decorations, a two-tiered cake, and hiring kids from the Lincoln Culinary Institute in nearby Columbia to make and serve hors d'oeuvres.

"You could say that."

"Wish I could come."

"I wish you could, too."

Brant, leaning casually in the doorway, said, "We'll talk to Doctor Kay about it."

Sally pouted. "Don't bother. He'll just say no."

Lillie gently pinched her pink-socked toe. "Let's stay positive. He might surprise you and say yes!"

The girl smiled. Barely. "Maybe. I guess."

Brant came closer to the bed. "Would you girls mind very much if I ran down to the cafeteria?"

"Will you bring me back a fudge pop?"

Lillie saw the indecision on his face: fulfill her request and risk an upset stomach, or deny her and deal with her disappointment.

"You bet, darlin'. One for you, too, Lillie?"

"Who can say no to a fudge pop!" she said, laughing a little harder than necessary. "Take your time. I'm not going anywhere."

"Thanks."

He hadn't been gone a full minute when Sally said, "Did Dad tell you about Jason?"

"Yes, he did. Bummer, huh?"

Bending low over the picture, Sally's forehead furrowed as she concentrated on filling in a stripe on a chipmunk's back with a crayon labeled Burnt Sienna. "He could die this time, Lillie," she said without looking up. "I mean really, *really* die. I heard his mom and dad talking. Then I heard them making phone calls." She met Lillie's eyes to add, "They were telling their friends and family to pray, 'cause this might be it."

Lillie wished she'd thought to buy a bottle of water at the gift shop, because suddenly, her throat was bone dry.

"What do *you* think?" Sally pressed.

Lillie didn't know how to respond, if she *should* respond. Wasn't it a question better left to Sally's dad? Or her oncologist? One look at the girl's wide-eyed, hopeful face prompted Lillie to take a deep breath. *Lord, if You're up there, I sure could use some guidance right about now.*

She scooted closer, until their knees were touching and took Sally's hands in her own. "Jason is getting the very best care," she began. "This is one of the finest hospitals in the whole world, and he has some of the most talented doctors. So let's keep a good thought, okay?"

"That's pretty good advice."

Sally looked toward the sound of the deep voice. "Hi," she said. "Who are you?"

He squirted a dollop of hand sanitizer into one palm and rubbed it in. "I'm Jase," he said. "And you must be Sally."

"What're *you* doing here?" Lillie asked.

He smiled. "I was in the neighborhood, so…"

Leaning closer, Sally whispered, "Is he your boyfriend?"

Lillie seemed too stunned to answer, so Jase said, "Well, I'm a boy—or was a boy, anyway—and I'm Lillie's friend. So yeah, I guess you could call me her boyfriend."

The girl leaned closer still, and in a hushed voice, said, "He's really, *really* handsome, Lillie."

And Lillie whispered back, "Don't let him hear you say that. His head will swell up so big, he won't be able to fit it through the doorway. Then he'll be stuck in here for who knows how long!"

Giggling, Sally accidentally kicked over the box, and colored pencils spilled from the box, rolled under the bed, toward the bathroom, near the night table. She started to get out of bed, but Jase stopped her, one hand in the air like a traffic cop.

"You stay put, li'l miss," he drawled. "Lillie and me, we'll fetch them colorin' sticks for ya."

"He's funny, too," Sally said.

Jase and Lillie bumped heads in the corner near the closet. "She's the bride?" he whispered.

Lillie answered with a nod.

"Okay to talk about it?"

She shook her head.

Ten minutes later, they'd refilled the box, leaving only one open space.

"Don't worry," Lillie assured Sally, "we'll find it. Eventually."

Jase agreed. "Or the custodian will."

"It's right here." Sally held up the brown crayon she'd been using. "It's the only one that *didn't* end up on the floor!"

"She's pretty tricky," he said, winking at Lillie. "But you two were busy when I barged in. Get back to whatever you were doing. Or talking about. I'll just sit over here like a good… *boyfriend*."

"Move the chair closer," Sally said, "and help us finish this picture. Then we can all sign it and tack it to my bulletin board."

It was already covered with so many cards and drawings that none of the cork showed through. Jase decided he'd ask a nurse for tape to stick the picture to the wall beside the corkboard, instead.

"So," he said, sliding a red crayon from the box, "what were you talking about when I got here?"

"Jason. He's getting an operation, right now," Sally answered. "We were just wondering what would happen to him…after…"

He met Lillie's eyes. What she'd said about the hospital, the doctors, keeping a good thought, made sense now. Though how she'd managed under the circumstances, he couldn't say. In her shoes, he'd probably have stuttered and stammered…if a response had come to mind at all.

A tall, lanky guy entered the room. "Fudge pops all 'round!" he said. "Eat 'em before they melt!" He handed one to Sally and another to Lillie, then stuck out his right hand. "Name's Perry. Brant Perry. And this li'l angel is my girl."

Jase shook the hand and said, "Jase Yeager."

"Guess what, Daddy? Jase is Lillie's *boyfriend*."

"Is that right? Well, now. You're one lucky man. Lillie, here, why, she's a real treasure."

Pink-cheeked and blinking fast in reaction to the compliment, Lillie hid behind one hand. "Hush, you two. You'll make me blush."

Too late, Jase thought. And it made him want to hug her. Eyes still locked to hers, he said, "Yup, she's a gem, all right."

"Isn't he handsome, Daddy? Just like a movie star!" She held up a crayon. "His eyes are as blue as *this*!"

Lillie came out of hiding. "Is it just me, or do we sound like actors in a 1940s movie?"

"I've never seen a 1940s movie," Sally said.

They shared a good laugh over that, and then Brant looked at Jase. "So you're the guy who volunteered to help Lillie with the wedding music?"

"Yes, that's me." Jase hoped there'd *be* a wedding. "Lillie and I ran through a few songs just this morning. I think the kids will like them."

Sally looked at her. "Did you bring your guitar?" She glanced at Lillie's bandaged hand. "Oh, guess you can't play with that, right? What happened, anyway?"

"Got clumsy, doing dishes."

When Lillie's eyes met his, Jase's pulse raced. They'd been head to head as he'd worked on the bandage. Close enough to…

He cleared his throat. "I have mine… It's in the truck…"

Sally's faint eyebrows rose high on her pale forehead.

"Oh, wow, will you get it!"

"Sure thing. Be right back."

Jase was in the hall, then in the elevator, then in the parking garage before he had a chance to think about what he was getting into. If it hadn't been for Deke's suggestion to come right out and ask Lillie about rehab, about her plans, he wouldn't have called her. And if he hadn't called her, she wouldn't have told him about this visit to the hospital. *Doggone that Deke, anyway.*

He retrieved the guitar and slammed the door. Hard. "What kind of jerk blames an aging war hero for his own stupid choices?"

The woman in the SUV beside his pickup

rolled down her window. "What's that, sir? Is everything all right?"

"Fine, fine. Everything's fine. Sorry," he said, and before she could reply, Jase half ran back to the hospital. *What. Have. You. Gotten. Yourself. Into?* he chanted with each step.

He'd gotten himself into spending time with Lillie, that's what. He'd sit beside her, strum the old Yamaha, sing a few songs, and then, finally, when they were alone, he could take Deke's advice.

If he was lucky, she'd repeat that defiant line from this morning: "I've *already* beat it… I've been clean for more than a year!"

He'd almost believed it then. Maybe tonight—

The last thing Jase expected when he rounded the corner was to see Sally, forehead resting on Lillie's shoulder.

It could only mean one thing.

He put down the guitar and went to them. "Lill…?"

She extended her uninjured hand and, without thinking twice, he took it.

"Where's her dad?"

"Down the hall."

He mouthed, "Not with Sally?"

"She asked him to find out why Jason's mother was crying."

As if they didn't already know. He'd say something comforting…if he had any idea *what.* Lillie cared about that boy. Jase knew by the way she'd brightened, just talking about him. Lillie needed more from him now than hollow platitudes. Besides, anything he said or asked would upset Sally further.

Jase settled for giving Lillie's hand a squeeze. She squeezed back, just as she had when they'd been a couple.

Brant walked in, tucking a starched hanky into his breast pocket as he moved closer to Sally's bed. He put a hand on Sally's head. "Is she okay?"

"A little calmer now."

"That's good. A relief." He punctuated the sentence with a craggy sigh. "Thanks, Lillie," he said, his voice softly coarse. His eyes were puffy and bloodshot when he glanced at Jase. "You guys don't need to hang around," he added, looking back at Lillie. "Sal and me, we'll be okay."

He didn't blame the man for not wanting an audience when he told his little girl that her pal had died. Jase pitied him. In Brant's shoes, he'd be a falling-down wreck, wondering if—or when—his little girl might suffer the same fate.

The adults exchanged stiff-lipped goodbyes, and Brant promised to call Lillie with any updates.

Jase grabbed his guitar case, and they left the room, still hand in hand. They'd made it as far as the nurse's station when she said, "I'll just be a minute." He watched her approach a weeping nurse and wrap the woman in a hug.

He couldn't hear the specifics of their conversation, but he didn't need to. Lillie's sympathetic expression and the way she rested a hand on the woman's forearm told him everything he needed to know. She was doing what Lillie did best, meting out comfort.

A minute passed, and as the nurse ducked into a room across the hall, a second staffer approached Lillie. Yet another nurse joined the hug. *So much for the theory that medical personnel didn't get involved in their patients' lives*, Jase told himself.

As they made their way toward the exit, doctors, interns, even custodians exchanged condolences with her. She cared about them, and they felt the same way. And not just because of young Jason.

It didn't surprise him. Lillie never had trouble getting along with others. It was what made it so easy for her to command attention whenever she had a mic in her hand.

She returned to his side, knuckling tears from her eyes. "For such a little guy, he made a big impression on a lot of people."

Look who's talking, he thought.

"Let's get out of here," he said. "We'll grab a sandwich or something." He'd table the question for now—Lillie needed better from him on that score, too.

He placed a hand in the middle of her back, and she pressed into his side as he led her to the elevator. Eyes on the numbers above the door, Lillie exhaled slowly. "I wish you could have met him. In a lot of ways, he reminded me of you. He was..."

Tears choked off her words. What could he do but puller her closer?

As they made their way past the information counter and the security check-in, silence settled on them like a comforting blanket. It tightened as he guided her through the hospital's enormous revolving doors.

"Where are you parked?" he asked.

"Top floor of the garage."

"I'll walk you up."

"You don't have to do that. I'll be fine."

"I know, but I want to."

A shaky little smile was her only response. Once they'd reached the top floor, Lillie pointed toward the concrete half wall that surrounded the space. "I'm over there. No need to lose the elevator car. I'm fine. Honest."

"How about if I follow you home? That way, you can drop off your mom's car. I know a nice quiet place where we can talk about Jason." He watched as one well-arched brow rose slightly.

"Or not," he quickly added. "I have questions. About the boy. The wedding. And stuff."

For now, it seemed best to let her believe *he* needed to talk.

"Okay."

She took a few steps closer to the car, then stopped and faced him. His heart sank.

"Don't you feel weird?"

"Sometimes..."

"Not weird in general. I mean, you're following me back to my folks' house. Don't you feel weird, being friends with someone my age who still lives with her parents?"

Was she kidding? As long as she stayed at the inn, he knew she was safe.

"Not at all."

"You're sure you wouldn't rather I just meet you someplace?"

And miss the chance to ride to and from the restaurant with her?

"I'm sure."

He watched her drive away. In twenty minutes, tops, he'd be with her again. So why did he get the feeling it would seem more like two hours?

CHAPTER THIRTEEN

"I'M SORRY MOM and Dad aren't home," Lillie said, climbing into the passenger seat. "They would have loved to see you."

"Yeah?" He chuckled. "Well, *I* think they're avoiding me."

She laughed, too. "No, of course not. They've always loved you. Tonight, they're spending some time with the Sams."

He rested a hand on her seat back to look over his shoulder and back out of the drive. "Somebody's birthday?"

"Just a simple supper, and if I know the twins, some gin rummy."

"They're the reason I can't play cards anymore. Those little con artists completely destroyed my confidence, I tell ya."

"You're not fooling anyone. They won every game because you *let* them."

He tried to deny it, but Lillie knew better.

"So am I dressed all right for this super-secret restaurant we're going to?"

"Absolutely. It's quiet, nothing fancy. And it's

a nice night, so I'm hoping they'll have a table outside on the deck. The view is—"

"Let me guess…the Waterfront Kitchen."

Jase thumped the steering wheel. "Man. You sure know how to spoil a surprise."

Had he forgotten that he'd made arrangements to leave the pub early the night he'd proposed to her…to celebrate with a quiet dinner at the Waterfront? Lillie didn't know if she could handle the memories. And it seemed wrong to celebrate so soon after hearing that Jason hadn't survived his surgery.

"Be honest now…how are you doing? With the Jason thing, I mean."

"Mind reader," she said under her breath.

"Nah. It just happened. Doesn't take psychic abilities to figure things out. Besides, you lit up like a Christmas tree talking about that boy, so…"

Lillie's eyes filled with tears. "Mom warned me not to get emotionally involved with the kids."

"If you hadn't gotten involved, you wouldn't be you. And I saw the way everyone reacted to losing him. Seems to me even the pros find it tough to take that advice."

They spent the remainder of the short drive to the restaurant in comfortable silence. It gave her time to remember a few more good things about Jase. That *way* he had of getting straight to the point. And his talent for reading people's moods, hers in particular. It had been one of the reasons she'd never been able to fool him when she was high, once he'd figured out that she was using.

Just as he'd hoped, there was room on the restaurant's deck. The hostess led them to a table along the rail and left them with menus. As Jase opened his, a light breeze riffled his hair and the collar of his shirt. Watching him made it difficult to enjoy the hazy orange glow of the setting sun, sailboats and schooners, smokestacks and barges out there in the harbor. Now, more than ever, Lillie wished she'd been stronger, that she hadn't put pain management above her love for him—and his for her. Dealing with the nonstop ache in her leg taught her that she *could* cope with pain. If only she'd known that then.

"Don't look so sad, Lill. I know how much you cared about Jason."

Until he spoke, Lillie hadn't realized her thoughts were visible on her face. Thankfully, the waitress showed up, sparing Lillie the need to reply.

Jase ordered sweet tea for both of them. Flashing his best onstage smile at the young woman, he added, "Give us a few minutes with the menu, will you?"

He scooted his chair closer to hers. "I'm sorry about Jason."

"Yeah, he was a really special little boy."

"Wish I'd known him."

"He was always looking out for everyone's feelings." *Like you*, she thought. "Did I tell you why he wanted the wedding?"

"I'm not sure. Remind me."

How like him to pretend he hadn't heard the story before, simply because he suspected she needed to talk about it. She told him the story, near tears at the end.

"Some good came of it, though," he said, looking at her. "It gave him something positive to focus on for a change. Gave him the feeling he was in control of something."

He was right, of course, and she said so.

"Sweet tea times two," the waitress said, delivering their glasses. "Ready to order your entrée yet?"

"Haven't even cracked the menu," Jase told her. "Sorry."

"No hurry. I'll be back."

"So," he said, pretending to read the list of options, "what're you in the mood for? Ratatouille? Pan-seared tuna? Steak?"

"The crab cake was good, last time we were here."

Although he didn't look up, something told her he, too, remembered everything about that night. She suddenly wondered how Whitney would feel about this dinner... In the shock of Jason's death, and then her gratefulness for Jase's presence, she hadn't considered how *he* might be feeling. No doubt conflicted—wanting to comfort Lillie but not wanting to hurt Whitney.

"You're right," he said. "That's what I'll have, too." Jase set the menu aside. "How are they in New York?"

Keep it casual. "Oh, they're edible, but the chefs could take a few lessons from Baltimoreans."

"Our chefs do some things right, for sure."

She laughed. "I remember once, when my agent set me up in a pub in Richmond, I ordered steamed crabs from this little sidewalk-type café. They were boiled, not steamed. Soggy. No spice. Bleh!"

"That violates just about every culinary rule on the books. Boiled? Why would anyone *do* such a thing!"

"The cook didn't know any better, I guess," she said as the waitress returned. They ordered, and Lillie watched Jase. He had something on his mind. She could tell by the set of his jaw.

"Are you thinking about Whitney?" she asked.

A strange look crossed his face before his brows drew together. "Whitney? No…it didn't work out between us, actually."

They'd broken up? When? Why? She had so many questions, but his closed-off expression told her maybe it wasn't the best time to ask. She had no idea he'd been dealing with a breakup. Lillie wanted to comfort him.

"Jase, I'm so sorry." And she meant it. He deserved to be happy, but…that glimmer of hope that he'd be happy with *her*…feelings she'd been trying to smother…flared within her. Was that awful?

Jase gave a warm smile. "It was for the best. But thanks, Lill." He directed his attention to the water, seemingly closing the subject. And she let him. He pointed out some boats and landmarks, visible across the harbor, commenting on the sights.

"How's your tea? Sweet enough?" he asked.

Lillie took a sip. Evidently, he was more comfortable with small talk, and for now, she was too. It had been a good idea, coming here. The ache of little Jason's passing had dimmed a bit.

"It's perfect." He was still smiling when she said, "Thanks for suggesting this, Jase. It's just what I needed tonight."

"Me, too."

As they enjoyed their meals, Jase talked about the TV show. His mom's latest creations. The host he'd requested during his last trip to Florida because the guy didn't dominate every second of airtime, pointing out overly obvious things about the products the way his last host had.

"She never lets the callers get a whole sentence out before interrupting them," he said. "I remember one lady—from California, I think—who said something along the lines of 'You must have been a middle child.' I didn't get it until after the host admitted it was true. It was all I could do to keep from laughing out loud when the caller said 'No wonder you're never quiet.'" Even now, leaning back in his chair, Jase chuckled.

It was good to see him looking so rested and relaxed. "Did that quiet your host down?"

"'Fraid not."

This time, Lillie laughed with him, and decided not to spoil the moment by guiding him toward the real reason—or reasons—he'd invited her here.

The waitress stacked their plates. "Dessert tonight?"

"Cheesecake," Jase said. "And cappuccino." He looked at Lillie. "Want your own, or can we share?"

The way we used to do... She remembered the times they'd had mock battles, using their forks as swords, fighting over the last bite. "I'd love to share." And the truth was, she'd love to share far more with him than a slice of cheesecake.

LILLIE CLIMBED INTO the truck. "I don't think there's so much as the hint of a breeze."

"Good thing it didn't decide to take a break while we were eating. It might've cooled the food faster, but it kept the flies away."

Jase closed the passenger door, knocking on the hood as he made his way around to the driver's side. Lillie had barely had time to process her feelings about Jason's death. So he'd avoided explaining about Whitney, and the question Deke had suggested, and kept the conversation light and upbeat. Not that he'd had to try very hard, looking across the table at her pretty face and listening to her lovely voice.

In ten minutes, they'd arrive at the inn, and he dreaded saying goodbye.

"How would you feel about taking a drive?"

"Where?"

"No place in particular. I just…it's such a nice night…"

Lillie sighed, and Jase prepared himself for her to recite a list of reasons why not: It was late. She had to work early. What would her parents say. Jason's death.

"It's nearly ten o'clock…"

Nodding, Jase prepared himself to set his disappointment aside and agree with her. And then she turned to face him.

"It *is* a nice night. How about if instead of a drive, we go back to the inn. My folks will be out until at least midnight—they had tickets to a play at the Hippodrome after supper with the Sams, and planned to stop for ice cream after that—so we'd have the gazebo all to ourselves."

That beat the alternative by a long shot.

"We've got cheese and crackers. Chips and salsa, too. And this morning, I made lemonade. Fresh squeezed!"

"I couldn't eat another bite, but who could say no to your fresh-squeezed lemonade?" As if he needed an enticement.

Her smile, illuminated by the green glow of the dashboard dials, touched a long-forgotten place inside him, a place he wasn't sure he wanted to fully expose to the light. At least, not yet.

He smiled, too, as she talked about the clouds that had moved in, as she hoped forecasters had been wrong, because she'd just dusted the roses with insecticide, "…and that stuff is expensive!"

Minutes later, he waited patiently as she searched her tote bag for her keys. For as long as he'd known her, Lillie had carried enormous purses. *A smaller pocketbook would be easier to carry*, he'd once suggested. Her reply? *Right. And then where would you be if you needed a tissue. An aspirin. A bandage*. The memory made him grin. He'd dubbed her Ready for Anything Lillie, and she'd *liked* it!

She hung the enormous purse on a peg near the door, and Jase snickered to himself, hoping it wouldn't pull down the whole wall.

"Let's grab our drinks before we go out back," she said, leading the way down the hall.

The inn was dark and quiet, except for the small lamp on the foyer table and another beckoning to them from somewhere in the kitchen. He liked the way she looked, silhouetted by the light.

He watched as she puttered around the kitchen, finding tumblers, adding ice, pouring their drinks. He considered offering to help, but that would mean taking his eyes off her. It worried him a little, recognizing how *much* he liked watching her.

"What's wrong?" she asked, wiping down the counter.

"Nothing. Why?"

She handed him a glass. "You look…concerned." And she'd looked concerned as she said it.

He had to think fast, because if he admitted the truth, Jase risked having her wonder if he'd taken up peeping-Tommery as a pastime.

"You, uh, you think it's a good idea, leaving your purse out in the open that way?"

Lillie glanced toward the foyer. "I've been putting it there for…" She paused, as if trying to focus on a specific date. "Since I was old enough to carry a purse."

The image of a knee-high Lillie, hauling around a bag that could have held *her*, inspired a smile.

"But the door isn't even locked. You're not worried someone will waltz right in and grab it?"

Lillie faked a frown and made her way back

to the entryway. “Well I am *now*,” she said, flipping the bolt into place. “Better?”

“As a matter of fact, yes.”

He followed close on her heels as she opened the French doors and, as an afterthought, reached into a drawer for a box of kitchen matches. Lillie handed him her drink and proceeded to light the votive candles on the coffee table, on the railings, even hanging from fishing line, attached to the ceiling. They flickered in multicolored glass candleholders, reminding him how the city lights looked when he was on a night flight. Their glow shimmered from every auburn-colored strand of her hair, too.

Jase chose one end of the love seat and waited for Lillie to settle onto one of two matching chairs that flanked it. Instead, she plopped down beside him and placed her drink on the glass-topped table.

“Need a cushion behind your back?” she asked, kicking off her sandals.

Her toenails gleamed with pink polish that exactly matched the rosebuds decorating her sundress. He noticed her fingernails boasted the same shade. Her left hand was splayed across the cushion between them, making him intensely aware of the twelve inches separating them. Jase fought the desire to grab that hand and pull her closer, reducing the distance to zero.

A train whistled in the distance, its forlorn

notes harmonizing with the chirrup of night birds and tree frogs.

"I'm going to miss this place," she said.

"Wait…what?" He tuned out night sounds and studied her face. "Where are you going?"

"Oh, not far. But I've saved up enough to get my own place. *Finally.*"

"Yeah? Where?"

She laughed. "I haven't even started looking at ads yet. The goal is to find someplace close, so I can keep walking to and from work."

"You'll hold on to both jobs, then?"

"Have to. For the time being anyway."

Was she ready for that much independence? Especially so soon after the emotional blow of losing the little boy she'd been so fond of? Jase pictured the sidebar of the article he'd read in *The Addictive Mind* magazine, featuring a quote from a well-known actor: "Finding sobriety was the hardest thing I've ever done." The star had been in rehab…and relapsed half a dozen times.

"Why not just stay here?" he asked. "I'm sure your folks love having you."

Her eyes narrowed slightly. "You aren't implying that as long as I'm here, they can keep an eye on me, to make sure I'm not using, are you?"

Jase bristled a bit before saying, "No! 'Course not. But since you brought it up, why put all that pressure on yourself so soon after coming home? Why not give it another couple months?"

Now her lips narrowed, too. "I appreciate the concern, and how hard it must be for you to buy into this, but I'm handling things well. Fully adjusted, as they say. I don't like to advertise it, but I attend meetings every day. *Every day.* Talk with my sponsor at least twice a week. I have a lot to prove, which is one of the reasons I don't broadcast my attendance at meetings. You'll just have to trust me when I say I'm fine. And I'm going to stay that way." She leaned back and crossed both arms over her chest. "I'll do it all on my own, of course, but it'll be easier if people like you at least *pretend* to have some faith in me."

He'd rarely seen her angry, but he recognized the signs: stiff back, shoulders tight, chin lifted…

"I'm sorry. You've worked hard to get where you are, and I respect that. I didn't mean to insult you." Left hand resting atop hers, he raised the right. "Honest."

She exhaled a long, soft breath. "I know. I'm the one who should be apologizing."

"No way. You didn't do anything." Except sit there looking vulnerable…*and gorgeous and 100 percent kissable.*

She continued as if he hadn't spoken. "I get it. And I don't blame anyone for being apprehensive. I did a lot of awful things, things that hurt a lot of people. I can't expect anyone to just forget about all those disappointments." Her shoulders rose, then fell. "It's going to take time. I've changed, but how do they know that, right?" Another sigh, and then, "I just need to be more patient. I owe everyone that, and then some."

She'd hit on every point of concern he had. And she was right. The people closest to her needed to show her that they believed she'd beat addiction, permanently.

"You don't owe anybody anything, except to keep right on being *you*."

With no warning whatever, Lillie jumped up and hurried toward the walkway that connected the gazebo to the kitchen. "I'll be right back!"

Jase didn't think he'd said anything that might have inspired tears, but then, what he knew about coping with a former addict could fit in one hand. He thought about going after her but decided she'd earned a moment or two of privacy to gather her thoughts, to collect herself.

But which comment, specifically, had inspired her hasty departure? Jase honestly couldn't say, but one thing was certain...if he wanted to keep seeing her, he needed to stop referencing her drug abuse.

Did he have what it took to support the new-and-improved Lillie? To *believe* she'd changed? During those first lonely months without her, he'd read up on addiction. The one thing that stood out was that months of taking prescription painkillers—and substitutes when they were no longer available—had altered her brain chemistry. That fact alone explained the futility of blaming weakness or willfulness for the stubborn drive to stay high.

He'd read about recovery, too, and from what he recalled, it appeared that Lillie was doing everything right. Without intending to, he'd put himself smack in the middle of a quandary: Stay with her, and prove he was on her side, or fade into the background, and hope she wouldn't read it as abandonment?

Lillie burst into the gazebo, breathless, smiling, and carrying a package the size of a trade paperback. So. She hadn't run off in a huff to whimper and stroke hurt feelings, after all.

"I was going to wait to give this to you," she said, returning to his side.

"It isn't my birthday, so..."

"I know that. Just open it, okay?"

Jase untied the white satin bow, then removed pale blue paper.

"Omigarsh! I'd forgotten how you like to take forever, opening gifts!"

He did his best to look offended. "I like to savor moments like this."

She gathered up the ribbon and wrapper as he held up a plaque of some sort. Even in the dim lighting, he could see her signature in the lower right corner. Tilting it for a better look, Jase saw that she'd whitewashed a half-inch-thick slab of wood. Tastefully arranged in tidy, hand-painted letters, he read.

> "I'm sorry" is an empty statement;
> "I won't do it again" was a broken promise;
> How I'll make it up to you is my responsibility.

A mix of relief, affection and pleasure threatened to overwhelm him. Jase swallowed. "Lillie," he said, facing her, "this is…it's gorgeous. But, but when did you have time to make it, holding down two jobs, volunteering at the hospital, helping out around here?"

One corner of her mouth lifted in a tiny grin. "I don't need a lot of sleep."

His forefingers brushed something on the back, so he turned it over. "What's this?" he said, inspecting an envelope, taped to the wood.

To Jase, it read, *with much gratitude and fondness*.

Jase peeled it off and, after carefully placing the plaque on the table, broke the seal. Inside, wrapped in a sheet of pale blue paper, was a check, made out to him.

"No way," he said, his voice foggy and low. She'd been saving to get her own place. A car. How much longer would she have to wait, because of this?

"You don't need to do this. I…I can't take this…"

He tried to hand it to her, but she held up both hands. "You can, and you will. It's everything I… Everything I took. Plus interest."

"But you worked so hard to dig out from under. Take it," he tried again, "and put it toward a down payment on a car or rent or something."

"I have enough for a car."

She looked so proud that he nearly gave in to the urge to hug her.

"I just haven't had time to shop for one."

He fixed his gaze on the check again. "I don't know what to say."

"Don't say anything." She relieved him of the check, folded it in half, and slid it into his shirt pocket. Patting it, Lillie said, "You've heard of do-overs. Let's just call it that, and put everything else in the past."

Jase picked up the plaque. Reread what it said.

"Don't put it someplace where you'll see it every day."

"Why not? It's beautiful."

"It'll only remind you of…" The shoulder lifted again. "You know…"

Nodding, Jase clumsily rewrapped it, put it back on the table. "You're something else, you know that?"

Lillie looked at some unknown spot on the

other side of the gazebo's screens. Oh, what he'd give to read her thoughts right now.

"You didn't have to do this." And before she could disagree, Jase placed a silencing forefinger over her lips. "I understand why you did it. So I'm not going to insist that you take back the money. I just want you to know I never considered it a debt. Not ever. Not even for a minute."

"I know that. I always knew it. Which is exactly why I needed to make things right. I hated taking advantage of your generosity, and destroying your opinion of me in the process. *Hated* it."

He studied her face, her big eyes and stunning, expressive features, then grasped her hand, guided it up and down, side to side.

Her quiet laughter soothed him.

"What're you doing, you big goof?"

"Erasing the board. It's blank now. There's nothing on it."

Although tears shimmered in her eyes, Lillie smiled. "Need me to freshen your drink? The ice has probably melted, watered it down."

"Everything I need," he admitted, "is right here." He slid an arm behind her, pulled her closer still, and she rested her head on his shoulder.

"You say the slate is clean," Lillie said, "but I need to tell you something."

He didn't want to hear that she'd keep working to earn back his trust and respect. She had that…for the most part. All he wanted now was to encourage her to stay on this path, for her sake and his.

"I'm still so ashamed," she whispered. "That'll pass in time, I hope, but I never want to forget what caused it. Remembering, that's what will ensure I'll never make the same mistakes again."

"Shh. You're cluttering up our clean board."

He didn't have to see her face to know she was smiling.

"One reason I'm ashamed…"

Jase opened his mouth to remind her that whatever it was belonged in the past.

"…is working with those kids. Seeing how they cope with incredible pain, every minute of every day. What I went through after the crash can't compare to what they're going through. And yet they tough it out, like the little champs they are, rarely complaining, never whining. If I'd had a tenth of their strength, I wouldn't have put everyone through—"

"Let's not forget that you went through it, too. Don't be so hard on yourself."

"You're sweet to say that, but there's no such thing. We both know that."

"I don't know anything of the kind. I'm just relieved things turned out the way they did."

"And I'm glad that despite everything, we're still friends."

Jase felt the same way. But he wanted more than friendship. So much more.

The knot in his throat prevented him from admitting it, so he told her with a kiss, instead.

And thankfully, she melted like snow on a sunny spring afternoon.

CHAPTER FOURTEEN

THE DAY BEFORE yesterday when he'd set up this meeting, Jase had felt anything but positive. Carl Daniels had never been an easy man to work with, particularly when he had the upper hand.

Colette's Crafts had grown to the point of needing a second manufacturer. He'd gladly throw all their orders to the Burton company, but his mom's business wasn't their only account. With any luck, lunch at the five-star Capital Grille would butter Daniels up just enough to inspire some mutually beneficial contract talk.

Jase asked for two orders of shrimp cocktail and listened patiently while Daniels went on and on about the case of pinot noir given to him by another client.

"It delights the palate," he said, "while layers of sandalwood and sassafras add intensity and depth. You really should try some. They serve it here."

"Maybe some other time," Jase said. "I have to work this afternoon." *And I need a clear head to deal with the likes of you!*

"I'll order it, then, and enjoy it enough for both of us."

Jase sat back, unfazed by the man's pretentiousness. Thanks to the mood Lillie had set last night, it was surprisingly easy to endure Daniels's pomposity, to allow him to push the envelope by ordering sliced filet Oscar with lump crab and Béarnaise sauce—the most expensive item on the menu. An old French proverb came to mind: "Patience is bitter, but its fruit is sweet." Sometime during dessert and coffee—and Daniels's insistence on filling his wineglass—Jase had opened the subject of what Daniels Fabrication could do for his mother's company. Suitably sated, the CEO might just be more flexible than normal.

Between the salad and main course, Carl excused himself to take a call. And as he stepped away from the table, Brant Perry walked up.

"Jase," he said, "how goes it."

Accepting the offered hand, Jase invited him to sit.

"Just for a minute." Brant glanced at his wristwatch. "Meeting a business associate in a few." He nodded at the empty chair across from him. "I see you're doing the same." Brant got real serious, real quick. "Tell me, what do you think of the deal I offered Lillie?"

Jase had just lifted the coffee cup to his lips, which spared him having to reply.

"She's the whole package, voice, looks, personality. I just know my guy out of Nashville plans to spend a couple weeks in Charm City, soon. I know I told her to take her time making a decision, but he's chompin' at the bit to meet her. Like I told Lillie, the guy's a pro, and honest as the day is long. He'll take her through the whole process, from choosing material to recording and going on tour to market the stuff."

Jase froze. This was potentially life-changing news. Why hadn't she told him about it?

It was her life. Clean slate and all that. What she did and who she saw wasn't any of his business. It shouldn't matter that she'd chosen to keep the information to herself.

But it did. It mattered a *lot.* And Jase knew, then and there, that he wanted to be a bigger part of her life. Maybe even a permanent part of her life.

If she'd have him.

"Remind me what you do for a living?"

Brant handed him a card, and Jase turned it over, then over again.

"Just between you and me, Lillie doesn't seem all that interested," Brant said. "I had to settle for her promise to think about it and get back to me. So far, not a peep. I'm hoping that's only because of everything else that's been going on."

"And this pro you mentioned?"

"Rusty McCoy. A&R rep for the Only Gold label."

Jase got the message, loud and clear: Rusty was like Only Gold's talent scout. The guy who found and developed new talent for the label.

"Yeah, Lillie's had a lot on her plate lately." He didn't feel right, giving away any information about how she was trying to get back on her feet. "Her schedule is pretty hectic, and she's trying to help her folks publicize the reopening of their bed and breakfast, so…"

"Yeah, that's pretty much what she told me."

"When?" Maybe Brant had made the offer last night, or early this morning, and Lillie hadn't kept the information from him, after all.

"At the hospital, couple days before Jason…" Frowning, he shook his head.

The reminder put a whole new spin on things. "How's Sally coping with that?"

"Not great, but as the saying goes, this ain't her first rodeo. She's been in and out of Hopkins a dozen times, and knows all too well what can happen to some of the kids."

"That's rough. Especially for a kid her age."

Then the suspicious side of his mind woke up. The way he understood things, Brant was a single dad with a very sick little girl. Yet between work and caring for Sally, he'd taken time to turn Lillie into the next singing sensation?

"If this deal between you and Lillie and McCoy goes through, you'll get a percentage?"

"No, I keep my ear to the ground and my eyes open. If I run across somebody like Lillie, I arrange a meeting. And Rusty returns the favor by recommending me as the agent."

It made sense, and yet Jase's doubts remained. He supposed it was because Lillie knew about all this and hadn't thought to tell him about it. Correction. She'd thought about it, and decided *not* to tell him. Was she afraid he'd try to stop her, citing her addiction as a reason not to sign a contract?

Carl returned, and plopped onto his seat as Jase made rudimentary introductions.

Brant stood. "Will you be talking with Lillie today?"

Oh, you bet I will.

"Probably."

"Ask her to give me a call, will you, so I can fill her in on what happens after I meet with Rusty today?" He glanced at his watch again. "Better run. Good seeing you again."

Carl watched until Brant disappeared into the bar. "Talent agent, huh? You thinking of tuning up the old git-fiddle, are ya?"

"No." Guys like Jase, who could hold a tune and act as front man for a band, were a dime a dozen. Women like Lillie on the other hand… Funny, but he didn't feel envious. Rather, Jase felt left behind. This time for a different kind of addiction: potential stardom. He hoped she'd turn McCoy down flat. Because he knew only too well how things like that worked in the industry. More often than not, no matter how much time and effort singers put into advancing their careers, they couldn't break into the big time. And a disappointment like that—

"Dessert today, gentlemen?"

"Still serving that warmed-up chocolate cake with wine-infused cherries and ice cream?"

"Yessir."

"I'll have that." He sat back as the young man collected his lunch plate and flatware.

"Anything for you, sir?"

"Just coffee, thanks."

It was time to get serious with Carl, and Jase leaned forward to outline his plan. As he talked, he opened a folder and showed the CEO color photos of the candle holders, serving bowls and figurines he wanted the company to produce. Nodding, Daniels examined the profit-loss statement, then gulped the last of his wine.

"You gonna drink that?" he asked, pointing at Jase's still-full goblet.

"Be my guest." He shoved it closer, and Daniels downed it in one swallow.

"I like your idea, Jase. I think we'd come away with a tidy sum…provided you can charm all the soccer moms who watch that crazy shopping show that they need this stuff in their homes."

"Carl. Trust me. Soccer moms can't be so easily dismissed. They know the value of a dollar and quality merchandise when they see it. That's why of all the companies I could choose for our latest line, I chose yours."

The man sat back, studying the contents of the folder and nodding thoughtfully. Jase hoped he hadn't laid it on too thick.

"Yeah, yeah, I like what I see," he repeated, closing the folder. "I think we can do business. I'll have Legal write up a contract. How soon do you need it?"

"Yesterday," Jase said, grinning.

"I hear ya, bud. Okay, soon as I get back to the office, I'll start the wheels turning."

He downed his cake in three big sloppy bites, and it was all Jase could do to mask his disgust.

"So," Carl said around a mouthful of chocolate, "you're really not interested in a recording contract for yourself?"

He hadn't been joking when he told Lillie that he didn't mind performing for small audiences. Working to make a name for himself required opening for established artists…in front of thousands.

"Not even a little bit."

"That's a shame. I've heard you sing. And so has the little woman. She talked about you for days after she heard you at Three-Eyed Joe's. If you cut a record, she'd be first in line to buy it. She'd talk her bridge biddies into buying one, too."

He sighed. If Daniels's company didn't have a reputation for turning out top-rate products in record time, he'd take his business elsewhere. Still, Jase pitied any female in his life, especially those who worked for him. The guy was the stereotypical chauvinist pig, and didn't even have the good grace to hide it. It made him glad Lillie had met him only in passing.

Lillie.

Whose kisses had told him she'd missed him, that she'd missed *them.*

And who'd kept her interaction with Brant a secret. Jase knew if he didn't get to the bottom of things, soon, it'd drive him to distraction. Signaling the waiter, he requested the check.

"Good seeing you, Jase," Carl said, pumping his arm. "I'll have the paperwork delivered to your office by morning at the latest. You still over on Aliceanna?"

"Yup."

Daniels said his goodbyes, and while the waiter rang up the order, Jase dialed Lillie's cell number. He hoped, as he counted the rings, her voicemail would pick up. He needed time to sift through what Brant had told him.

"Lill," he said after her recorded message played, "it's Jase. Give me a call when you get a minute. I need to run something by you." He decided against providing more information. She'd thought nothing of lying to him during her addict days. Why force her to tell another one, now? "Talk soon," he said, and hit End Call.

It felt good, he thought, signing the tab, having made a deal that would nearly double Colette's Crafts' annual income. The only thing that could make this day better? Hearing that Lillie hadn't mentioned Brant because she had no intention of signing with McCoy.

While buckling into his seat belt, his phone rang, and he answered without even checking the caller ID screen.

"Yeager…"

"Jason, hello!"

"Hey, Whit. How's Hollyweird?"

"San Francisco, silly, and it's fine. Better than fine, actually. The weather is glorious, and I love, love, *love* my condo. I'm sure once our clients see the office suites, they'll feel we're worth our fees."

"Good. Great. Happy for you." And he meant it.

"My house sold for the asking price. So did my car." Whitney rattled off the dollar amounts, and Jase was glad they were on opposite coasts. Even with his limited knowledge of real estate, Jase knew her town house was worth at least fifty grand more than she'd accepted. And that little puddle jumper of a car? These days, with every parent looking for a well-maintained vehicle that was easy on gas for their teens, she could have easily pocketed an additional three thousand. *Guess she was more anxious to get out of Dodge than she let on,* he thought.

"Glad to hear it. So tell me, how's the new staff?"

"It's too soon to tell, really. But there's one woman who's already on her way out. I don't trust her, and if I'm going to be in charge of these people, I need to trust them."

Trust. The word was getting a lot of use these days.

"I'm thinking of getting a dog," she said, giggling. "A Yorkie, so I can bring it to work with me."

"They allow dogs in court?"

"No, of course not. But I'll have assistants. Associates. And a secretary. Plenty of people to take it for walks."

The telltale *ding* of call waiting sounded in his ear.

"Somebody's calling, Whit. Can you hold, or should I call you back?"

"I should go. I only wanted to say hi, see how you're doing."

"All's well here, and I'm glad you're doing well out there."

She promised they'd chat soon, and he clicked over.

"Yeager..."

"Hello, my hardworking son. How did things go with that big blowhard? You kicked him to the curb, I hope."

Chuckling, Jase said, "It went well. Great, actually. Carl left with a promise to draft a contract and have it delivered by morning."

"Uh-oh…"

"What does that mean?"

"I never expected him to agree to your terms. Not that they were unreasonable. It's just, well, he's *Carl*."

"What does that have to do with your uh-oh?"

"I invited Bill Reeves over for coffee yesterday. We had a lovely visit. And I signed a contract with him, instead."

Jase ground his molars together. "You did *what*? Seriously, Mom? *Reeves*, the guy who routinely distracts people from the fine print in his contracts?"

He heard her disapproving sniff.

"His offer was more than fair."

Yeah, right. Fair according to *Bill*. Jase couldn't believe she'd close a deal this big and important—one that affected her *and* him—without letting him look over the paperwork first. Too late now, he thought. He'd blame the stroke for this latest off-the-cuff decision, but she'd been doing things like this for years. He only hoped he could iron out all the wrinkles.

And if history was any predictor, there would be wrinkles.

"Oh, guess what? Dora sold that rare book you gave her."

Nicely played, Mom, he thought of her distraction.

"Sold it?"

"Yes, to one of the partners at the firm."

It had been a gift, so it shouldn't bug him. Jase remembered how, after hearing his sister-in-law wish for a copy of Charlotte Brontë's *Shirley* to add to her collection, he'd spent weeks searching for a copy online. He'd found one in mint condition for $350. And he'd snapped it up. Dora had been overjoyed on Christmas morning, although, even as she unwrapped it, he hadn't understood why, in this day and age, she wanted to read a book that questioned men's power over women in the workplace. Now, however, the question brought Carl to mind, and Jase admitted that her interest in the subject might not be so far offtrack, after all.

"Dora *traded* it with the partner, you mean."

"No, no, she sold it. For $125."

During his book hunt, he'd learned a thing or two about rare book collectors. Just as a philatelist is always on the lookout for his next great stamp, and baseball card collectors were in constant pursuit of Babe Ruths or Mickey Mantles, people like Dora were never satisfied with the tomes on their shelves. She'd known its value, because weeks into January, she admitted having looked it up, and what she discovered had led to a whole new flurry of hugs and thank-yous aimed at Jase. If she'd traded it for something of equal or greater value, he would have understood. But to accept less than *half* what he'd paid for it? Without checking to see if he'd mind?

"You're awfully quiet. You're not angry, are you, son?"

"Angry? Me? Why would I be angry? It was her book, and it's your company."

What was it with the women in his life, striking deals without his input and keeping secrets from him!

His mother began to ramble, repeating that for all intents and purposes, *Jase* was the boss, and had been since he'd first made the deal with the cable shopping network. She went on to explain that with everything else on his plate, the agreement with Reeves had one purpose: to spare him the trouble of hammering out a deal with Daniels.

So he'd just spent $300 on a lunch intended to soften up the arrogant gasbag, and now, thanks to his mother's reckless move, he'd have to call and renege on the deal. Worse, Reeves's reputation couldn't compare to Daniels's. Jase leaned into the headrest and clapped a hand over his eyes, wishing he could say something like, *You want to control stuff like this?* You *call him!*

Jase sat up and started the truck.

"Oh, I didn't realize you were on the road."

"Just leaving the lunch meeting with Carl, remember?"

"Oh. Yes. Of course."

If she thought for a minute that he believed she'd forgotten about the meeting, she had another think coming. His mom was a lot of things, but absentminded wasn't one of them, despite the stroke. It was only because of the TIA that he chose not to pursue it. At least, not right now.

"Are you coming by soon?"

"Not tonight. I have some things to take care of." He'd deal with Reeves later. But he needed to call Carl. And Lillie.

Jase had a sinking suspicion that the first conversation would be a whole lot easier than the second.

CHAPTER FIFTEEN

LILLIE WANDERED AROUND the used-car lot, inspecting SUVs, sedans, coupes and small pickup trucks, but nothing in her price range appealed to her.

"Have you seen the vehicles on our south lot?" the salesman asked.

"Didn't even realize there was a south lot!" she said, following him. Once there, Lillie saw dozens of cars. They all looked good to her.

"Do you have a particular make or model in mind?"

The guy reminded her a little of her dad, but she knew better than to let her guard down.

"My criteria are pretty simple. Good gas mileage, easy to parallel park, one owner, no accident history." She named her price range, then waited for him to roll his eyes.

He patted the hood of a gray sedan, and after a quick trip around it, Lillie saw no evidence of damage.

"Want to take her for a spin?"

Yes, she'd like that very much. But first things first. "It comes with a warranty?"

"All our vehicles do," he said before listing what it covered.

"And verification that it hasn't been in any accidents?"

"That's our policy for everything we sell."

"How much do I need to put down?"

He told her, then said, "We have an excellent payment program for first-time purchasers…"

She'd never owned a car before, thanks to being on the road, then accepting jobs that allowed her to use public transportation or her own two feet.

The salesman gave her a quick rundown on gas mileage, then they took it out for a test drive.

She quickly made up her mind. And when all was said and done, there was still enough left in her savings account to pay for taxes, registration and insurance. Best of all, she didn't need to finance the vehicle. Now if only she could summon the patience to return her mom's car and ask one of her parents to bring her back to the dealership. When she explained the problem to the salesman, he waved to two mechanics on the other lot.

"This young lady needs someone to follow her home so she can return her mother's car," he hollered.

The men headed over to a huge pickup truck.

"Maury, here, will drive your new car," the salesman explained as one hopped down from the passenger seat, "and once you've delivered your mother's, he'll ride back with James."

An hour later, when the men left the inn, Lillie stood in the driveway, admiring her car. She waited until four o'clock, then called Jase. She knew he'd had an important lunch meeting today, and she was bursting to tell him her news.

He picked up on the second ring. "Yeager…"

"Rourke," she replied.

"Hey, Lillie. What's up?"

She could have said "You told me to call." Instead, she blurted, "Guess what I just did!"

"Who knows," he growled.

That must have been some lunch meeting, she thought.

"I bought a car. Can you believe it? I've never had my own car before."

"Nice. Real nice."

Something—anger, perhaps?—simmered in his tone. Lillie chose to ignore it.

"If you aren't busy, c'mon over. I'll take you for a drive. We can ride into Ellicott City, try out that new soft ice cream place."

"I dunno, Lillie. I won't be very good company."

"If a hot-fudge sundae doesn't sweeten your sour mood, a ride in this baby will." She reached through the open driver's side window and tooted the horn.

No response. What could it hurt to give it one last shot?

"I know you're tired. I won't keep you out long. Twenty minutes to, twenty minutes back, fifteen to eat. You'll be home before it gets dark, I promise."

His heavy sigh filtered into her ear.

"Okay."

And then he muttered something that sounded an awful lot like "might as well kill two birds with one stone."

Lillie tensed. "I'm sorry you had such a rotten day, Jase."

Another long pause, and then, "Be there in ten."

Much as she wanted to stand there, admiring her new ride, Lillie hurried inside to run a comb through her hair and freshen her makeup. While upstairs, she might as well change into something to match *her* mood.

Lillie had worn a lightweight suit and low-heeled pumps to the dealership. After tromping around the dusty lot, her shoes could use a good buffing and the outfit ought to be dry-cleaned. Everything ended up in a small pile in the corner of her bedroom. After slipping into a full-skirted sleeveless dress, she put on white sandals. Leaning into the mirror over her dresser, she added a yellow hairband—one that matched the centers of the daisies on her dress. Jase had never been a fan of too much makeup, so she opted for the au naturel look and headed downstairs, stopping only long enough to grab her purse on the way out the door.

"Where are you off to in such a hurry?" her dad wanted to know.

"Jase is coming over to see my new wheels. We're going to take a drive to Ellicott City for ice cream."

"You two have fun," her mom said.

"But drive safely."

And as if they'd rehearsed it, their voices harmonized, "Say hi to Jase for us."

Lillie tossed the bag onto the back seat just as Jase pulled into the drive. He'd always been so easygoing, even when she'd given him reason not to be. But even through the slight glare of his windshield, she could see that his disposition hadn't improved.

Lillie remembered plenty of times when she'd slipped into a grouchy state of mind, and usually it only upset her more if people asked what had caused it.

"So what do you think?" she said, striking a Vanna White pose beside the car. "Isn't she gorgeous?"

Hands in his pockets, he walked around it. "She?"

"Isn't that what people call cars? And boats? Airplanes? I don't know why, but—"

"You'd better hope it's a *he*, because *she's* will drive you crazy."

Maybe he and his mom had exchanged words. It wouldn't have been the first time. The woman had strong opinions and wasn't afraid to voice them. Not even to Jase, who'd doted on her since his dad died, who'd literally saved her company from bankruptcy, and now ran it with such precision that Colette's Crafts was one of the top twenty-five of its kind in the nation.

"I've been thinking of hot-fudge sundaes ever since we hung up." She smiled, a little too wide and a little too long, but maybe, just maybe, it would coax him out of the doldrums.

One look at his serious expression told her she'd failed. No matter. He'd called her stubborn and single-minded. This seemed like the perfect time to prove him right.

"Are you ready?"

"I guess."

She climbed in behind the wheel, and as he opened the passenger door, Lillie said, "You'll probably need to slide the seat back."

He got in, and as an afterthought, she said, "Would you rather drive?"

Jase shot her a *you're kidding* look. "No way. It's your car. And didn't you say you didn't even get to drive it home?"

"Right..."

"Then this is your first time behind the wheel?"

"Yes."

"Then why would you give me the virgin drive?"

Because I'm crazy about you, and I hate seeing you so miserable.

Lillie shoved the key into the ignition and fired up the engine.

"Sounds good. And that's good," he said with an approving nod.

Lillie moved the shift lever to Drive. "Better buckle up, cowboy!"

"Cowboy? Me?"

That, at least, got a chuckle out of him.

"Of course you. Cowboys are big and strong. They defend the weak, and they're honest and true. And that, Jase Yeager, describes *you*."

She half expected him to tease her for the pathetic attempt at poetry. Instead, he fiddled with the radio buttons and turned up the volume on an old '50s song.

As they made their way west, the crowded city streets gave way to heavy traffic, then to a two-lane country road.

She looked his way for a second. "Why? Have you heard something?" The question didn't make any sense, even to her. How would Jase have heard something? He'd been to the child's room at Hopkins *once.*

"Just wondering is all."

"Well, let's keep a good thought, shall we? I don't think I could handle it if Sally had a setback. I know I'm not supposed to get close to the kids, but I can't help it. That kid is amazing, and I adore her."

"What's the deal with her mom?"

"I don't know much about her."

Jase snorted.

"What. You know something I don't?"

"Forget I said anything." Then, "Told you I wouldn't be good company."

She almost replied "You weren't kidding!" Instead, Lillie took advantage of the space alongside the road and pulled over.

"All right," she said. "Talk to me. What's going on?"

He didn't answer right away. Instead, he stared out the window. Unbuckled his seat belt and got out of the car, leaving the door open. For a moment, he paced the roadside gravel. Then he got back in and, facing her, said, "Sally's mother… you're giving her way too much credit. She's in Paris with some famous tenor."

"Oh. My. *Gosh.* Where did you get all of *that* information?"

"Brant."

"Brant."

"Is there an echo in here? Yes, Brant. Ran into him at lunch today. The guy I was meeting with stepped away, and Sally's dad sat down. We got to talking and, well, some stuff came out."

"Stuff?" The way he'd said it told Lillie Jase wasn't just referring to Sally's mother. That could mean only one thing. "Stuff, like the guy who's supposed to turn me into a megastar?" Lillie laughed. "What a joke."

"What's that mean? You aren't interested?"

"I'd be lying if I said I wasn't. But I can't take him up on an offer like that."

"Why not? God knows you're talented enough. What if this meeting is your only chance to make your Nashville dream come true?"

If she quoted what he'd said, just last night, *then* would he understand?

"Everything I need is right here."

"Then why keep it a big secret?"

Ah, she thought, so *that* was what had riled him.

"It just seemed silly, talking about a meeting I'm not going to take."

A confused frown lined his brow. "I got the impression that he believes you're thinking about it."

"I should never have said that. I just wanted to end the whole conversation about..." Exasperated, she sighed. "I don't even remember the producer's name."

"Rusty. Rusty McCoy."

"So let me see if I have a handle on this. You're mad at me because I didn't tell you about Brant's offer?"

"Well, when you put it that way, you make me sound like a petty control freak."

Since her return to Baltimore, Lillie had been walking on eggshells around everyone. She'd cut them all a lot of slack for watching her every move, for questioning her whereabouts, for looking suspicious if she so much as winced because her leg hurt. And it was time for it to stop.

It didn't escape her notice that he hadn't said he *wasn't* angry.

"Look," she began, "I'm fully aware that writing that check doesn't come close to repaying you for everything you've done for me. Those times I overdosed, before the big intervention? You saved my life! You think I don't know that? I went to Rising Sun, where they browbeat me every day until I admitted I was an addict, until I started doing the hard work to turn my life around. But even before that—deep down inside—I knew what a mess I was. That's why I ended our engagement. I couldn't in good conscience drag you down with me. Because what if I went to rehab and failed to get clean? That would have been completely unfair to you! I guess you think the hardest thing I've ever done was giving up my precious drugs, don't you?"

Jase's eyes widened, and she read his silence as a resounding *yes.*

"Well, you're wrong, buddy! *Wrong.* Even in my addled state I knew that I wasn't good for you, that you deserved better than the likes of me. I'll bet you also think I ended our engagement because you issued that..."

Lillie stopped herself from saying *that sanctimonious ultimatum.*

"Leaving you," she said, "*that* was the hardest thing I've ever done."

Jase, nodding slowly, stared at his hands, resting on his thighs.

"That said," she continued, "you need to know that while I respect your opinion, I don't need your permission or your approval. For anything. I'm like an ex-con. I served my time and paid for my crimes. And whether you agree or not, I deserve a second chance."

Jase continued to sit, forefingers tapping his knees, eyes down.

"Now, I'm going to turn this engine back on and drive us to Ellicott City. We'll order hot-fudge sundaes—because they're your favorite—and afterward, we'll drive straight back to the inn."

Lillie leaned forward, forcing him to make eye contact.

"And if you aren't out of this foul mood by the time we get there, I'm going to... I'll... I don't know what," she said, thumping the dash, "but you won't like it!"

Finally, he said, "You're wasting gas."

They rode in silence to the ice cream stand. She ordered their sundaes, and they found a picnic table and ate in silence, too. By the time they returned to the inn, she'd had enough. Lillie hit the childproof door locks, effectively imprisoning him in the car.

"Let me tell you a thing or two, *Jase Yeager.* I think it's terrible, the way you're behaving. After last night…" She'd thought of little else but the warm, sweet way he'd held her, kissed her… "I guess you're confused by what *seemed* to be happening between us, and that's why you're behaving like a rude, spoiled child. I guess I have it coming, but I don't mind admitting, it isn't easy putting up with all of this. Especially after—"

He reached for her hand, and she pulled it away.

He finally spoke. "Look, I'm sorry. It wasn't fair, taking my bad day out on you. Not that this excuses my behavior, but… Mom made a lousy business decision, and I'll have to eat crow and jump through hoops and who knows what else to straighten things out. Then I found out that after I'd spent a small fortune on a book for Dora, she sold it for next to nothing. And Whitney…"

At the mention of her name, he stopped talking so suddenly that it scared Lillie.

"What about her?"

The instant the sarcastic words were out, Lillie regretted them. Hiding behind one hand, she said, "Oh, good grief. Did that make me sound like a jealous shrew?"

He sent her a half-hearted grin. "Nah."

"So what happened with Whitney?" Last night, Jase had told her about their rather sudden breakup, how she'd taken a job in California. Now, if he said she'd invited him to join her on the west coast, Lillie didn't know what she might do. Or say.

"Nothing, really, except she's just one more example of the women closest to me, making decisions about things that involve me without talking to me."

Now Jase hid behind a hand. She saw one corner of his mouth lift in a small grin.

"Good grief. Did that make me sound like a whiny child?"

"Nah."

Following a moment of tense silence, she said, "I guess after a day like that, I can cut you a little slack. But… I'd have to turn in my Girl Power card if I didn't repeat that women no longer need to run every idea past a man. We vote now, and everything."

"Touché," he said. "And you know what?"

"I'm almost afraid to ask."

"I barely tasted that sundae."

"Me, too."

He smiled. It was a relief, knowing they'd worked things out.

This time.

CHAPTER SIXTEEN

JASE DIDN'T THINK he'd ever seen her that angry. Part of him had silently cheered as her eyes flashed. *Good for you, Lill*, he'd thought. *Stick up for yourself!* Lillie had been right when she'd said people still didn't trust her. People, meaning *him*. And she'd been right to think her recent past motivated his suspicions.

He wanted to trust her. God knew he did! Still, he couldn't help questioning Lillie's claim that she was clean now. He'd heard it all from her before. Too many times. Like the night she'd swallowed a handful of pills, and slipped into near-unconsciousness, unable to utter an intelligent sentence, drooling, incapable of staying on her feet. While waiting for the paramedics to hook her up to an IV, he'd overheard one EMT—who'd transported her to the hospital several times before—tell his partner, "If this one was a cat, she'd only have a life or two left." The day after, while signing her release papers, the doctor had taken Jase aside. "Next time," he'd said, "she might not be so lucky." Eight words that had shaken Jase to his core, awakening a keen awareness that because he couldn't say no to her, he had unintentionally contributed to her condition. Guilt and fear merged, inspiring the toughest resolution of his life: he'd insist that Lillie get professional help, *or else*. The demand started the dominos toppling… First, her tears. Apologies and pleading. The return of his ring. The train to New York. And the last domino… Jase, burying the diamond in his sock drawer.

Anger-turned-self-pity pushed him through those first tormenting weeks, and by the time it dulled, he'd fully engulfed himself in running his mother's company. He couldn't hold Lillie accountable for his mother's controlling behavior, for her unwillingness to respect his life choices.

Concentrate on the positives, he told himself. Life hadn't been perfect, but he'd survived.

Until, on a whim, he'd gone to the inn, where one look at her freckled face, smudged and streaked by hard work, put him on the path that led to the unexpected meeting at the music store, which led to his invitation to join him for coffee and pie. It had been his idea to stop by the hospital, his idea to have dinner at the Waterfront afterward, and his decision to say yes when she asked him to join her in the gazebo… where those delicious, tantalizing kisses had left him feeling weak-kneed and longing for more. And despite all the reasons he should run in the opposite direction, Jase knew he was in too deep. What choice did he have but to believe that this time, she was telling the truth?

Lillie had changed a lot during her months in New York. She'd cut her hair—something she'd sworn she'd never do—and set her sights on repaying every debt, on saving enough money to survive on her own. Volunteer hours at Hopkins served as clear evidence that her "doing for others feels good" declaration had been genuine.

His dad had a long list of sayings that he could recite to fit just about any circumstance, such as "if something seems too good to be true, it probably is" and "good things come to those who wait." What advice would he give if Jase recounted everything that had happened between him and Lillie?

He missed his dad every day, but oh, what he'd give to have a good heart-to-heart with the man at times like this.

Drew had always been levelheaded and honest with him…

He dialed his brother's number.

"Yeager."

Chuckling at the fact that his brother answered the phone the same way he did, Jase said, "What's new, dude?"

In place of an answer, his older brother said, "So how are things between you and Lillie?"

"How about if I buy you a beer, and I'll tell you all about it."

"Uh-oh, that bad, is it?"

"No. Maybe." Jase groaned under his breath. "I dunno. Are you free for lunch?"

"How 'bout noon, Sur les Quais. I haven't seen Ian since the firm booked his banquet room for the holiday party last year. It'll be good, seeing the guy."

He wondered how much their old pal had changed since the night he'd gotten down on one knee and, oblivious to the curious stares of nearby diners, asked Maleah to marry him.

An hour later, Jase sat across from Drew and grinned. "What does Dora think of the new look?"

His brother scrubbed a hand over his goateed chin. "She's not exactly wild about it. Yet. But it'll grow on her."

"Either that, or you'll wake up with just enough of that scruffy 'stache missing that you'll have to shave the rest of it off."

The brothers laughed as a bow-tied waiter delivered lemon-sliced ice water and took their order.

"Where's Ian?" Drew asked him.

"In the back. But please don't ask me to disturb him," the young man kidded. "He's doing payroll!"

"Knowing Ian, there aren't many zeroes on

those checks," Jase said, "so that shouldn't take long. Give him ten minutes, then tell him that his ol' buddies are here to collect on a whoppin' fat loan." Snickering, he added, "That's a whoppin' fat fib, but it's guaranteed to get him out here!"

Once the waiter was out of earshot, Drew leaned both forearms on the table. "All right, let me have it. What's going on with you and Lillie?"

Jase sat back, ran a hand through his hair, then recited the essentials, from the initial meeting outside the jewelry store, to her physical and emotional transformation, to the visit in her folks' gazebo. He left out the *I kissed her and I liked it* part.

"Sounds like she pulled herself together. She paid us what she owed, plus interest, months ago. From what I hear, she paid back all the guys in your band, too."

"Yeah…"

"Hey, nobody can blame you for keeping your guard up. She put you through hell. You'd be crazy if you *weren't* a little edgy."

Nodding, Jase sipped his water.

"Here's a dumb question for ya, bro. Do you *want* to pick up where you left off with her?"

More than anything, Jase thought. But he said, "I'm not sure."

"What's the main bone of contention? She still owes you money?"

Jase paused as the waiter delivered their meals.

"No, she paid back every cent, with interest." He pictured the plaque she'd made him. The sentiment sure seemed sincere. So far.

"How long has she been back now? Three months?"

"She got home the week of Mother's Day." Easy to remember, since he'd avoided talking marriage with Whitney, even as Lillie and her dad talked about gifts for Amelia.

"Sounds to me like you two need a good old-fashioned sit-down. Lay your cards on the table, as Dad used to say, and hope that when the game's over, you're both holding a winning hand."

That's just it, Jase thought. This wasn't a game. He winced, recalling her recent outburst.

"Afraid she might go back to her old ways, huh? Well, like I said, who wouldn't under the circumstances?"

"I guess."

"Sit her down. Get specific. Talk until she convinces you that won't happen."

He didn't feel like repeating the many times and ways she'd delivered the "drugs are in the past" speech, because Drew had been the go-to guy when Jase needed help picking up the pieces.

"I hate to sound like a cynic, but when all's said and done, there are no guarantees. You're gonna have to trust your gut."

"I guess," Jase repeated.

Ian pulled out a chair and joined them. "Well as I live and breathe, if it isn't the Yeager brothers."

The men exchanged handshakes and "what's new" conversation.

"Enjoying the meal?" Ian wanted to know.

"As always," Drew said.

Ian rested tattooed forearms on the table and studied their faces. "Why so serious, guys? Somebody lose their job?"

Drew chuckled. Jase did not.

"Lillie's back," Drew said.

"Ah. That explains a lot."

"Little brother, here, can't decide whether or not they should pick up where they left off."

"*I* changed," Ian said. "Maybe she has, too."

Jase had heard stories about Ian's background—serving ten long years in prison for joining his pals in a convenience store robbery before he'd even turned twenty. It couldn't have been easy, joining society again, not with a thing like that hanging over his head, but he'd done it. Couldn't have been easy convincing Maleah, the love of his life, that he wouldn't hurt her again—especially not with a decade-long gap between his release and their reunion, but he'd done that, too.

"Give her a little credit," their friend said.

Jase only nodded.

"What's the worst that can happen?" Ian pressed.

"Drugs," Drew offered.

Jase's heartbeat picked up as he added, "And this time, they could kill her."

"Neither of those things are very likely." Ian studied Drew's face, then aimed his gaze toward Jase. "You know that, right?"

Again, Jase only nodded.

"Let me ask you something..."

Jase braced himself to hear what he'd been asking himself since Lillie came home: *Do you have what it takes to help her stay straight?* Better still: *Are you man enough to handle it if she can't?*

"If you two get back together, what's in it for *her*?"

Guilt shot through him, because until that moment, he hadn't given a thought to whether or not *Lillie* wanted to start over. Or if that would be best for her, for that matter. *Guy has to be pretty selfish not to consider a thing that important...*

Memory of those moments in the gazebo rumbled in his heart. If that was how she behaved if she *didn't* want to renew what they'd had—

"Sounds corny, I know," Ian said, "but I'll be forever grateful to Maleah, to her family and mine, for giving me a second chance. Without that, who knows where I would have ended up."

Drew snorted. "Gimme a break, pal. You put in ten long years of clean living before you two hooked up again. That hard work is responsible for the success of this place, and for your close ties to your aunt, your dad, your employees."

A waitress stepped up and whispered something in Ian's ear. Nodding, he got to his feet. "Sorry, guys, but duty calls. Good to see you both," he said. "Don't be such strangers, okay?" He gripped Jase's hand a tick longer than before. "If you want to talk, you know how to find me."

"Thanks."

And with that, their host left them alone to finish lunch and discuss their respective jobs, their mother's health and the upcoming surprise birthday bash Colette's sorority sisters would throw in a few months, right here at Sur les Quais.

Jase's attention on the conversation was half-hearted at best, because already he'd started thinking about how he'd convince Lillie to sit down for that much-needed heart-to-heart.

CHAPTER SEVENTEEN

"I HAVE GOOD NEWS!" Lillie's sister said. "You're not going to believe this!"

Molly had a reputation for exaggerating, so Lillie smiled as she dropped onto the nearest kitchen chair. "How many guesses do I get?"

"One." Shoulders raised with excitement, she folded her hands on the table.

"You and Matt decided to stop globe-trotting?"

"No! You know how much we love traveling."

"You're adopting a dog? A cat? A parrot?"

Frowning, Molly said, "You're so far off base, it isn't even funny!"

"Then...you're selling the house so you can afford that place at the beach you've been dreaming about?"

Brows high on her forehead, Molly gave that some thought before saying, "No, but that isn't a half-bad idea." She knocked on the table. "C'mon. I'll give you one more chance..."

"Matt got a promotion."

"No! It isn't good news for Matt and me, it's good news for *you*! Great news, actually."

What her sister needed, Lillie thought, was a kid or two. Or at the very least, a cat or a dog, a bird, some fish even, to give her something to focus on besides planning the next exotic trip. And maybe then she wouldn't be so inclined to turn everything into a never-ending game.

"Molly, you know I love you to pieces, but I don't have a clue what you're talking about."

"I ran into Jase's girlfriend this morning."

"But… I thought she moved to California…"

"She's only back for a week or so, to pack up her town house and arrange to have things shipped to San Francisco. I barely recognized her! Her hair is almost white-blond, and she's as tan as a caramel. One loose end to tie up, she told me, and she's done with Baltimore for good."

"Well, good for her," Lillie muttered. And then it dawned on her that the loose end might be Jase.

"Stop looking like you just saw a ghost. It didn't take her long to replace Jase. She's dating some hotshot restaurateur with—as she put it—'establishments in LA, Vegas, Sacramento *and* San Francisco.'" Molly rolled her eyes. "I have no idea what Jase ever saw in her. He's always been so down to earth. Even after all those hours on TV, with women calling in and blatantly flirting and show hosts falling all over themselves around him, he's still the most grounded guy I know."

Lillie couldn't get her mind off Whitney's last move.

"So here's the best part," Molly continued. "She's moving her family to California. Found an assisted living center for her mother, and a one-bedroom apartment nearby for her sister, whom she's paying to—" Molly drew air quotes "'—to take care of Mom, because I'm way too busy to oversee things, myself.'"

"Well, to give credit where it's due, at least she's seeing to their needs."

"Lillie, Lillie, Lillie." Molly sighed. "She gets no credit from *me*. Think how hard that'll be for her poor ol' mama, packing up, flying all the way across the country, adjusting to a one-bedroom apartment after living in a big house on an acre of ground, leaving all her friends behind. Same goes for the sister. Nope, nope, nope. Whitney gets no credit from me. She's doing this to make her own life easier, not her family's."

"She shared all that with you during a chance meeting?"

"You'd be surprised what I can get out of people when I set my mind to it." Helping herself to a glass of iced tea, Molly turned from the sink. "Can I pour one for you, sis?"

"Sure. I could use a little caffeine kick. I have some final touches to put on the grand opening flyer. After my shift at the hotel, that is. I might need a little help, staying awake."

After delivering the drink, Molly sat across from Lillie again. “How are things with you and Jase these days?”

“I wish I knew.”

“I heard you two rehearsed for some shindig at Hopkins?”

“That isn’t going to happen. Little Jason died.”

“Oh, Lill… I’m sorry to hear that. I know you really cared about that boy.”

Lillie sipped the tea.

“Don’t let it get you down. He’s in a better place. No more suffering. No more tests. No more hospitals.”

She knew her sister meant well, or Lillie would have pointed out that those were precisely the things people *didn’t* need to hear after experiencing a loss. Why couldn’t people just say “I’m sorry” and be done with it?

“Mom said you turned down a great offer from some fancy record producer. She was mistaken, right?”

“I didn’t hear an offer. The father of one of the Hopkins kids thought he could make a deal if I wanted him to, but—”

“You didn’t want him to?”

“Too many other things to adjust to right now.”

“But, you’ve had your eyes on that prize for as long as I can remember!”

“Yeah, well, that was then, and this is now.”

“Oh, c’mon. What kind of gobbledygook is

that? You don't really expect me to believe you don't want to at least *try* to make your Nashville dreams come true."

"Believe it or not, that was more Dad's dream than mine. I sort of bought into it, for a little while. But my dreams have changed."

Molly scrutinized her. "It's because of Jase, isn't it?"

She shook her head. "Jase is… He and I… We…" Lillie honestly didn't know how to explain things.

"If you want him, go after him."

"It isn't that simple. I'm sure the things I put him through are front and center in his mind. In his shoes, I wouldn't trust me either."

"First of all, you couldn't wear his shoes if you tried. Size 12 on a size 5 foot?" Molly laughed. "Now, there's a picture for the Rourke family photo album!" One look at Lillie was enough to sober her. "He's not a fool, I'll give you that. But you two had something truly special. He's footloose and fancy-free now, so…" She paused before adding, "Unless…unless you don't care about him anymore."

Lillie didn't trust herself to speak. Not with a huge sob stuck in her throat.

"I can't say as I blame you. He was pretty tough on you before you left for New York. For a long time, I blamed him for making you leave."

"Nothing that happened was Jase's fault. Nothing."

"Okay, then what about that mean-spirited speech you told me about when I visited you at Rising Sun?"

"I drove him to it."

"Excuses, excuses. What's your sponsor say about you and Jase getting back together?"

"I haven't made a big deal of it, because it isn't a big deal."

Molly harrumphed. "In other words, you haven't told him."

"Not in so many words."

"Because you know what he'd say."

Lillie glanced at the clock. Why did the hands seem frozen in place?

"You can fool your friends, maybe even Mom and Dad, but you can't fool me. You're still head over heels for the guy. It's written all over your face, and I can hear it in your voice. Seems to me if you hope to stay off the pills, you need to make life as easy as possible. Reconnecting with Jase will accomplish that."

How would living with his doubt and mistrust make life as easy as possible?

"Okay, all right, I'll butt out."

"Too late for that," Lillie teased. "But I appreciate what you're trying to do. I love you for it."

"I'd do anything for you, sis. Anything. If only I could think of something." She swiped condensation from the sides of her glass and wiped it on a paper napkin. "Hey, here's an idea… I'll track him down and knock some sense into him."

Laughing, Lillie patted Molly's hand. "You'd have to catch him first, and with those long legs, that's all but impossible. But even if you got lucky, like you said, size 12 shoes versus size 5…"

"Good point. I suppose." Her sister fell silent for a moment. "I just want you to be happy, you know? You've worked so hard, you deserve every good thing life has to offer."

"Oh, my life is pretty good, even without Jase," she admitted. "I have a great family, a safe place to live, jobs that pay fair wages and my health." Sitting up straighter, she added, "Did Mom tell you I finally bought a car?"

"Yup. I saw it in the driveway. Pretty cool, sister dear. Pretty cool." She chugged down the last of her tea, and while putting the glass into the dishwasher, said, "What can I do to help with the grand opening?"

"Just show up on Saturday. There's bound to be something I've forgotten."

Molly shouldered her purse and, one hand on the back doorknob, added, "Is Jase coming?"

"He knows about it, but I haven't shared the specifics."

"Call him. Spell 'em out. Trust me, he'll be here."

"Wish I had your confidence."

Molly winked and sent Lillie a knowing smile. "I have it on good authority that he cares more than you think."

"Oh, yeah? What authority?"

"Whitney. She said if you hadn't come back to town, Jase never would have let her move to California alone. Said he can do his mother's bidding from anywhere in the world, so he would've followed her out there in a heartbeat."

"She makes him sound like a well-trained pup. I think you're right. Jase *is* better off without her."

But was he better off with *Lillie*?

Only one way to find out, she thought, waving to Molly. The instant her sister's car was out of sight, she dialed his number.

Voicemail. Lillie cleared her throat and said, "It's me. I know I told you about the inn's reopening party, but I don't remember if I gave you any of the details. Mom and Dad—and the rest of the family—would love to see you here." Lillie hesitated. "I'd like to see you here, too, so if you have time on Saturday, between noon and six, bring your appetite."

She pressed End, then kicked herself for not saying "Call me if you can make it." The way she'd left things, he could show up, unannounced. Worse, he wouldn't show up at all, and say it was because he didn't know he was supposed to RSVP.

Lillie looked out the window, where the big white gazebo loomed in the backyard. Inside, on the bench farthest from the double screen doors, Jase had taken her in his arms and kissed her so tenderly, so longingly, that Lillie worried she might melt, slide from his lap onto the floor, like unpredictable mercury that had escaped a broken antique thermometer.

"It's a beautiful sight, isn't it?"

Lillie startled at the sudden sound of her mother's voice. She turned and smiled. *It's more beautiful than you know, Mom.*

"I hope a lot of wonderful memories will be made there."

Lillie's heart beat a tick faster. "I have a feeling it'll be the favorite place of lots of people." *It's already one of my favorite places!*

"Working tonight?"

"'Fraid so. I'm on duty until 2:00 a.m."

"Goodness, Lillie. That isn't very safe, is it? All alone there at the desk at that hour?"

"There are always a few maids on duty, and the night manager. Nothing has ever happened, but if it should, help is as close as the phone."

Frowning, Amelia propped both fists on her hips. "If you can get to the phone, that is."

If only she knew how many crazy risks Lillie had taken walking the dark, gritty streets in search of her next fix.

"Love you, Mama." She gave her a big hug. "But please don't worry. Trust me, I can take care of myself."

"Supper will be ready any minute. Will you be able to eat with your dad and me?"

She glanced at the clock. "I can. But I'll have to hit the road as soon as we're finished, so leave the dishes soaking in the sink, and I'll do them when I get home."

"We'll do no such thing! You've worked miracles in the flower gardens. I can't even count how many neighbors have told me they look like something from a landscaping magazine." Amelia took Lillie's hands in her own and inspected the palms. "No girl should have hands like this. What if you wanted to give Jase's cheek a gentle pat? Why, you might scratch him with these calluses!"

The image of Jase holding *her* face in his big hands—seconds before he kissed her—came to mind. Oh, what she wouldn't give for a chance to repeat that sweet and intimate moment!

Liam strode into the kitchen and, standing between them, pulled his wife and daughter into a hug.

"What're my girls talking about?"

"Supper. Dishes…" Amelia laughed. "And Lillie's man hands."

"Man hands!" Liam inspected her palms, too. "Well now, don't know as I'd call 'em *man hands*, but my, my, my, you sure couldn't get a job modeling rings, now could you!"

Lillie kissed his cheek. "Good thing modeling has never been on my bucket list, then."

He patted his ample belly. "When do we eat? I'm starved."

"Scrub up, Mr. Rourke, and set the table. Soup's on!"

They ate in companionable silence for a minute or two before Liam said, "What do you hear from Jase these days?"

Were all these Jase-related questions the result of a conspiracy? "Not much." What would he say if she told him how many hours it had been since Jase kissed her, right out back, in the gazebo? "Why do you ask, Dad?"

"Oh, no reason."

"Your dad's probably just wondering if Jase will be here on Saturday."

They exchanged a look that told Lillie there was more to the story.

"I left him a message a little while ago, letting him know what time things start, but he hasn't called back."

"He will," Amelia said.

"No doubt in my mind," Liam agreed.

"How can you be so sure?" Lillie asked.

Liam wiggled his eyebrows. “Let’s just say we know what we know.”

If she hadn’t seen them checking on their tickets to the theater the other night, Lillie would have sworn they’d been present when she and Jase went to the gazebo. Had they come home early? No…she would have seen their car in the drive when she walked Jase to the door.

Unless they’d parked out back…

One look at her mother’s twinkling eyes told her that was exactly what had happened. The heat of a blush made its way from her shoulders to her cheeks, and the only way to hide it was to make her way to the sink.

“I need to get to the hotel,” she said. “Your father and I will clean up.” Amelia looked at her husband. “Won’t we, Liam?”

He looked less than enthused when he sighed and agreed.

Just a few more minutes, Lillie thought, and she’d be out the door, safe from any questions or conversation about that night with Jase.

“That boy is still sweet on you,” her dad said. “If you ask me, he’d be lost without you.”

“Oh, I know.” Amelia sighed. “Every time he stopped by to see how you were doing, it was written all over his face.”

“Yup. Even when he brought a young lady with him.”

"Just how many women did he parade past you, anyway?"

"Three, counting Whitney."

Her mother clucked her tongue. "So sad for those young ladies, because not one of them was Jase's type."

What *was* Jase's type? A year or so ago, Lillie would have said "Me!" But as she'd told Molly, that was then, and this is now.

Jase will call, no doubt about it, they'd said. Lillie got in her car and caught herself smiling. Smiling *wide.*

"Straighten up, girl," she muttered. So what if he'd kissed her. It didn't mean he felt anything beyond friendship for her. Jase probably hadn't given it a moment's thought, since.

And why would he? She'd brought nothing but misery to his life during their final year together. Jase hadn't come right out and said that he didn't trust her, but then, it hadn't been necessary.

Eventually, she'd prove to everyone that her work at Rising Sun had made her trustworthy again. So the real question was, could she trust *Jase* not to hurt her the way he had on the night she returned his ring.

Lillie would fight for him, if she believed there was anything to fight for. But what if he still saw her as a weak, sniveling, drug-addicted parasite?

That little speech on the way to the ice cream stand? At first, she'd felt empowered. Now, Lillie felt embarrassed by every word. She'd let her feelings push her into a corner, where anger and disappointment forced her to defend herself.

She'd learned a few things about herself in rehab, among them that her battle for sobriety had made her strong. Stronger than she'd ever been. That alone was reason enough to feel proud of herself, too proud to allow a repeat of that scene!

Let it go, she told herself. *Let go and move on.*

The glimmer of hope that had burned in her throughout her time at Rising Sun, that continued to flicker during the months of scrimping and saving while working for Pete, had given her false hope. Running into Jase at the jewelry store had fanned the coals, and every meeting since only added fuel to the fire. What rational person would allow a couple of kisses—however wonderful they had been—to lead her to believe that after all they'd been through, a reunion was possible?

She'd been silly. Immature.

But that was then, and this is now.

It wouldn't happen again.

Not if she had anything to say about it.

CHAPTER EIGHTEEN

"ARE YOU GOING to the White Roof Inn reopening?" Colette asked.

Jase had batted the question around for days and still hadn't made a decision. For every good reason to go, he'd come up with two to stay away.

"I doubt it." He glanced at the small envelope in her hand. "Why? Are you?"

"I'm giving it some serious thought." She placed the invitation on the table beside her chair. "I always liked Liam and Amelia. It isn't their fault that Lillie turned out the way she did."

"C'mon, Mom. That's not fair. She paid a price for her actions. A big one."

Colette sniffed. "That remains to be seen."

"If you feel that way, why are you going? Lillie arranged the whole shindig, practically single-handed, so she'll be there."

"How would you know the amount of work she put into the party?"

He didn't like that suspicious glint in her eyes. "I get around, and I hear things."

"Get around, as in around Lillie?"

Sometimes, her ability to make him feel like a misbehaving brat amazed him. He had two choices: admit that he'd seen a lot of Lillie since she got back to Baltimore, or find a way to sidestep her question.

"So if you go to the reopening, what will you wear?"

"I haven't the foggiest idea."

"Your invitation doesn't say? I only ask because I didn't get one." She didn't need to know that his invite had come by way of a voice message. A message he'd listened to at least ten times.

Colette patted the envelope. "I suppose it's one of those gatherings where guests are expected to use their own good sense. But it does make one wonder."

"Wonder what?"

"Why Lillie the Great Organizer didn't think to specify proper attire. Perhaps it means—"

"She's working two jobs, three if you count all the things she does around the inn. Plus she volunteers at the Hopkins children's ward a couple times a month."

A daunting thought crossed his mind: if she attended without him, chances were better than good that she'd put Lillie to some sort of sobriety test.

"Here's an idea," he countered. "Let's not go.

I'll find something else for us to do. Maybe Drew and Dora can join us."

"Something else. Such as?"

"Such as one of those lighthouse tours up the Chesapeake. They sound interesting."

"Oh, please. Something like that would take days. There must be fifty lighthouses in the bay. We'd have to stay overnight to fit them all in."

"So? Let's do it. The way Drew and Dora love to travel, I'll bet they'd have fun."

A lighthouse tour seemed fitting, considering her attitude toward Lillie was stormy at best. Maybe a trip like that would guide her into calmer waters.

And guide him to a decision—

"She forgot something else."

Jase stifled a groan of frustration. He didn't like being in this position, wanting to defend Lillie but not wanting to offend his mother. It reminded him that he needed to find a way to disconnect from her, gradually.

"There's nothing here about how a person should RSVP."

"Because it's an open house kinda thing, come if you can, stay as long as you like."

She flicked the envelope's flap. "I have to admit, I *am* curious to see the place again. I haven't been there since your engagement party."

The word felt like a slap. That party had been *her* idea, and he still felt that he owed Amelia an apology for all the work and expense that went into it.

Jase finally diverted the subject to business. She showed him drawings of her newest design and he feigned more interest than warranted to get Colette off the subjects of Lillie and the opening. He hoped she wouldn't revisit her crazy, off-the-cuff deal with Bill Reeves, still a sore subject in his mind. It hadn't been easy, smoothing things over with Carl Daniels. One of these days, when he felt more confident that she'd fully recovered from the TIA, he'd get into that with her.

She walked him to the door. It wasn't like her to do that, and it made him automatically uneasy. He steadied himself in preparation for another shocker.

"Pick me up a little past noon. We don't want to be the first ones there, but it would be rude to get there much later."

"We? I didn't realize we'd made a decision."

"You might be old enough to put CEO on your business cards, but I'm still your mother. Wear your Oxford shirt. It brings out the blue of your eyes. And if you stop looking so stunned, I won't make you wear a tie."

Jase leaned in and pressed a kiss to her cheek. "I'll give you five bucks, right now, if you can name one time when you *made* me do anything."

She held out one hand, palm up. "I made you admit you were in over your head with Lillie."

Unfortunately, he couldn't deny it. The morning after Lillie's last OD, he'd stopped by his mom's, shaken and angry.

She had him dead to rights, and knew it. Colette wiggled her fingers, and grinning, he peeled a five from his wallet. "You didn't *make* me break it off."

"I *made* you see that you should," she said, snapping it from his fingers. "Same thing." Winking, she added, "See you at noon. Blue shirt. No tie."

One good thing came of this, Jase thought, firing up the truck. The 'go—don't go' question had been answered.

The feeling that rose up inside him reminded Jase how he'd felt as a boy, going to bed extra early on Christmas Eve to help time pass more quickly until the morning.

Tonight might just be a good night to turn in early.

JUST AS HE'D EXPECTED, Jase spent the night tossing and turning. During the few hours when he managed to nod off, his mind churned with dreams.

Dreams of Lillie, broken and bandaged and fighting for her life after the bus flattened her car. Lillie—days after the first surgery—easing battered fingers through his hair as he slept in the chair beside her hospital bed. Lillie, opening one swollen eye to look into his. Lillie, trying to coax her bruised mouth into a smile.

He'd chugged a mug of coffee and ate a slice of dry toast, hoping to shake the cobwebs from his brain. An exercise in futility, he realized, when his mom plucked a tiny scrap of tissue from his chin.

"Nicked yourself shaving, did you?" she said, examining the already-healed scrape. "Your dad used to do that. More mornings than not, I had to remove little white patches before he left for work."

Now, as they stood in the White Roof Inn's turret, she admired Amelia's paintings. Jase was more interested in the gazebo.

"Is it my imagination, or is Lillie favoring her right leg?"

It took a second or two to shake free of the memories. Jase followed his mother's gaze to the foyer, where Lillie had linked arms with a guest, then guided her into the parlor. Yes, she was limping. Knowing her, she'd put every bit of energy and muscle into making this event the best it could be, and overtaxed herself. Despite it all, though, she looked wide-awake and cheery in a gauzy black-and-white polka-dot dress. And with her hair pulled back from her face by a matching ribbon, she looked like a teenager.

"Stop staring," Colette said, gently smacking his forearm. "People will notice."

Jase aimed his gaze at the gazebo again.

"How long since her accident?"

He did the math in his head. "Almost three years, give or take."

"What do her doctors say about that leg?"

"Never asked her about it." Because he'd been too busy looking for signs that she might backslide.

Now, Lillie laughed as she pointed toward the dining room, where the caterers had laid out enough food to feed a horde.

"It's a good thing she has a pretty face. People are less likely to stare. The way you are."

He didn't think anyone else had noticed, but just in case, he looked toward the terrace, where hundreds of rose blossoms of every color bobbed in the warm breeze. He knew Amelia had a knack for painting flowers, not growing them. This was Lillie's work.

He thought of the goldfish he'd won for her at a carnival. It grew to ten times its original size before a guest's kid dropped a ginger snap into the fishbowl. And the fledgling that, after leaving its nest a bit too soon, caught a lucky break when Lillie picked it up. After weeks of her loving care, it flew south with its peers. She'd found homes for abandoned puppies, and if not for allergies to pet dander, she would likely have been dubbed Fells Point's crazy cat lady for taking in every kitten discarded at the docks. She even took care of Jase, who had been prone to bronchitis until Lillie came into his life, insisting on vaporizers and humidifiers, chest wraps and her recipe for robust chicken soup.

Now, huge, long-lashed brown eyes locked with his, sending his heart into overdrive. Jase questioned his sanity, because what man in his right mind would give a moment's thought to distancing himself from a woman like that?

"Oh, no," Colette said, elbowing him. "Now see what your gawking has done? She's coming over here."

"She's the hostess, Mom. Did you really think you could avoid talking to her?"

"Mrs. Yeager," she said, grasping Colette's hand. "What a relief to see you looking so hale and hearty."

His mom's back stiffened. "Thank you. You look well, too."

Jase held his breath, hoping his mother wouldn't bring addiction into the conversation or, God forbid, the time she'd caught Lillie digging around in her purse.

"Very nice affair," Colette continued. "Your hard work shows."

"Why, thank you."

Lillie's posture told him that she remembered

how withholding his mom could be with compliments.

Lillie surprised them both by linking arms with Colette. "Have you found the food table yet? We have something for every taste," she said, laughing, "from vegan to the most devout carnivore."

She didn't lead her to the table, though. Instead, Lillie guided his mother onto the terrace. Jase followed a comfortable distance away, wondering what, exactly, Lillie had up her sleeve. It didn't take long to find out.

"Mrs. Yeager, I've been meaning to apologize. For so many things. For taking advantage of your kindness. For trying to steal from you. For destroying our friendship. I miss that more than you'll ever know."

His mother stood gaping as Lillie's eyes filled with tears.

"I don't deserve your forgiveness, but I'm asking for it, anyway."

A long time passed before his mother said, "Don't make a scene, Lillie. What's done is done. I harbor no ill will toward you."

She surprised him again by drawing Colette into a loose hug.

"Thank you," she whispered. "Thank you so much."

His mother's eyes connected with his as Lillie released her. He moved closer.

"What're you two chatting about?"

Colette took a careful step back as a wavering smile crossed her face. "Lillie was just thanking us for coming." The smile softened. "Now then, where can I find your parents, so I can say hello?"

Lillie pointed to where they stood, smiling and nodding in response to a news anchor's questions.

"Mercy me. I had no idea the media would be here." Fluffing chin-length white waves, she giggled. "I might have worn something fancier if I thought I'd be on camera."

"No worries, Mom," Jase said. "The reporters aren't here to interview the guests."

"That may not have been in the initial plan, but when they find out the creator of Colette's Crafts and her TV star son are present, they'll polish up their lenses!"

Lillie sent him an almost sympathetic look. "Actually, your mom makes a good point. It'll be good for business when people find out the likes of Colette and Jase Yeager are among the inn's admirers." She patted his mother's forearm. "Stay right here, and I'll bring them over."

She turned to leave, but Colette grabbed her hand. "I'm glad we had this chance to talk. I've… I've missed you, too."

Lillie's grateful smile could have lit a dark room. "Thank you, Mrs. Yea—"

"Colette."

"Thank you, Colette." And with that, Lillie made her way to the other side of the room.

He was proud of his mother. Soon, he'd find a way to let her know just how proud. For now, he simply draped an arm across her shoulders.

"Good grief, Mom, have you no shame?"

She answered with an expansive shrug. "As Lillie so astutely pointed out, the connection is good for business. Ours *and* theirs." Elbowing him again, Colette added, "Bet you're wishing you had taken my advice."

"What advice?"

"To wear the long-sleeved Oxford, because it brings out the blue of your eyes. The viewers would have swooned. *Swooned* I tell you!"

"Guess they'll have to put their imaginations into action, then."

A balding, bespectacled fellow approached.

"Ron Matz," he said, extending a hand, "WJZ-TV."

"Oh, no need to introduce yourself," Colette crooned. "We've been fans for *years*."

If Matz picked up on the blatant flirtation, it didn't show. His questions were friendly but on-target, and he kept Jase's mother focused on the inn's new look. She was beginning to show signs of frustration when he held the mic out to Jase. Following a few questions about the TV show and Colette's Crafts, Matz winked. "How many marriage proposals from your adoring fans?" he joked.

"Only a few, mostly from ladies who are already married."

Matz laughed. "So you're safe. Lucky you!"

He signaled his cameraman that the interview had ended, and this time, shook Jase's hand. "Thanks for your time. And you know what? You look taller in person."

It's what everyone said, so Jase chuckled as his mother asked when the interview would air.

"Unless something big breaks, tonight on the evening news."

The crew moved on as Lillie returned. "You two are naturals. What a great idea," she told his mom. "I can hardly wait to see the story."

"We can hope it will inspire reservations and word of mouth, right?"

"She's right," Jase agreed. "Businesses, people celebrating anniversaries, or putting up out-of-town guests, you'll probably have a waiting list that goes years into the future."

Liam and Amelia made their way to where they stood.

"So glad you could come," Lillie's mom said, grasping Colette's hand. "You look just wonderful!"

"Thank you," Colette replied. "Maybe someday, you'll have to share your fountain of youth secret. You don't look a day older than you did on the night of…" Blushing, she caught herself and looked up at Jase, then continued with, "You look wonderful, too!"

Liam, Jase noted, hadn't joined the conversation. He knew the man had never been overly fond of his mother. He gave it ten seconds, tops, before Liam mentioned other guests he and his wife needed to greet.

Less, as it turned out…

"Well, we'd better say hello to the mayor before she has to get back to the office."

It wasn't like his mom to be at a loss for words, but there she stood, clearly searching for a topic that would break the difficult silence.

Lillie solved the problem by stepping between them. "Come with me, you two," she said, "and we'll get you something to eat." On the way to the dining room, she chattered about the weather, the bird feeder that had been raided by squirrels, a potted plant she'd forgotten to water in her hurry to get ready for the festivities. Once there, she gestured toward platters of meat and bowls filled with every imaginable side dish.

"There are dips and chips, and fresh veggies on most of the end tables. Desserts are in the kitchen," she said. "Everything from pudding to cheesecake." Lillie looked up at him and, smiling, said, "Eat up, or I'll have no choice but to send you home with doggie bags."

And when she left them to direct other guests

to the spread, Jase felt a noticeable chill where her warm hand had touched his elbow. He regretted wearing the short-sleeved polo shirt after all, because long sleeves would have put something between his skin and hers.

You're behaving like a love-struck schoolboy, he admonished. The feelings underscored his need to make a decision, and make it soon. Otherwise, thoughts of her might distract him to the point of walking into the harbor.

After finishing their meal, Colette ushered Jase through the inn's first floor rooms, pointing out American art pottery, vintage glassware and china stored in glass-doored antique hutches and classic prints and maps that decorated every wall.

"How old *is* this place?" she wanted to know.

"If memory serves, Liam said it dates back to the 1790s."

She grinned. "Oh, my. Do you suppose there are ghosts?"

Only the ghost of what Lillie and I once had...

Gaze flicking around the rooms, he spotted her in the turret, introducing a silver-haired couple to her mother's artwork. He searched his mind for an appropriate word to describe her, something that wasn't trite, like pretty or beautiful, gorgeous or lovely. No question about it, she was all those things, but she was more. So much more. The only word that came to mind was also a cliché, but like Lillie, herself, it defined her: *perfect*.

She'd often joked that there was an invisible thread connecting them, something ethereal, even metaphysical. It explained why she would call him right when he was thinking about and missing her, and why he'd so often finished her sentences. Whatever it was, Jase had a feeling it was what inspired her to turn around at that moment and single him out from dozens of others milling through the rooms.

From time to time when he was a boy, Jase had wished for supernatural powers. To fly. To see through walls. To make things disappear. He felt that way right now, because nothing would please him more than to be alone with her again.

"Jase, for goodness sake. What's gotten into you today?"

Eyebrows raised, he looked at his mother. "What?"

"I raised you better. Stop staring at that girl!"

"Sorry. Didn't realize that's what I was doing." *But can you blame me? Just* look *at her!*

Maybe he was seeing things. Had Lillie just beckoned him with a sideways nod? Jase couldn't imagine what she'd want to say, but as she disappeared around the corner, he faced his mother.

Colette smiled. "Lillie is so different now, I saw it in her eyes. Like the pretty young thing you first introduced me to. I saw something else, too."

"What?"

"She's still in love with you." Colette gave him a gentle nudge.

He hoped so. Oh man, did he hope so.

"Have you heard of *kintsugi*, the method of repairing broken ceramics with a mixture of lacquer and gold? The Japanese believe it's best to incorporate the repair into the vessel, instead of trying to hide it."

The metaphor wasn't lost on him: Lillie had a few scars—some visible, others that didn't show. And after one brief conversation with her, his mother believed he could mend the remaining breaks.

She nudged him again. "Go to her."

He hesitated, and she added, "Don't you see? You're the gold, son. *You're the gold.*"

"I'll be right back," he said, and started for the kitchen, where Lillie had just plated up a slice of cheesecake.

"Did you get enough to eat?" she asked, grabbing a fork.

"Plenty. Everything was great."

Using the fork, she gestured toward the table, crowded with desserts. "Can I get you anything else?"

"Thanks, but I'm stuffed."

She handed him a wedge of chocolate cake

anyway. "I've been thinking. This isn't the time or place to discuss…things…so maybe if you're not too busy tomorrow night, we can get together? Somewhere private? To talk?"

"I don't want to wait a whole day to hear what's on your mind. Why not tonight at my place?"

She'd just slid a bite of cheesecake into her mouth, and replied with a nod.

"I can pick you up. Parking is the pits in my neighborhood."

"I remember. But there's too much going on here tonight. We'll be at the Sams' tomorrow for a cookout. So, afterward?"

It wasn't what he'd wanted to hear, but he said, "What time?"

"How's seven?"

Not nearly as good as *now*, but it would have to do. "Sure."

Someone from the other room called her name, and they simultaneously turned toward the door.

She dropped the plastic plate into the recycling bin.

"See you tomorrow. At seven."

"I'll be waiting out front."

"Can't wait."

And he meant it.

CHAPTER NINETEEN

LILLIE WAS GLAD that she'd decided to take a day off from the restaurant. It felt good, being surrounded by family again. Her nieces each took a hand and led her to the big wooden swing set their dad had erected in the shade beyond their backyard pool.

"Remember when you used to push us way high," Katie said, taking hold of the chains, "and tell us to touch the sky with our toes?"

"You bet I do. And I remember that you thought you could, too!"

Kassie said, "We were five, so of course we did."

"Six," her twin said, "but who's counting."

"Hard to believe you'll be eleven on your next birthday. What sort of a party are you planning?"

"Mom wants to go to Swim World. Dad wants to take some of our friends camping." Kassie rolled her eyes. "A bunch of us in an RV that sleeps ten?"

Katie giggled. "No kiddin'! He'll go crazy in the first half hour."

"I think we should have a sleepover right here." Kassie pumped her feet, taking her swing high into the air. "We have a pool. Games. And a nice big basement where everybody could spread out their sleeping bags…"

"Good luck with that. Mom says slumber parties are too much work."

"What if I helped?" Lillie said. It was the least she could do, since she'd missed their last two birthdays.

"Really? You'd do that?" Kassie asked.

"I'd love it."

Both girls squealed.

"It'll be fun. We can plan it together. And I'll do all the work, so your mom can just relax, like any other guest."

"What'll we do with the dogs? They'll bark and eat all the snacks."

"We'll put the snacks out of reach," Lillie said, "and after a while, they'll get tired of yapping and find a quiet spot to snooze." She stooped to pat their fuzzy heads, wincing slightly when she straightened.

"What's wrong, Aunt Lill? Is your leg hurting again?" Katie asked.

"Just a little. Nothing to worry about. I should have iced it down after the opening yesterday, but I was so pooped that I just fell into bed." Like Kassie, she rolled her eyes. "And now I'm paying for it. But don't worry. It'll be fine by tomorrow."

Her leg had been bothering her a lot lately. After a lengthy discussion with her sponsor earlier in the month, she'd agreed to see her surgeon. The appointment had left her rattled, because another operation was the last thing Lillie needed, just when her life was getting back on track.

"Daddy said you're going to the hospital again, so the doctor can fix it."

"I didn't realize your folks told you about that."

"We're not babies, Aunt Lill."

"Sorry, Katie. I keep forgetting that. But don't worry," she repeated, "afterward, I'll be good as new."

The girls exchanged a concerned look, and then Katie said, "Were you really a drug addict, Aunt Lill?"

The question hit like a punch to the chest. Lillie wasn't sure how to answer. No one had said it in so many words, but she got the impression her brother and his wife had skirted the issue, to protect the impressionable children from the ugly truth. Had they overheard something to prompt the inquiry now?

"What have your parents told you?"

"Daddy says you had a hard time after your accident, and took pills to make things easier."

"Lots of pills," Katie added.

"Mom said you slid down the rabbit hole for a while—whatever *that* means—but you're better now."

Down the rabbit hole. What an interesting way to put it, Lillie thought. And since it seemed her nieces already knew the worst of it, she saw no reason to avoid the truth.

"Your dad's right. I had a hard time for a while there. And your mom's right, too. What started out as a few pills to ease the pain turned into a whole bunch. So yeah, I was a drug addict."

Their wide-eyed, serious faces made her quickly tack on, "But that's why I went to a special hospital in New York. I worked really hard, and I'm not addicted anymore. In fact, I haven't taken any pills in a long, long time."

Her explanation didn't seem to satisfy them. Maybe she'd provided too much information. Maybe they weren't old enough to process it all.

"Won't the doctor prescribe more pills after the next operation?"

"Maybe, but I won't take them."

"But…won't it hurt when they cut you?"

"Probably," she said, "but I'd rather deal with a little discomfort than go through rehab again."

"We can help," Katie offered.

"Right. We'll visit you. A lot. And make you play all those stupid games that Daddy calls *bored* games."

Katie joined her sister's laughter. "If that doesn't get your mind off the pain, nothing will!"

Lillie stood between the swings and pulled

them to her in a sideways hug. "You know, I'm almost looking forward to the surgery now!"

"Almost?"

Laughing, Lillie said, "Well, I know I call myself your crazy aunt, but I'm not really crazy!"

She kissed Katie's cheek, then Kassie's. "I want you to promise me something, girls."

"Sure, Aunt Lill," Kassie said, and Katie added, "Anything."

"This is serious. Real serious. And I'm going to hold you to this promise, all of your lives."

Again, the twins exchanged a puzzled glance.

"Promise me you won't ever make the same mistakes I did. If your doctor prescribes medicine, follow the instructions to the letter. But never, *ever* take any other drugs, no matter what your friends do or say."

She met their eyes, first Kassie's, then Katie's. "So? Do I have your promise?"

The twins raised their right hands, fingers forming the Scouts' salute. "Promise," they said in unison.

"It's time for dessert," Lillie's brother called. "Get in here, or I'm eating your share!"

Her nieces hopped down from the swings. "He isn't kidding," they said, each taking one of Lillie's hands again.

"I remember," she said, ignoring her throbbing leg as they raced across the yard. "When we were little, I used to call him a big horse with a feed bag over his face."

"Oh, he is *so* gonna hear that next time he tries to steal a bite of pie," Kassie said.

"Or a spoonful of ice cream."

"What's so funny?" her brother asked as they entered the kitchen.

"Oh, nothing—" Lillie winked at her nieces "—Flicka."

The girls wrapped their arms around his waist, giggling too hard to speak.

"Flicka is a girl horse, Aunt Lill!" Katie said.

Sam, still looking confused, said, "Yeah. Flicka is a girl."

Her addiction had deprived Lillie of scenes like this one, and for what was probably the thousandth time since entering Rising Sun, she sent a silent thanks to Pete, whose advice and connections had freed her in every imaginable way.

After a make-your-own-sundae dessert, the girls dragged Lillie to the sun porch, where they assembled the materials needed to construct wind chimes from old keys. Surprisingly, Molly—not one to join any game or project that involved children—sat down and asked how she might help. Kassie and Katie handed her a stack of newspapers, and once they covered the table's surface, gave her two cans of spray paint.

"These need to be pink," Kassie said, spreading an assortment of keys across the paper, "and these need to be blue."

After an hour of tying fishing line to twigs, then tying keys to each strand, they'd produced half a dozen noisemakers…one for each of the girls, one for their mom, one for Molly and one for Lillie.

"Who gets the last one?" Molly asked.

"Aunt Lillie gets an extra one. This was her idea, after all."

She met Kassie's eyes. "I can't believe you remembered after all this time."

"Are you kidding? We've been saving keys for*ever*, just so we could do this craft with you!"

Lillie knew exactly where she'd hang hers… and exactly what she'd do with the extra chimes.

"Sam told me that one of your Hopkins kids died," Molly said.

The girls' cheery faces turned sad. "Oh, no," Kassie said. "Which one?"

"Jason."

"The one who wanted to marry that little girl?"

Nodding, Lillie wondered how they'd learned about all that.

"Daddy says he always liked you, but never more than since you got back from New York."

"Yeah," Katie agreed. "Mom says the same thing."

"'From the mouths of babes,'" Molly quoted.

Another scene for the memory book, Lillie

thought. She ought to start a journal, chronicling every warm and happy moment she experienced now.

She'd keep it nearby, so that when the post-op discomforts seemed too tough to bear, she could flip through the pages and remind herself how very blessed she was...with*out* drugs.

Jase's truck was parked out front when she stepped onto the porch at five minutes to seven. He leaned against the passenger door, one booted ankle atop the other, arms crossed over his chest. All he needed, Lillie thought, was a cowboy hat, and he could pass for a romance novel hero.

"What're you grinning about?" he asked, opening her door.

"Can't a gal just be in a good mood?"

"I suppose," he said as she slid onto the seat.

Lillie hoped he hadn't noticed that even that minuscule action made her wince.

"The twins said to tell you hello," she said as he buckled up.

"Yeah? Cool. How are they doing?"

"They're terrific. So smart. And sweet. And inquisitive..."

"Oh?"

"They came right out and asked if I was an addict."

Jase inhaled. "Way to put you on the spot, huh?"

"I didn't see much point in dodging the question. So now they know. And the conversation gave me the perfect opportunity to make them swear they'd never do drugs."

"Still, had to be tough."

"Funny thing is, the more times I tell the story, the easier it gets."

He nodded at the package on her lap. "What's that?"

"Oh, just a little something the girls and Molly and I made yesterday. I thought you might like it for your back porch."

Jase laughed. "What back porch? It's stairs leading to a five-by-five platform. Barely enough room to turn around, especially when the screen door is open."

"It was plenty big enough for a few things."

He licked his lips, and she could tell he was remembering how, at the conclusion of one of their first rehearsals in his living room, he'd kissed her good-night on that very porch. She wondered if the elderly woman across the way still lived there. She'd banged a ladle on a soup pot, yelling, "Take that craziness back inside, fools! Nobody wants to see the pair of you lockin' lips!"

"Yeah, every now and then when I toss a bag of trash into the garbage can, I can still hear Mrs. Aikens, calling us fools."

It was a good memory. Bittersweet, too, since

it reminded her yet again of all they'd had—and lost—because of her habit.

During the remainder of the short drive to his row house, Jase talked about the party. He complimented the tasteful decorations, the food, the catering crew, even the music, provided by a DJ.

"Your mom surprised me," Lillie admitted.

"Not nearly as much as you surprised her."

"I should have apologized a long time ago."

"Still, it couldn't have been easy. You earned some serious brownie points."

"Good. I've always hated the way we left things."

"I have soda, iced tea and bottled water," he said, leading her into the tiny galley kitchen.

"Water sounds great." Lillie unwrapped the wind chimes and held them up for him to see. "The girls started saving keys before I signed myself into Rising Sun. Yesterday, we finally put them to good use."

He thumped the closest key, and like a tiny pendulum, it careened into the one beside it, setting off a cacophony of tinny notes.

"Not exactly melodic," Lillie said.

"I'll focus on who made it for me, and it'll sound like a symphony."

She smiled and told her water bottle, "The man's a poet."

Jase pulled out a stool and gave its seat a pat.

"Take a load off," he said. "Tell me what you've been thinking about that required total privacy."

"I could have put that better. It's true, I've been thinking about this for a while, but the reality of it is, I've made my decision."

"Jeez, Lill. I don't know if I want to hear this..."

The last time she'd seen that expression on his face had been the night she gave back his ring. She spoke quickly to relieve his anxiety.

"I'm having surgery next week."

He exhaled audibly. "Good. Great. I'm glad. It's about time."

"What did you think I was going to say?"

"I dunno, could have been any one of a dozen things."

"Well, that's it. They'll scrape away any scar tissue, maybe insert a pin into the bone and stitch me up. They'll try to convince me that I need pain meds afterward. I just want you to know, I'm not going to do it. No matter how bad it gets. Just a word of warning, in case you decide to visit while I'm recovering."

"In case? Of course I'll visit. But Lill...that's not smart, is it? From what I hear, pain can cause all sorts of damage. It makes you tense up and clench your muscles. Won't that put stress on the bone? Plus, it keeps you awake when you need sleep the most. Messes with your mind. Affects your ability to do physical therapy."

"I know, I know. The doctor already gave me that lecture. So it'll take a little longer to recover. I'm resigned to that fact. It beats the alternative."

He inspected the water bottle's label, turning it right and left before meeting her eyes. "You're that worried you'll get hooked again?"

"No. But why take chances?"

"*Now* I see what you meant when you said you'd been thinking."

Lillie played with the bottle cap.

He hadn't recited any of the usual things: *If you need me, I'll be here. Let me know how I can help. I'm pullin' for you.* It hurt a little, knowing he didn't trust her to make it through the surgery and rehab without drugs. Still, Lillie felt certain that this was the right decision. If she could make it through this without pills, she could make it through anything.

She hopped down from the stool, picked up the wind chimes and flung open his back door.

"Going to hang that up?"

"Yep, scoping out the perfect spot."

"Ah," he said, following her.

"Think Mrs. Aikens will get out her ladle when she hears it?"

Jase's forefinger traced the contours of her cheek. "I have a drawer full of old keys. If she does, you and I will make another one, just for her. What's that old saying?" He struck a pose, like a stage actor. "'*Musick has charms to soothe a savage breast, to soften rocks, or bend a knotted oak.'"*

"Wow. I'm impressed."

"What, that I can quote William Congreve's *The Mourning Bride*?"

"You're full of surprises, Jase Yeager. Now let's figure out how to get this symphony hung."

If things worked out between them, life would be a lot of things…

…but boring wouldn't be one of them.

CHAPTER TWENTY

LILLIE DIDN'T LOOK anywhere as banged up as she had after the accident. Then, she'd been bandaged head to toe, with multiple splints and slings, monitors and tubes. Now, although it was worrisome that she hadn't regained consciousness yet, she looked peaceful.

He'd sent her parents to the cafeteria, promising to text them if she woke up. Grabbing one of the magazines her mom had placed on the rolling tray table, Jase settled into the gray chair beside her bed and did what he could to get comfortable. Might be easier, he thought, if Amelia had brought a newspaper or a crossword puzzle book. Anything but a stack of how-to-crochet books.

He held out a forefinger, trying to duplicate the article's instructions. "'Make a slip knot on the shaft of one needle,'" he said, reading aloud. "'Place this needle in your left hand and move left fingers over to brace right needle. With right index finger, pick up the yarn and—'"

"Are you trying to keep me asleep indefinitely?"

The magazine hit the tray with a *splat*.

"Lill… *Lill.* You're awake!"

"No thanks to you."

Her voice, groggy and gruff, was music to his ears.

"What's that you were reading?"

"Your mom's crochet book. Darned if I know how she can figure out how to make sweaters, reading instructions like that."

Laughing, Lillie pointed to the water cup on her nightstand, and as he held the straw to her lips, Jase said, "Don't mind saying, you had us all worried there for a while."

"Worried? Why?"

"You didn't come around as quickly as the doc thought you should."

"He would've stayed asleep, too," she said, nodding at the magazine, "exposed to a recitation from *that*."

"Well, it's good to know you're all right." He patted her hand. "Are you in much pain?"

"Nothing I can't handle."

It was likely the anesthesia hadn't completely worn off yet. Would she answer the same way when it did?

"I promised to text your folks when you came to."

"Where are they, anyway?"

"Cafeteria. They've been here from the get-go, and by the time I got here, they looked a little rough around the edges. I sent them, along with the Sams, the twins and Molly and Matt, down to grab a sandwich."

He pulled out his phone, scrolled through the numbers in his contacts list.

"Don't. Not yet. Please?"

"They're worried about you, Lill."

"I know. I just need another minute or two to get my head straight. So that when they get back, they'll see there really isn't anything to worry about."

She ran a hand through her hair. "I must look terrible."

"I can't remember when I've seen a more beautiful sight..." The words were out before he had a chance to think about what they'd mean to her. Jase blamed it on relief, because it had been pure hell, repeating the doctor's words in his head: "It doesn't happen often, but once in a while, a more sensitive patient never comes to. And it's possible that instead of repairing the bone, we'll make it worse."

Her family had drawn together, but Jase was alone. Uninvited. And while they'd all been cordial enough during the surgery, the awkward silences and quick glances were evidence of their uncertainty: How did he fit into the picture now?

He dug around in the duffle bag perched on the wide windowsill and came up with a hairbrush; then he hit the up arrow on the bed's controls and slowly brought her to a more upright position. One knee beside her, he did his best to tidy her hair. When he finished, it didn't look much different than before.

"There," he said, "you're a cover model."

She laughed and squeezed his hand. "All right. Shoot them a text. And when you're finished, maybe you can poke your head into the hall, see if there's a nurse out there who can help me get to the bathroom."

The black-on-white name tag read Tina St. Claire. "You'll have to wait outside for a few minutes," she said, pulling the curtain around the bed.

"Oh, no," he heard Lillie groan. "Not a bedpan!"

"Just this once," Tina said. "The doctor will want you on your feet ASAP. Next time, we'll let you use the en suite."

Jase stopped pacing when the elevator doors opened. "Give her a minute. She's with the nurse," he said, barring the door.

Amelia hugged him. "Thanks for staying with her, Jase." Holding him at arm's length, she said, "How did she react, seeing you first thing when she opened her eyes?"

He didn't want to admit that he hadn't noticed at first because he'd been trying to figure out the crochet stitch, but when he told them, everyone, the twins included, laughed.

"Oh, to have been a bug on the wall," Lillie's brother-in-law said.

"No kiddin'," her brother agreed.

"Wonder what your TV ladies would think if they heard that."

"Are you kidding?" Liam said. "They'd swoon, picturing this big handsome hunk, doing dainty things with those big ham hocks of his!"

A second round of laughter preceded Tina's exit from the room. "Try to keep it down a little, folks," she said, winking. "She's awake but still groggy from the anesthesia."

Amelia and Liam flanked Lillie, and the rest of the family surrounded the bed. Jase could have shouldered his way in, but he thought it best to let her family stand close. Later, after visiting hours, he'd sneak back and have her all to himself.

"Let me get out of your hair," he said from the doorway. "I'll catch y'all later."

"No… Jase, wait…"

Lillie reached for his hand, and Liam stepped aside to make room for him.

"Thanks for being here. Will you come back tomorrow?"

He couldn't very well admit his intentions of returning when the rest of them had gone, now could he? "Have to catch an early flight to Florida in the morning," he admitted. "But I'll call every chance I get."

"Promise?"

"You bet."

Jase ducked out of the room, pretending he hadn't noticed the warm smiles beaming from every family member's face. It buoyed him, knowing that if he and Lillie managed to work things out, her family would be all for it.

When he climbed out of the truck, quiet tinkling greeted him. Pink, blue and green keys. Red and yellow keys. He got the distinct impression someone was watching. Mrs. Aikens, if he had to guess. And Jase resisted the urge to peek over his shoulder. Why spoil his good mood by looking into the face of disapproval?

"I like it," the older woman yelled across the way. "I wouldn't complain if you made one for me."

"It was a gift," he called, turning after all, "but I'll see if I can scrounge up some materials and reproduce it for you."

"You'd do that?"

"Why wouldn't I?"

She swatted at a fly, then disappeared into her kitchen.

"Don't make mine all them rainbow colors," she hollered through the screen.

"What's your favorite color?"

"Lavender."

With that, she slammed the interior door, startling the robin that had perched on his porch rail.

He'd already booked his flight and hotel room.

If he skipped supper, he could pack and load the truck, which would save time in the morning rush, leaving a couple of hours to spend with Lillie before a nurse booted him out. She'd get a kick out of hearing that Mrs. Aikens had requested a lavender wind chime.

Jase had just zipped up his duffle when his cell phone rang.

"Got a huge favor to ask you," Drew said. "We had a…an incident, and we're stuck on I-95. Can you come pick us up?"

"That's one heckuva long stretch of road. Can you be a little more specific?"

"Were just past the ramp to Caton Avenue."

"Exit 50. I know right where you are." It shouldn't take long to reach them. There would still be plenty of time to pay Lillie a quick visit before hitting the hay.

"Looks like rain, so don't piddle around, okay?"

"Give me five to ten minutes," Jase said, laughing. "And you're very welcome."

It surprised him to find his brother and sister-in-law sitting on the tailgate of their SUV, covered in something that looked like tar. He pulled up behind them, and the instant he set foot on the pavement, realized the black stuff wasn't tar. "Holy smokes, dude. What did you hit? A septic tank truck?"

Drew snorted. "Close. We were behind some

sort of garbage truck, and believe it or not…" He pointed at a gigantic metal barrel on the side of the road. "That thing rolled off the truck bed and bounced around a couple of times. I swerved to miss it but failed. Stupid thing scraped up the whole undercarriage. Tore holes right through to the floorboards."

"And splattered God-knows-what all over us in the process," Dora whimpered.

Jase held his nose. "Holy smokes," he said again, "what a stench. So where's the garbage truck?"

"He never even slowed down!" Dora said, pointing north. "I snapped a picture of the license plate, for all the good it'll do."

Jase met his brother's eyes. "Have you called for a tow truck?"

"Should be here any minute."

Jase walked around the car, then rejoined Drew and Dora, shaking his head. "Chances are good your insurance company will stamp this baby *totaled*."

Dora made a feeble attempt at wiping sludge from Drew's cheek, but only made a bigger mess. "It'll be okay," she said, pocketing the shredded tissue. "I'll borrow my mom's car until the insurance company comes through."

The tow truck pulled up in front of their car. Thumbing the baseball cap to the back of his head, the driver said, "Name's Jim. Dispatch said you hit a barrel?"

Drew pointed into the roadside ditch.

"Oy-polloy! What's in it? Rotten eggs? A skunk? A skunk that ate rotten eggs?"

There wasn't a trace of humor in Drew's voice when he said, "Let me guess, you work at the Comedy Club on weekends."

"No disrespect intended, sir, but there's nothin' funny about that smell." He looked at Jase. "You're driving them home?"

"'Fraid so," he said, grinning.

"Better you than me," the man said, handing Drew a clipboard. "Fill that out and sign it while I hook 'er up."

Once finished, he took one look at thc smudged clipboard and tugged on a pair of work gloves. "If you're picking up your car anytime soon, tell the lady at the desk that your vehicle will be out back." He hoisted himself into the driver's seat. "*Way* out back."

Jase, Drew and Dora watched him drive away, then climbed into the pickup. Even before starting the motor, Jase realized that the stench clinging to their shoes and clothes and hair would permeate his upholstery.

"If this ain't love," he joked, throwing the truck into gear, "I don't know what is."

So much for visiting Lillie tonight. He dialed

her number, and when she said a groggy hello, relief pulsed through him.

"How's it going?"

"If you're asking if the stuff they gave me in the OR has worn off, yes, it has."

"So you're hurting pretty bad, huh?"

"It's no picnic, but it's not anywhere near as bad as it was after the accident. Besides, they've got me on something called an ice therapy machine. It's supposed to reduce swelling and prevent muscle spasms."

"Is it working?"

"Seems to be. But I'm freezing!"

She laughed, then told him that the surgeon explained that he'd had to crack only one bone to correct the problem.

"That's gotta be a relief."

"You sound tired," she said.

He told her about Drew's call for help, and hearing her laugh as he relayed the rest of the story energized him.

"And your truck will smell even riper after sitting all night with the windows up in this heat and humidity. Looks like you'll have to take a cab to the airport."

"Yup. And it'll be worse when I get back. So it looks like there's a rental car in my future, too. I'd tell my insurance agent about it in person, just to get a look at his face when I explain things... if I had a way to get to his office."

"A rental car? Jase, that isn't necessary."

"'Course it is. There's no telling how long it'll take a detail shop to get rid of that smell."

"What I mean is, why rent something when you can borrow mine? I won't be able to drive for weeks, a month, maybe. Wish I'd known that before I bought it."

It made perfect sense, and yet, Jase couldn't see himself taking her up on the offer.

"You'll be doing me a favor."

He chuckled. "How do you figure that?"

"It isn't good for a vehicle to sit idle for weeks on end. Dad says things get gummed up in the engine."

"I'm sure he wouldn't mind taking it for a spin every couple of days."

"Dad has a lead foot. And he rides the brakes. I'd rather have you watching over Mona."

"Mona?"

Soft laughter filtered into his ear. "When you were a kid, didn't you ever look at car grills and imagine the headlights as eyes, the split of the hood as the eyebrows, the bumper a mouth?"

"Yeah, I guess…"

"In the used car lot, while I wandered around inspecting vehicles, that one smiled at me. A tiny Mona Lisa smile."

Leave it to Lillie to give an inanimate object a personality…and a name to fit it.

"Please tell me that isn't the reason you bought…her."

More laughter, and then, "She fit perfectly into my budget. She's small, so gas won't be an issue. Front-wheel drive means I can maneuver better in the snow. And…"

"And she smiled at you," he finished. It was his turn to say, "You sound tired."

"A little. Maybe."

"Get some sleep, kiddo. I'll call you from Florida, okay?"

"When do you get back?"

"Day after tomorrow."

"Have the cab drop you off here so I can give you my car keys."

"I thought your folks drove you to the hospital."

He still didn't feel right, using her car, and he said so.

"Look at it this way—I owe you far more than that paltry check I wrote you. I know you erased a symbolic slate, but still. Use the car. It'll make it more like we're even."

Life would be easier if he said yes. Plus, he'd have the pickup and drop-off as legitimate excuses to see her.

"Okay, but only on one condition."

Silence.

"This *really* wipes the slate clean, totally, once and for all."

More silence, and then, “We’ll leave that discussion for another day.”

She *did* sound exhausted. And who wouldn’t be following a surgery like that? *You bet we’ll take this up another day*, he thought, and launched into the goodbye routine he’d started so long ago. Would she remember her part?

“G’night, Lill.”

“Sleep tight, Jase.”

“Happy dreams.”

“Catch you on the other side of the moon.”

Thirty seconds after she hung up, Jase was still staring at the handset.

In bed that night, he scrunched the pillow under his neck and flicked through the TV channels. “Three hundred and some channels, and there’s nothing on,” he groused, and hit the off button. Then, as shards of moonlight painted white streaks on the dark ceiling and drowsiness overtook him, Jase did something he hadn’t done in far too long.

I’m not usually a praying man, You know that. This thing with Lillie... I want it more than I’ve ever wanted anything. If it’s the right *thing, well, I sure could use some guidance here...so if You’re listening, I’d appreciate a sign.*

CHAPTER TWENTY-ONE

AMELIA HAD TURNED the turret into a bedroom to spare Lillie clomping up and down the stairs in her cast. She'd been using a walker for nearly a week when Jase stopped by.

"Looks pretty good," he said, admiring her temporary bedroom. "What did your mom do with all the antiques that were in here?"

"Dad and Matt put some in the basement and some in the garage. Temporarily. Just to make room for this hideous hospital bed."

Faint furrows creased her otherwise smooth brow, proof enough to Jase that she was in considerable pain.

"You don't like it in here?"

"It's cramped and noisy, and with all these windows, it's too bright to sleep well, especially if the moon is out. And the guests…" She heaved a frustrated sigh. "They waltz in and out of here, interrupting when I'm trying to write." She sighed again. "See? Told you I might get surly after the operation."

"Those sound like legit complaints to me. You

just had major surgery, don't forget. But wait. Did you say writing?"

"I did." She pointed at the green spiral notebook atop her guitar case. "Nothing earth-shattering. Just a few simple melodies to go with some lyrics I pulled together."

"How 'bout singing a tune or two for me?"

"They're not even close to being listen-ready yet."

"Well, let me know when I can hear them, okay?"

Jase counted the tiles on the turret's floor. "I can see how, even without an official door, the walls might feel like they're closing in on you."

"I don't really mind the size. It's the no-door thing that drives me batty."

"I hear ya. And I'll bet you'd sleep a whole lot better in your own bed. How much longer until you can maneuver the stairs?"

"I could do it now...if they'd let me."

"Are they here?"

She looked surprised. "Well, no. When they found out you were coming over, they decided to run some errands."

"Well?" He held out a hand, and that, at least, produced a smile.

He helped her up and slid an arm around her. "Lean on me," he instructed. "We'll just take it slow and easy, right here beside the bed, one small step at a time."

"So how'd you get here today?" she asked, moving slowly forward.

"Rented a big ol' boat. Mom calls it an old lady car."

He laughed. She did not.

"I don't know why you have to be so stubborn. You could be driving my car for free."

"This is free, thanks to insurance."

She waved the explanation away with her free hand, then licked her lips.

"Thirsty?"

"No, I'm good. What about you? Are you hungry?"

"Just had breakfast, but thanks."

"At eleven o'clock!"

"Jet lag. Always messes with my feeding schedule."

"Very funny. You know better than most people that Florida and Maryland are in the same time zone."

"True, but I don't sleep much when I'm doing the show. Same aftereffect as jet lag."

"So how long will you need the old lady car?" They continued to shuffle around the room together.

"It's gonna take the detailer another week. If I'm lucky."

"Wow. That must have been some polluted barrel. Any idea what was in it?"

"To tell you the truth, I'd rather not know."

Jase decided to end the small talk. But first, he wanted to get her off her feet and back into bed.

Once he got her settled, Jase said, “Still no pain pills, huh?”

“Not so much as an aspirin.” Eyes narrowed, she said, “So you really *didn’t* believe me when I told you that before.”

Hopefully, he could avoid the question by pretending to search for a light quilt. And it worked. Sort of.

“Sorry I’m such a grump.”

“Hey, I wouldn’t be at my best either, if a surgeon cracked my thigh bone and put it back together with pins and screws.”

She grew quiet. And serious. Jase steadied himself for bad news of some sort.

“While we’re on the subject of pills,” she began, “and as long as I can blame the leg for my less-than-pleasant attitude—”

“Uh-oh…”

“Stop trying to entertain me for a minute, will you? You need to hear this, and I need to say it. I’m not the same person who was all wigged-out on drugs. If you can’t accept that, we’re doomed, even as friends. Because frankly…”

She looked at the ceiling, as if the rest of what she’d planned to say was written up there, like lines from a script.

“Frankly, I’ve had it with your lack of faith. How long have I been home now?”

Since Mother's Day, he thought, but before he could say so, she continued with, "Months, Jase. *Months.* And I'm still clean. So deal with it!"

"Okay."

"Now you have a choice to make."

"A choice…"

"I'm sure it's no surprise to hear that I love you. That I always have and always will. But I won't live with your judgment hanging over my head like a guillotine. It's high time you showed some confidence in me, time for you to take me at my word. Because honestly? That's all I've got."

"You must be exhausted," he said, evading a response. "I should let you get some rest. Need anything before I hit the road?"

"Oh. So now you're leaving? Just like that."

"You're tired." *And I'm tired of you labeling me the bad guy, just because I'm taking my time about—*

"I'm not tired, but if you want to go," she gestured toward the leg, "I'm certainly in no position to stop you."

You could ask me to stay. You could suggest that we start this whole visit over again, on an up note this time…

He'd never understood the phrase "silence is deafening" before. Well, he understood it now.

Minutes passed before he said, "I'll check in with you soon." He started for the door, stopping long enough to add, "Forgot to mention, I have a three-week stint in Florida, starting tomorrow. Meeting with a couple of local manufacturers down there about adding my mom's designs to their production lines. It'll save us the freight charges."

"Three *weeks*?"

Deke had often accused him of burying the lede, and he couldn't deny it. He'd always been a "good news first" sort of guy. Would it have been smarter to mention the extended trip right up front? *Yeah, but you know what they say about hindsight.*

Lillie's lips had formed a taut line as she reached for the paperback she'd been reading when he arrived.

"Safe travels," she said, opening it to a bookmarked page. "And if you happen to think of it, give me a call."

He took it to mean "Time's up, pal. Hit the road."

"Take care of yourself, okay?"

"You do the same."

He quietly let himself out and wasted no time making his way to the rental. He slid behind the steering wheel and shook his head.

It hit him like a punch to the jaw: Lillie had come right out and said that she still loved him, and instead of admitting that he felt the same way, he'd stood, staring and openmouthed.

Too late to go back in there and make things right?

Who knew what *right* was anymore! Everything had changed since she got back. More and more, Jase felt like a passenger on a carnival ride, the one that spun people around so fast that they stuck to the wall, even as the bottom dropped out from under them. He'd been hanging on, barely, but only because he'd chosen not to get off.

Maybe it was time to do just that.

LILLIE RAN THROUGH the he said–she said, over and over, always coming to the same conclusion: Jase had saved the news about his long Florida trip until the last minute to underscore how he'd felt when Brant dropped the producer bombshell on him. It had been a petty, immature thing to do, and look where it left them: nearly a month without so much as a text message.

She couldn't afford to stress out over it and chose, instead, to throw herself into physical therapy. The result? Her leg was healing faster than expected. She'd traded the walker for crutches, then the crutches for a cane. Soon, she'd be able to walk without aid. And since Jase had made it clear that he could get along without *her*, Lillie resolved to start fresh.

And she started with the phone call that she'd put off for far too long.

"Hey, Brant."

"Lillie! It's good to hear from you."

"How's Sally?"

"Doing well. Doing great, actually. She's been home for a month. Her oncologist reduced chemo treatments to one, every other week. If her numbers continue to improve, she'll be off it altogether, and they'll remove the port."

"So she's close to remission, then?"

"Real close."

"That's wonderful news. I need to make time to see her, soon. I really miss that big smile of hers!"

"She misses you, too. In fact, she mentioned you at breakfast the other day."

"Is her immune system strong enough to eat out?"

"Not just yet. But you're more than welcome to come to the house. If you're up to it, that is."

Lillie explained that she hadn't quite recovered enough to drive, but promised to stop by the minute her surgeon gave her the go-ahead.

"Happy as I am to hear that Sally's doing well, I have an ulterior motive for calling."

"Let me guess. You're finally ready to meet Rusty."

She'd turn twenty-eight on her next birthday. She missed singing. Missed interacting with audiences. And since there wasn't anything—or anyone—holding her back, why not reach for the brass ring after all? If she missed it, she'd be no worse off than she was now. And at least then, she could say that she'd tried.

"Yes, I'm ready."

"Let me make a couple phone calls and get back to you. Will you be home tomorrow?"

"Yes, all day."

"Just so happens he's in town. If he has an hour or two in the afternoon, can we hold the initial meeting at your folks' inn? His hotel is nearby, and that'd spare you having to hire a taxi."

With just one couple in the Constellation Suite and still no word from Jase, there would never be a better time.

The next day, at two sharp, Brant parked a sleek silver van in front of the White Roof Inn. Lillie's mouth went dry when he slid the door open and five men hopped down onto the horseshoe drive. Two grabbed instrument cases, one hoisted an amplifier and another carried a gooseneck microphone stand, and they all followed Brant onto the porch.

"What's all this?" Liam asked, stepping outside.

"We have a two o'clock with Lillie. I'm Brant Perry," he said, handing over a business card.

Her dad held open the screen door. "Ah, the fella with Nashville connections…"

The second man in line grinned. "Just one connection," he said, extending a hand. "Rusty McCoy." He, too, gave Liam a card.

Lillie, standing beside her father, trembled… and tried to hide it. This was it. The true test. The make it or break it moment. If she didn't pass muster with Rusty…

"And you must be Lillie of the lovely voice," he said, bowing slightly. He sandwiched her hand between his own. "Brant has been singing your praises for months, if you'll pardon the pun. I'm looking forward to hearing it for myself."

Brant dropped a hand onto Rusty's shoulder. "Where can we set up, Ms. Rourke?"

"Follow me," Lillie said, hoping her still-weak leg wouldn't collapse under her as she led them into the turret.

It reminded her of that day, more than two months ago now, when she and Jase ran through half a dozen songs in preparation for what would have been the kids' wedding. After all this time without a word from him, the memory shouldn't hurt this much. But he'd made his choice, and just as she had on the night she left for New York, Lillie respected it…and forced herself to move on.

Rusty barked orders as he pointed at the equipment. "The amp is for the mic, not the guitars." He found a socket for a bulky, reel-to-reel tape recorder. "It's old-fashioned," he said, "but it can't be beat for portable sound quality."

Brant frowned. "Sorry, Lillie. Let me make a few introductions. I guess you've figured out which one is Mr. McCoy…the guy with the rusty manners. Gene, here, will back you up on keyboard, Hank's on the twelve-string. Why don't y'all take a couple minutes to tune up."

"Speaking of tunes," Rusty said, facing Lillie, "do you know what you're singing?"

She didn't like the man. Not even a little bit. But if he could help pave the road to Nashville, she'd tolerate a little rudeness. She handed him a short stack of sheet music.

But he was far more interested in the green spiral notebook *under* the sheet music.

"*You* wrote all these?"

"I did." During her first week home after the operation, she'd come to grips with the fact that Jase wasn't going to call. She shouldn't have been surprised. The look on his face as he backed out of the room had been identical to the one permanently imprinted in her memory. Those weeks she'd spent waiting for him to visit or call turned into months. Wasted time that would have been far better spent focusing on recovery rather than lost romance. She wouldn't make that mistake again, and the decision resulted in several maudlin melodies that served no purpose than to provide a way to vent.

"But I think it's best if we start with something everyone's familiar with," she concluded.

"Let me be the judge of that." Rusty pointed to the nearest mic stand, then at the first song in the notebook. "Grab your guitar and let's hear it." He turned to the musicians. "You guys jump in when you feel like it." And then, pointy-toed boots planted shoulder width apart on the tiles, he crossed his arms over his chest. "Well, hit it, girl!"

Against her better judgment, Lillie stepped up to the mic, fingers forming the D7 chord on the fretboard. Following a short six-chord intro, she closed her eyes and sang.

"I think of you as time slips by.
"As I stare into the inky sky.
"I plead my case to the hands of fate.
"And I wait… I wait…
"From twilight black to morning light.
"Mem'ries hold you in my sight.
"Through the lonely hours I hate.
"And I wait… I wait…
"I'll wait forever, forever if I must—"

"Cut," Rusty said. "I've heard enough."

Lillie gripped the mic stand so tightly, her fingers ached. She'd hit every note…or thought she had. Too much vibrato? Not enough? Or were the lyrics of interest to no one but herself?

"Was it us?" Gene asked. "How 'bout if we start over, cut back on the treble, give it more bass. 'Cause it's good. Real good."

Hank agreed. "Yeah, let's run through it again."

"I'd like to hear it with Gene's suggestions in place," Brant said.

"Relax, guys, ever'body did fine. Real fine," Rusty drawled.

He stood beside Lillie. Stood so close that she thought maybe he intended to harmonize with her.

"And you," he said, drawing out the word, "you're a natural." He motioned for the performers to pack up their instruments. "We need to talk, so make yourselves comfortable."

Once everyone found a seat, he outlined his plan: get Lillie into a recording studio, stat. "Soon as I've put the tape into the right hands—DJs, booking agents, promoters—I'll send her on the road, let her open for acts like Wes McNeal, Haley Nichols, Dusty Parker to get her name out there."

He owned an RV, Rusty told them, large enough for a five-man band, equipment, costumes and some rudimentary backdrops. "Won't need fireworks and big screens. She's exactly what I've been looking for, and I have a feeling fans will see her as I do—a powerhouse. At least, that's the hope, right?"

She heard him, loud and clear.

"So if the audience doesn't react well to me,

the guys, the setup crew, RV driver...we'll all be out of work."

Rusty shrugged. "Pretty much, yeah." He smirked. "Think you can handle that?"

She looked at Gene, then Hank. It wouldn't have been a question if she could work with the Muzikalees. But the guys were married, with kids and full-time jobs. She couldn't ask them to risk it all on a *maybe*.

"Are you on board?" she asked the guys.

They looked at each other and, grinning, Gene said, "You bet."

"Where will you be? While we're motoring from town to town in your RV, I mean?" she asked Rusty.

"At the office, where I belong, talking to club owners and bar managers and trying to convince them you're worth the pay." He arched a brow. "Where did you think I'd be?"

"Well, it's your vehicle, so..."

"It's obvious you don't know this guy very well," Brant said, grinning. "He owns the rig but hasn't driven it."

"Yet," Rusty said. He took his time, studying her from head to toe, then turned to Brant. "Got those papers? And a pen?"

Brant opened his briefcase and withdrew four documents, each affixed to the traditional blue file jacket. "You might want to meet the drummer and the bassist," he told Lillie, "make sure their sound is—"

"I'm sure they're good at what they do. What we need, before any of us signs anything, is a name." She met each man's eyes. "Try this on for size—Turret." She waited as they silently repeated it. "It means tower. The first turrets were attached to castles and provided cover for medieval soldiers. It's also what they call the rotating thing on top of military tanks, so it symbolizes strength and power."

The guys exchanged amused glances.

"Sounds like you've given it a lot of thought," Gene said.

"Yeah," Brant said, "how long have you been planning this?"

Since the day Jase walked out of here and left for Florida without even looking back.

"Well? What do you think?"

Rusty said, "I like it. Especially the strong and powerful stuff. Guys? What say you?"

Murmured agreement moved around the space.

"And what about the whole 'everything rests on my ability to wow audiences' deal?" she asked. "What do you think of *that*?"

"Dunno about Gene," Hank began, "but I've been around long enough to recognize a good sound when I hear it. I'm all in."

"Ditto," Gene said.

Rusty passed out the contracts. "These are preliminary. Just something to show that we're all on the same page, literally and figuratively. When you meet drummer and the guy who plays bass, I'll issue new ones, with dates, your names typed in, and..."

She didn't hear what he said next, because fear had wrapped around her brain like a big cold fist, blocking out everything else. She'd been only too eager to tell anyone who'd listen all about the new Lillie. Suddenly, facing this sink-or-swim scenario made her wonder if she'd been fooling herself. *Was* she strong enough to shoulder this much responsibility?

"Lillie...?"

The sound of her name snapped her to attention. "Sorry...what?"

Brant sat beside her and calmly explained, "We were discussing whether to go the jeans and T-shirts route, or take a step back in history and wear suits and ties."

"You mean like '50s bands?"

"Exactly."

Lillie didn't like the idea, but because she hadn't had time to come up with logical reasons *why*, she said, "This is all happening a bit fast. I need a few days to mull it over. Last thing I want to do is rush into a commitment, only to let all of you down."

The way she'd let down her family, her friends and Jase.

Rusty handed the pen back to Brant. Returned the contracts, too.

"How about a trial run, then, right here in Baltimore? Brant can set up a few shows, give y'all a chance to get used to working together."

"Does anyone mind if I take a couple of days, a week maybe, to think about it?"

Rusty glared at Brant. "Thought you said she was unattached."

"She is, far as I know."

"Brant is right. I *am* unattached." Lifting her chin, Lillie added, "I don't need to get permission from anyone." Although she wondered what sort of advice Jase might offer…if she told him about the deal.

"I'm okay waiting," Hank said.

Gene nodded. "Ditto."

"Then it's settled," Brant said. "We'll table the discussion for now. What say we meet again in a week. Same time. Same place."

The men shook hands with her, said their goodbyes and piled back into the big silver van.

She should have been honest with them. Jase had already taken care of that…his lack of communication making it known he didn't see a future for them.

CHAPTER TWENTY-TWO

"SERIOUSLY, DUDE? YOU two haven't talked in how long?"

"Going on two months now," Jase said.

"I thought you guys were doing well."

He frowned at his brother. "You didn't get that from anything *I* said."

"More like what you implied."

"What, by not relating a blow-by-blow description of a big argument?"

Drew didn't speak for several seconds. "Sorry, bro, didn't realize there you and Lillie had a big argument."

"We didn't, exactly." Lillie had gotten a lot off her chest, and like an idiot, he'd left in a huff without letting her know how he felt. He'd dwelt on it all through Florida, during three weeks' worth of meals consumed alone, time spent waiting for business appointments, and those long, lonely hours while sleep eluded him. His only consolations were the signed documents that assured swift turnaround for every product ordered. It made doing business on his mother's behalf better. He loved the work, even the on-air stuff, and as long as the company flourished, he had no intention of changing career tracks.

"So?"

Jase had been so lost in his thoughts that he'd missed some of the conversation.

"What're you gonna do about it?" Drew asked.

"What's to do? She's on the road somewhere, livin' her dream, and I'm here…" *Wishing she wasn't.*

He knew that was selfish. She'd always wanted to make a name for herself in the music industry. It just seemed a shame that, because of his doubts, Lillie was out there, reaching for her star…while he had zip.

"Dude, it's never too late."

"I appreciate your concern, but—"

"It's that thing Ian said, isn't it? That's why you're dragging your feet."

Jase didn't want to hear his brother recite "that thing." He'd been hearing it in his head for weeks now: *What's in it for Lillie?* He didn't like admitting that so far, he hadn't come up with a single thing.

"The longer you wait to talk to her, the harder it'll be."

Yeah, he'd considered that, too. "I don't even know where she is."

"Knock it off. You can find out, if you want

to. Who's that guy again? The one who put her in touch with the producer?"

"Brant Perry."

"Right. Him. Pick up the phone. Ask how *he* gets in touch with her." Drew paused. "What've you got to lose?"

Everything, Jase admitted. If he never called, he'd never have to deal with the possibility that she might say "too little, too late."

"Hang up. Call the guy, right now."

Jase heard Dora in the background, asking if Drew was ready to help with dinner.

"Let me know what he says."

The brothers agreed to talk later, and Jase decided not to waste another minute.

"She's in New York," Brant said after a few formalities, "performing at the Harmony Factory."

"Alone?"

"No way I'd let Rusty send her on tour without backup. She nearly called the whole deal off. Only thing that saved our bacon was that big heart of hers, worrying what would become of the guys if she backed out."

Even though he knew she wanted to perform, Jase was having a hard time believing she'd signed a contract, let alone agreed to go back on the road. She'd hated everything about that lifestyle.

"Have you seen her lately?"

“A couple weeks ago.” Brant paused. “Last time I checked in with her, she asked about you. No idea where she got the crazy idea that I’d know anything, but there you have it.” After a moment, Brant asked, “You two were more than just friends, eh?”

“We…we go way back,” Jase said. What did the guy expect? That he’d blurt “We’d be married now, if she hadn’t become an addict”?

“Where’s she going after New York?”

“Home. But not for…”

Jase heard the sounds of turning pages. So he wasn’t the only one who still relied on paper calendars.

“…not for a week and a half. She’s scheduled to meet with Rusty in Nashville, talk about signing a contract.”

“Wait. What? She went on the road without one?”

“Not exactly. Rusty got her to agree to a trial run, and she signed a three-month deal.”

“What’s your take on things? I mean, do you think the group will stay together?”

“You know her better than I do…”

In other words, he had a fifty-fifty shot at making things right.

“Where’s she staying, in case I want to surprise her with a visit?”

“Rusty’s RV is parked behind the club.”

Mighty close quarters in one of those rigs…

Jealousy was an emotion he couldn't afford to give in to right now.

Jase cleared his throat. "If you talk to her in the next couple of days, don't tell her we spoke, okay?"

With the difficult conversation behind him, Jase started practicing what he'd say when he got hold of her on the phone…

"Hey, Lill. It's me. Jase. It's Wednesday. Six fifteen. In the evening. Sorry I haven't called before now. It's been crazy around here. I've barely had a minute to myself."

If that sounded lame to him, how would it sound to her? He started over.

He cleared his throat and dialed her number.

"Just calling to say I'm sorry. I shouldn't have waited so long to get in touch. But what can you expect from an arrogant, self-centered, thinks-only-of-myself judgmental boob. I've had a lot of time to think, and if you'll let me, I'll repeat every word in person."

He'd never made a call like this before, and had no idea how to wrap things up.

"I hope your leg isn't giving you fits. Call me when you get a minute."

Jase hit End and hoped Drew had been right, that it wasn't too late.

It was time to come up with an answer to Ian's question. He'd lead with that…if she agreed to see him.

Jase pocketed his cell phone and passed a mirror on the way back to the set. He looked tired and agitated. And why wouldn't he, when Lillie had dominated his thoughts—night and day—for weeks?

What's in it for Lillie?

Answer: a guy who's so stuck in the past that he can't focus on the present *or* the future...walking, talking proof that she deserved better.

But things didn't have to stay this way. She'd changed. A lot.

And so could he.

CHAPTER TWENTY-THREE

AS SHE DRESSED for Friday's show, Lillie's phone beeped, letting her know it was fully charged. She still had a phone message. From Jase. The one she'd listened to a dozen times since receiving it.

She didn't know which surprised her more, that he'd called, or that he'd been so self-deprecating.

Her reasons for not returning his call had been solid: before making any decisions about him—about *them*—Lillie needed to figure out how to tell Brant and Rusty that she couldn't sign a long-term contract. And she had to tell the guys.

Touring had been exhilarating, and filled her with a sense of purpose and pride. But it hadn't been a good fit. Spending time in the studio, reacting to applause, being greeted by an adoring public that held napkins and envelopes and CD covers in the hope of an autograph had been fun. But it hadn't made her happy. Something was missing. Something big.

She counted her blessings: the operation had been successful, and soon all traces of the limp would vanish, this time, for good. Every debt was paid, and despite temptation on the road, she'd remained drug-free. There was a ready-made job and a home to return to, thanks to the secret her dad revealed during their last conversation: her mom wouldn't agree to a six-month world cruise to celebrate their fortieth anniversary until they found someone reliable to run the inn while they were gone. It seemed the most natural thing in the world, volunteering to take over. With all that going for her, she ought to feel content.

The missing puzzle piece had a name, she realized after hearing that message.

Jase.

For his sake and hers, Lillie needed to put things right, and that meant a call to Brant.

"At the risk of earning a reputation for being ungrateful," she began, "I wanted you to be the first to know, it isn't working out."

"I had a feeling you'd say that," Brant said.

"It was that obvious?"

"You have everything it takes to go to the top, except one thing."

She knew what it was: desire. Lillie no longer saw music as the road to her dream come true.

"Some folks take to the road like birds take to the air. Without that, you'd starve out there. I've seen it before, so I know what it looks like."

"No wonder you're such a great dad to Sally.

Not many people in your position would be as understanding."

"In my position?"

"You put your reputation on the line for me. And unless I'm mistaken, made a monetary investment, too. I can only guess the amount, but if you'll send me the numbers, we can work out a repayment plan."

"That's crazy talk. This is all part and parcel of the industry, and why I pay exorbitant rates for business insurance."

"But Brant…"

"But nothing. The only thing you owe me is to stay in touch with Sally and me. Well, there's one other thing. Reconnect with that boyfriend of yours. Get married. Buy a little house, have a couple of kids and spend the rest of your lives making beautiful music together."

He'd just described her *new* dream. "You've been a good friend, Brant. I don't know what to say."

"Say that you'll let Sally babysit those kids."

"I'd love that."

"Can I ask you something?"

"Of course."

"Have you talked to Rusty about this yet?"

Lillie winced. "No. I'm afraid I practiced the speech on you."

"Piece of advice? Just blurt it out. He'll try to interrupt, to make you change your mind. Don't let him. Just keep talking, louder if you need to, until he's heard you out. If he still insists on giving you a hard time, tell him to take it up with me. Then say thank you…and hang up."

She saw no reason to put off the inevitable, so after a heartfelt thank-you, she hung up and immediately dialed Rusty's number.

"Let me get this straight," he said when she finished her speech, "you're throwing your whole future away for some guy, when they're all a dime a dozen? Big mistake, Lillie-girl. Big mistake."

"My vision of the future is different from yours. That doesn't mean it's a mistake."

"Well, as they say, it's your life."

Yes, and if she didn't waste too much more time, Jase would be a major part of it.

"Thank you, for everything. The band, the bookings, the use of the RV… You've been more than generous. I'll never forget what you've done for me."

"We could've gone big places, kid. Country Music Award big. But like I said, it's your life. If you change your mind, you know where to find me."

Her mind was made up, but Lillie repeated, "Thank you, Rusty."

Now, there was nothing to do but check with Dora about Jase's schedule and buy a ticket to

Miami. If things worked out as she hoped, Lillie would be waiting for him in the studio lobby.

What happened after that was up to him.

And fate.

JASE HAD JUST rinsed the last of the thick stage makeup from his face when he heard a knock at his dressing room door.

"It's open..."

"Got a minute?" the producer asked.

Voice muffled by the towel, he said, "Sure, Phil. What's up?"

"Got a favor to ask you. Big one, considering how long you've been down here this time."

Tossing the towel aside, Jase sat on the edge of the vanity and waited to hear just how big this favor might be.

"There's a four-hour gap between the vitamin guy and the makeup show tomorrow. I'm hoping you can hang around to fill it."

Jase had booked the first flight to Kennedy, intent on catching Lillie before she walked onstage in New York.

"Sorry, man. Already have things lined up to head out early tomorrow."

"Cancel the flight. I'll pick up the penalty fees."

"No can do. I've left things at home unattended for too long."

Phil looked concerned. “Your mom’s okay, I hope…”

“She’s doing great.” And thanks to the heart-to-heart he’d had with her a week or so ago, their relationship had taken a turn for the better. “I have checks to write and invoices to send. And if I don’t keep tabs on that new manufacturer she lined up, we won’t have enough inventory to fill orders the next time I’m in town.” Before any of that, a surprise visit with Lillie…

“Aw, man. You’re breakin’ my heart.”

“Sorry, Phil. If I’d had a little more notice…”

Not a bald-faced lie, but not exactly the truth either. The producer would have had to catch him yesterday. Early. Before he’d made up his mind to head north and deliver his apology face-to-face. If things worked out as he hoped, by this time next week…

Don’t put the cart before the horse, he told himself.

First, he needed to make sure Lillie understood that she was more important to him than anything. He’d do everything in his power to ensure she’d never get away from him again.

The plan was admittedly scary, because while Colette’s Crafts came with guarantees, life didn’t.

Lillie had said so herself.

CHAPTER TWENTY-FOUR

"WHAT DO YOU MEAN, he isn't registered? Does that mean he's checked out?"

"It's against policy to divulge information about our guests," the desk clerk said.

Lillie had done this kid's job long enough to have memorized that line. She'd never been on the receiving end of it, though. Now that she knew how annoying it was, she'd work on finding more courteous ways to say the same thing.

"But if he checked out, he isn't a guest." Lillie pointed out. "Right? Can you at least tell me if he asked you to call a taxi to take him to the airport?"

"Yes, as a matter of fact, he did."

"How long ago?"

The clerk glanced at the computer screen. "About half an hour ago."

Meaning, if she'd hailed a cab instead of riding the much-cheaper shuttle, she wouldn't have missed him. Frustration flooded her being. She'd wasted most of the day—and hundreds of dollars—making her way here to surprise him. And he was gone.

Guess the surprise is on you*!*

"My cell battery is almost dead, so I wonder if you'd call a cab for me."

"No problem." He picked up the phone's handset. "Where to? Airport or train station?"

"Airport." The club had paid her and the band in cash. She considered it found money, and it didn't bother her a bit, spending a little more to make the trip in half the time.

She had just enough battery power to leave a message on the ride to MIA.

"Hi, Jase. It's me. Sorry it's taken so long to respond to your message. I won't recite a list of flimsy excuses. Instead, I wonder if you'd do me a favor. Meet me at Sur les Quais. Tonight. Eight o'clock. There's something I need to discuss with you, and since it's usually pretty quiet at Ian's on weeknights…" *Stop rambling, you ditz, and hang up!*

The flight got into Baltimore a few minutes before four, leaving her plenty of time to shower and change into something flattering. Because in order for this plan of hers to work, she needed to look her best.

A MECHANICAL ISSUE delayed his flight, and as the jetliner sat on the tarmac, Jase closed his eyes. An hour's delay wouldn't matter at all…if he hadn't planned to stop by the White Roof and whisk Lillie away for a private dinner.

The message light on his phone blinked. Funny, but he would have sworn he'd checked it while waiting to board the plane. Jase punched in his security code and put the phone to his ear.

"Hi, Jase," Lillie said, "sorry it's taken so long to respond to your message…"

She asked him to meet her at Ian's at eight. She'd sounded edgy, like she had the night she'd returned his ring. Lillie hadn't said, "Hope to see you there" or "It's okay if you can't make it." Not even goodbye. In his head, that could mean only one thing: she'd signed with Rusty and wanted to deliver the news in person.

The flight delay would put him home with barely enough time to shower and shave, but if he had to skip that to meet her, so be it. Maybe seeing him looking scruffy and exhausted would make it harder for her to break his heart.

It was nearly eight when he reached the bistro. But he'd had to stop at home first. There was something he had to do there. He was out of breath as he jogged up to the reservation desk.

"Jase Yeager," he said. The blonde's name tag said Terri. "I'm meeting Lillie Rourke at eight?"

"Oh, yes. Right this way," she said, and led him to a table in the far rear corner.

The same table they'd shared on the night Jase proposed.

Weird coincidence? Or had she planned it to hammer her point home: *We're through. For good.*

Lillie lowered the menu as the hostess approached. And when their eyes met, her smile sent his heart into overdrive.

Terri pulled out a chair for him. "I'll send your waiter right over."

"Thanks, but no hurry."

She'd looked happy to see him, so Jase bent at the waist and pressed a kiss to Lillie's temple. He wanted to do more. Lift her from that chair. Take her in his arms. Kiss her the way he had that night in the gazebo. *Then* launch into his apology. But there'd be time, later, to recite the speech he'd prepared.

"You look wonderful tonight."

"Better be careful," she said, "or Eric Clapton might sue you for using his song lyrics without permission."

She waited until he'd situated himself to say, "You're out of breath."

"My flight got in late. By the time I made it home and..." He trailed off.

"Are you hungry?"

"As a matter of fact, I'm starving. Haven't had a meal since this morning...if you want to call the hotel's continental breakfast a meal."

Eyes wide, her smile broadened. "I'm glad you showed up."

"Wouldn't have missed it for all the world. Somebody leaves a mysterious 'I need privacy to tell you something' message, I make sure to show up."

She closed the menu again, and the waiter appeared.

"Need a few minutes?" the younger man asked Jase.

"Yeah. But in the meantime, how about bringing us a bottle of Fillico."

Brows raised, the waiter leaned close and whispered, "Are you aware, sir, that it's $219 a bottle?"

"I'm aware."

Lillie gasped and held a hand to her throat.

"Jase, all that money, for *water*, just because the bottles look like chess pieces, studded with Swarovski crystals? Did you win the megalottery or something?"

"No. I just feel like splurging."

Lillie shrugged, then asked how his Florida meetings went, and he told her. He asked about the tour.

"It's over. I decided not to sign Rusty's contract."

If he'd ever felt more relieved, Jase couldn't say when. He wondered why, but only for a nanosecond. It didn't matter why. All that mattered was that she wasn't going away again. He hoped.

"I'll probably sound like a selfish jerk admitting it, but I'm glad."

Her eyes were twinkling when she said, "You're not a jerk."

"Oh," he teased back, "so I'm just selfish, huh?"

Lillie laughed, though she sounded nervous.

"How's your car?" he asked.

"It's great. I can't believe I got along without one for so long. It's liberating, being able to slide behind the wheel and just...*go*."

Suddenly, Lillie's brow furrowed. She took a sip of her water. A long, slow sip.

"I'll sound like an unsophisticated ninny admitting it, but this stuff tastes like...water."

It was his turn to laugh, and when he quieted, she met his eyes.

"I can't take it any longer, Jase. I need to say something, right now."

She repeated some of what she'd said that afternoon in the turret...how she was a different, more trustworthy person, that life didn't come with guarantees...

"Lillie..."

She stopped talking, clearly confused by his interruption. *Idiot*, he thought. *Why are you in such a rush to hear her break things off again?*

"Sorry. Didn't mean to interrupt."

"Don't worry about it."

"I'm sorry as I can be," he said, grabbing her

hand, "for leaving the way I did. You'd just been released from the hospital. In pain. Probably a little scared about whether or not the leg would heal. I should have been more understanding. Should've been more honest." He grabbed her other hand and sandwiched them between his own. "I want to be with you, Lill, now and always."

"Stop, Jase. Stop talking about things like that. What we need to talk about is my past. The lies. The stealing. Everything I did and said to get my hands on drugs, things that hurt you, that made you doubt and hate me."

"No, *you* stop. I'll admit, I was angry. Hurt. Scared. But never, not for a minute, did I hate you."

Tears shimmered in her eyes when she whispered, "I accused you of being too stubborn to accept things as they are instead of..."

Jase could tell that she was searching for the right way to let him off the hook. He filled the instant of silence. "You're right about a lot of things, including my stubbornness. But we *don't* need to talk about that stuff. I've already cost us way too much time, wallowing in self-pity, rehashing what was, instead of focusing on what *is*, and what could be...

"Being away from you, not hearing from you these past few months made me realize what a selfish, self-indulgent man I am. Don't look at me that way. It's true. I want what I want. And I don't want to be apart from you, ever again."

Before he could talk himself out of it, he got down on one knee and fished around in his pocket and did his best to ignore her tiny gasp. The ring box squealed quietly when he pulled open the lid.

"You…you kept it? All this time?"

"You know how hard it is to sell a used ring?"

She met his eyes, read the true meaning behind his words and pressed a palm to his cheek.

Tears puddled in her eyes as he grasped her left hand and slid the ring onto her finger. "I hope you're not one of those women who believes in long engagements."

"I haven't said yes. Yet."

"Does that mean what I think it means?"

Gently, she finger-combed his hair, and Jase closed his eyes, memorizing every touch, every gesture, every sound.

"I hope you weren't counting on a big fancy wedding. You know, for business purposes?"

"Say the word and we'll leave right now, and drive to Elkton."

"My mother will never forgive us if went to Maryland's 'quickie wedding' city and deprived her of planning the event."

Jase nodded. "You're right, as usual."

"Besides, I've barely worked my way back into

your mom's good graces. She'll have a whole new reason to hate me if we elope."

"Don't worry about her. Worry about me. *I'm* the one you have to live with."

A dreamy expression crossed her face. "Yeah," she sighed.

"Forever."

Her gaze flicked from his eyes to his lips and back again. "You're really not afraid?" she asked, her voice a mere whisper.

"Actually, I am, a little..."

She tensed.

"I'm afraid you're never gonna stop talking long enough to say *yes*. My knee is killin' me!"

Their noses were touching when she said, "Yes. Yes-yes-yes-yes, *yes*!"

When they kissed, nearby diners applauded and whistled.

He could feel the heat of a blush creep into her cheeks, and kissed them, first one, then the other.

"Do you have any idea how much I love you?"

"Oh, about as much as I love you, I suspect." Lillie leaned back, just far enough to say, "I need to have a talk with Ian."

"Ian?" he echoed. What a weird time to mention the bistro's owner! "Why?"

"Because—" she bobbed her head, indicating the still-staring, curious onlookers "—he promised me a quiet, private corner."

Grinning, Jase referenced a once-popular

song. “Should we give ’em somethin’ to talk about?”

And this time when he kissed her, Jase barely heard the congratulatory clamor.

* * * * *